Cold
Cases and
Second
Chances

J.M. DABNEY

Hostile
WHISPERS PRESS

COLD CASES AND SECOND CHANCES

J.M. DABNEY

HOSTILE WHISPERS PRESS, LLC

Copyright © 2021 by J.M. Dabney

Hostile Whispers Press, LLC

ISBN: 978-1-947184-45-9

Print ISBN: 978-1-947184-49-7

Photographer: Golden Czermak (FuriousFotog)

Model: Silal Shafqat

Cover by: J.M. Dabney at Hostile Whispers Designs

Edits by: AlternativEdits (Laura McNellis)

Proof Edits by: Maggie Decker and Kelly Miller

REMEMBER:

This book is a work of fiction. All characters, places, and events are from the author's imagination and should not be confused with fact. Any resemblance to persons, living or dead, events or places, is purely coincidental.

PLEASE BE ADVISED:

This book contains material that is only suitable for mature readers. It may contain scenes of a sexual nature and/or violence.

For my readers who make telling my stories worth it.

COLD CASES AND SECOND CHANCES

Life and Death sometimes made you believe in second chances

Robert

One thing I was sure of in my life was I'd never start over after my marriage of thirty years ended. Yet when our kids formed lives of their own, we'd grown apart. I'd signed the papers and tried to move on. My work as a Homicide Detective became my life. It left me with no time to think, but I couldn't exist for my job alone. All that changed when they assigned Remy Bosley as my new partner. He was too good to be true, but in a short time, he became my friend—maybe something more.

Remy

For twenty-eight years, I'd worked to leave my past behind. Although, when the horrors shaped you into the person you were, there was no escape. Being a cop for me was making sure no one else turned out like me. My partner, Robert Kauffman, made it clear how far I'd shoved my dreams down. I was too old and damaged for fairy tales, yet that's exactly what I wanted. In a few short years, his family became mine, and I couldn't lose that no matter how much I wanted more than friends. When he was in danger, I did what needed to be done, and nothing was ever the same.

When a serial killer makes Remy's old turf his hunting ground, how far will he go to protect the innocent?

(TW: Mentions of childhood sexual, physical, and mental abuses. Passive Suicidal Ideation, self-harm, and mental illness. These are off-page, but there are detailed flashbacks and conversations of said acts. Yet if these are triggering for you, please feel free not to read the story. Your self-care and mental health are more important. Thank you.)

ROBERT

I wore many titles in my life—husband, father, detective, and grandpa, and I felt all my fifty-five years. Sadly, I glanced across the living room to find my ex-wife, Gladys, doing everything not to look at me. We'd decided to spend our holidays together for the sake of our kids and grandkids, but the tension was killing me. We were friends before we married, and I'd hoped we'd reconnect that old friendship. That hadn't happened, and I didn't know how to fix what I hadn't realized broke.

She'd wanted the divorce. I'd come home from work one night to find her at the kitchen table with the papers already signed with her name. Out of all the emotions I'd felt, shock hadn't been one of them. We'd steadily grown apart until we were nothing more than roommates, rarely seeing each other more than three or four days a week. My career hadn't changed, and she'd married me knowing that I'd join the academy after college while she went to law school. We'd had our lives, and I'd thought, futures planned.

As a knock sounded at the door, Teddy, the ten-year-old and my oldest grandson, yelled he'd get the it. I heard *Police* bellowed loudly in a deep baritone and rolled my eyes. Remy Bosley, my partner of two years, was forty-six but was more like an overgrown kid than anything. He'd made life interesting.

I heard the door open, and heavy steps announced that Remy was inside. Teddy was giggling, and I shook my head as Remy appeared with the little boy hanging upside down over his shoulder. He had three large bags in his free hand.

"I come bearing gifts."

"Hey, Remy." Carol, my youngest, got up from the floor and kissed his cheek as the big man leaned down for her to reach.

"Beautiful as always, darlin'."

"What are you doing here, man?" I asked.

"Just finished serving Christmas dinner at the shelter and thought I'd drop off what Santa left at my place."

"Didn't go to your families?" Robert Jr, mostly called RJ, asked as he took the bags from Remy.

"Haven't seen them since I was eighteen. I usually just work serving food at several shelters on holidays or volunteer to work. Sometimes I'm at the crisis hotline answering phones. I sent a text, but you didn't answer, so I figured the kids were here."

He made it sound like no big deal, but I knew he still had some wounds even twenty-eight years later. The few times I'd asked about his family, he'd shut down. I'd always wanted to know what went down for the fallout. I couldn't imagine anything making me turn my back on my children.

"There's stuff for everyone in there. I may have gotten a little crazy with helping Santa out."

I chuckled roughly as he winked at me and then growled as he flipped Teddy over his shoulder to set his feet on the floor. The big man removed his leather jacket to expose the cream-colored sweater beneath it. He shoved the sleeves up to show off his fully tattooed forearms. Remy crouched down in front of the bouncy seat and the six-month-old secured inside; the man's long wavy hair fell forward to conceal his face.

"Hello, Love, would you mind if Uncle Remy picked you up?"

Her huge smile must have been answer enough. He dug into one of the bags and pulled out a pale blue elephant. "I washed it, and it's all soft and cuddly just for you."

"We haven't had dinner yet. You sticking around?" I asked.

"Nah, man, I had dinner with a few of the regulars I know. I spent two days packing care packages with socks, gloves, and toiletries, and a few personal items. I packed enough that there were some left over for them to keep for the ones who need them. I just wanted to drop the presents off, see the kids open them, and then I'm headed home."

I nodded. Remy always handed out condoms, lube, and gift cards to fast food places when we were on shift. For Halloween, he'd dressed up as a zombie and turned his SUV into a mobile haunted house to hand out candy and bagged meals to the homeless. Thanksgiving was a repeat of Christmas, shelter and then the crisis hotline. He was a good guy and a great partner. My last one had smelled of mints and toothpaste that never quite covered the liquor stench that seemed to permeate his skin.

"Remy!" I jumped as Carol screamed, and he barely moved Becca out of the way before he had one arm wrapped around her. "This is too much."

"It's just a weekend. The place is kid-friendly with stuff to do with them, but babysitting is on you if you decide not to take them. I'd watch them, but my schedule is kinda funky."

I sat back as I watched my partner get swamped by adults and kids alike as they opened presents. Even my ex-wife thanked him for the silky scarf she was running through her fingers.

"Dad, this one is yours."

I felt like a bastard because I hadn't gotten him anything. He wasn't looking at me as he was sitting crossed-legged on the floor playing with Becca as she clung tightly to her elephant. I opened the box, and it wasn't anything personal, new shirt, a more fashionable tie than I normally wore and a pair of new gloves.

"Noticed yours were frayed a bit."

3

The fact he still wouldn't look at me annoyed me. He was always over the top. I'd gotten used to surprise hugs, but it wasn't just me because he did it with everyone. Going out of his way for everyone made Remy happy. If he had it to give, he wouldn't hesitate. Time, money, nothing appeared too much for him. His selflessness had put me on edge at first. I wasn't accustomed to someone not having an angle; I'd spent too many years as a cop.

"You need to bring the kids to the house to play with Romeo. He's missed them."

"I'm sure the house horse was glad to see the kids go." Carol giggled.

"He likes kids. We go almost weekly to the hospital to visit the children's ward, but we've missed the last few weeks because of work."

"Is there anything sweet you don't do?" RJ asked.

"I gotta lot of time on my hands."

"Find yourself a boyfriend," RJ said with a smile, as he studied the video game in his hands that Remy had given him, and I stared at Remy.

He'd never said he was gay. Yet the rumors around the precinct said he was, but that chain of gossip wasn't always trustworthy. Between us, the subject never came up, but apparently, both my kids knew and didn't care. I wouldn't have cared if he'd told me. He was a great guy, and I loved him as my partner.

"I wish, but the one I want is kinda not interested. We've talked about this, RJ. Maybe one day. Forty-six is past the sell-by date anyway. Men my age kinda get left on the shelf."

"What about that guy I set you up with from the gym?" Carol asked.

"That was a no-go. Apparently, bellies aren't his thing. It was a fun date, though. Nice to get out of the house. Only so much you can read and clean or go over case files."

An annoyed sounding throat clearing had me jerking my

gaze to my ex-wife. The tension had amped up in her shoulders, and I knew her family had raised her in a strict Catholic home. I was surprised when they agreed to allow us to date in high school after our feelings had shifted from friends to more.

"I better get going. My house is a wreck from Christmas prep and all the care packages. There's a bottle of scotch calling my name, too. My ex sent it to me for Christmas along with pictures of his new baby."

"Harry had a new one? I thought they just had the one a few years ago." Carol frowned as she spoke, and I wondered who Harry was and if she'd met him.

"Yeah, look." He laid Becca in the cradle of his legs and pulled out his phone. He seemed to be scrolling through images until he got to the ones he wanted. "Isn't she amazing? A little over ten pounds. I felt so sorry for their surrogate. Harry and Tim can't produce a baby under linebacker status. They told me next vacation I had to go see them. Video calls just aren't the same." RJ snatched the phone before Remy could put it away and said how cute the baby was.

Remy played with and teased Teddy and Becca, but Samson, my middle grandchild was shy, and I thought Remy was a bit too loud for him, so he stayed close to my daughter-in-law. I saw how he reluctantly returned Becca to her seat. I opened my mouth to ask him to stay, at least to hang out. Except for his volunteer stuff, he always spent most of his time alone.

Carol rolled to her knees and wrapped her arms around Remy's neck. His eyes closed as if he were savoring the contact. "You already ate, but we have a ton of food. You can hang out; have dessert, and we'll send you home with leftovers. You'll be home in plenty of time to act all domestic. No reason for you to spend the holiday alone."

"If I wouldn't be a bother. Romeo should be good for a little while longer. We didn't make it to the park for his run this morning. So much to do, but I planned to go for a run this evening."

"Then it's settled." She kissed his scruffy cheek.

I covered my smile with my hand as he retrieved Becca from her seat, and that's where she stayed the rest of the evening cuddled in his arms. My grandkids were catered to, and he even helped feed them so their parents could get a break.

I'd never allowed a partner into my personal life before. Work was work, and home was home. It started with a beer after work, watching a game at my place, and an invite to dinner with my kids. How I'd missed how big a part of my family he'd become shocked me. My last partner I had, we'd been assigned to each other for a decade and never once had he even met my family.

What it meant I didn't know, but he always seemed alone. He went above and beyond for everyone. Treated every person he met with the utmost respect, no matter how filthy or foul-smelling, they all received the biggest and longest hugs. Yet while I'd allowed him into my family and started to consider him a friend, he didn't share anything with me.

That shouldn't matter, but it did.

REMY

COLD CASE
UNIT

I sat crossed-legged in the middle of the interrogation room table as we kept going over the same information on the case. The forensic evidence was taking forever to analyze. It didn't help I'd just pissed off the boss at the lab. Wouldn't be the first time. He and I butted heads since he put the evidence from one of my cases on the back burner because he didn't feel the victim was important enough to rush the tests.

"Call him?" I rested my elbows on the inside of my knees, cupped my chin in my upraised palms, and batted my lashes at my irritated partner.

"I think you trying to loosen his very expensive dental work at the Christmas party says we're not getting any favors. He lost a tooth, I think. That veneer sticks out like a sore thumb."

"I tripped. I had too much to drink. It was a complete accident."

"Remy."

I suppressed a shiver at his stern tone. "I hit him. You didn't."

"You're my partner and friend. I'm guilty by association." He lifted to sit on the table beside me, and I closed my eyes to inhale the scent of his body wash.

Robert never wore cologne at work, but whatever soap he used was sexy as hell. I wanted to ask what brand he bought. Normal men didn't ask their coworkers what scents they used with the intention of using the soap to get off in their shower. To be honest, I wanted his smell on me and not because I bought the one he used.

"He deserved it."

"You can't hit him every time they don't run your samples as soon as they hit the lab."

"He skipped Shine's rape kit to take on that higher-profile case with the rich boy." To be honest, it's a wonder I'd stayed a cop as long as I had. Hypocrisy was a major point of contention with the profession I chose. Sad thing was that's one of the reasons I decided to join the academy; I'd wanted to make a difference.

"I didn't say he was right. I just said you can't try to destroy his teeth."

I huffed and brought my attention back to the board. We had a double murder. They had long sheets for drug offenses, mostly distribution. We had several suspects, but we just needed the DNA run.

"What are we doing for dinner?" I asked.

"What do you want? It's Friday night. It's usually Chinese."

"My place or yours?"

"Wanna be fancy and eat there?"

"Really, like a real date? Aw, Daddy, I didn't know you felt that way."

He grinned and shook his head. "I'll even pay for dessert."

"Just to let you know, I don't put out on the first date."

"No dessert then." I gasped, and he chuckled. "Why didn't you ever tell me? We've been partners for almost two years."

"I don't know. It never came up. I haven't been dating anyone so it didn't seem important since you wouldn't be meeting a boyfriend or whatever." That was only partially true. I'd had a few partners in the past who had an issue working with a gay man. Attraction or no attraction, I liked him and didn't want him to treat me differently.

"You told my kids."

"They saw me coming out a bar one night with a date and saw us kissing." I didn't want to admit that I hadn't participated in said kiss and that me and the guy had parted ways right after the introductions. "Does it bother you that I'm gay?" I'd held my breath as I waited for his answer.

"No, why should it?"

"I had a few partners that asked not to work with me. I get along with you...we're friends, not just partners. And I like this. I didn't want to fuck that up."

"It's fine, Remy. Nothing changes. Did you know I was adopted?"

"No, you never talk about your parents."

"They were older, could never have kids, so they adopted me from Pakistan when I was a few years old. They were already coming up on fifty. The brown kid with the Jewish parents in a predominately white neighborhood, I kinda stuck out. I never got bullied in the community but outside it, let's just say it wasn't fun."

"I wondered where you got the name Kauffman from, and why do you celebrate Christmas?"

"Gladys isn't Jewish. She's Catholic."

"Married a Catholic girl. Had a thing for those schoolgirl outfits? I think my legs are too hairy for one, but I could—" I snorted as he pushed my arm.

"All I'm saying is I know what it's like to get ostracized for something you can't help. Me? It was the color of my skin, and for you, it's being gay. We're good, and if you do start dating someone, you can talk about him."

"Thanks. I'm not the dating sort. And like I told your kids, guys my age aren't exactly sought after in the gay dating game."

He rolled his eyes at me. "You're only forty-six."

"Way past my prime."

"Someone would be lucky to have you."

"Keep talking like that, Daddy, I'd think you were interested." I winked, and again, he snorted at me.

"This new flirty attitude of yours is going to get you in trouble."

"I don't know about that, sometimes getting in trouble has perks. There's spankings and..."

"And you can stop there."

"Such a prude, Daddy."

He just ignored me, and I wasn't offended at all. He'd always been that strong silent type; mysterious in a way. I'd found it strangely comforting since I met him. Handsome or not, he was perfect in every way, from his serene demeanor to his intelligence. If a man didn't have all the good things inside him, then he could be ugly. I knew all about how the physically flawless could be stained by depravity.

I pushed my past to the back of my brain before it had a chance to intrude. Other than my psychiatrists and doctors, I'd never spoken about my life to anyone. Not even with the men I'd dated for semi-long-term relationships. Harry didn't even know, and maybe that's why I hadn't experienced anything but a small hurt.

The only other people who knew my past were in the community I'd joined. People who were just like me. Runaways and outcasts who found their place—our family. Those connections had served me well, and I paid them back at every opportunity.

"Let's get dinner. Staring at this board isn't going to help us out any. I'll even spring for dessert."

"Now, you're speaking my language." I dropped my feet to the floor and stood up, then I stretched my stiff back. I grabbed our jackets, handed him his, and I followed him through the building. We didn't stop to talk or socialize with anyone we met up with. I think we were the most anti-social team in that precinct.

"We got time to stop and check up on Shine after dinner?"

"Sure. She still staying in the safehouse you arranged?"

"She'll stay there for a while just until the trial, or I can make better arrangements. I need to hit the store first, so if you want to just drop me off. We can just meet up when I'm done."

"No. We can take care of all that. No need for you to order a car to drive you everywhere. What does she need?" he asked as he pulled out onto the main road.

"She needs some dressier clothes for court. Some personal care items. I know she likes those dollar romance novels you can get at those everything for a dollar stores. Cheesier, the better. We used to joke about them while she sat in my cruiser while I was on breaks, and we were both reading one. So dog-eared and spines so split it was surprising they held together."

"You don't talk about your past."

"It's not worth talking about." I forced myself not to tense up at the phantom pains still as agonizing as they were when they happened. I didn't want to remember. Didn't want to deal with it, but I had no choice in the memories. They were always there. They'd etched themselves into my flesh and brain—in my nightmares.

"If you ever want to talk, you know I'll listen."

There was the quiet confidence that made everything better when I was with him. He'd become like a security blanket, safe and warm, something I'd never had growing up or even when I reached adulthood. Nothing had ever made the memories stop. Didn't cease the flinch of an unsuspected touch on my back.

"Thanks." It's all I could say. Explanations weren't possible with my past. No one would understand the hell I'd lived in until I was twenty-six and someone cared enough to step in. I hadn't lived the safest or law-abiding life, and Robert was so clean he squeaked. There were a lot of reasons for him to view me differently, and I didn't want that.

"So, you want to shop first or eat first?"

"Shop. Maybe I can get Shine something to go. She's been complaining her guard can't cook. She's starving. I'd agree with her. His cooking is barely a step up from possible food poisoning."

"Then we have a plan. Just tell me where."

I gave him directions to a thrift store that was near one of those discount places. They knew me by name since around the holidays and once a month, I pretty much bought out sections of their store. I was comfortable, but I wasn't rich, so sometimes I went without to make sure the street kids had what they needed. I could deal with it. I had a house, food in my fridge—I was fine.

ROBERT

COLD CASE
UNIT

Three hours of shopping and dinner, I was past ready to go home, but Remy had gone through the stores like a madman on a mission. He'd held up each item in the thrift store with a critical eye. Muttered to himself every couple of minutes. He said Shine could alter anything, but he just needed to find things that would hold up to being torn apart and made anew.

At the discount store we'd stopped at after the clothes shopping, every person in the place greeted Remy by name. He did the same, asked about kids, families, partners, and I could see that to them, he was more than a customer. He'd explained that's where he picked up the goody bag items he gave away at holidays and kept some in his trunk for emergencies.

He was an amazing guy, but every time I asked about his past, he'd visibly tensed. I wanted to push out of my natural curiosity but didn't believe it would do me any favors with him.

When we arrived, I'd seen a side of him I'd never noticed before. Yes, I'd seen the compassion and the connection he had with the victims—with the street kids we encountered, but this was different. I'd overheard bits and pieces of Remy's conversation with Shine.

"I feel dirty, but I can't..." Shine barely stroked the limp, oily strands of her dark, heavy hair.

I was shocked by her appearance. I'd seen her around; interacted with her. She was sassy and bold. Even in the hospital, she'd kept her chin up—defiant. Like with a lot of the survivors we met during cases, it doesn't hit them until later. We didn't even work sex crimes or the special victim's unit. She knew Remy and had called him.

"What do you say, love, if I stay with you? You can bathe, I can wash your hair. We can just lock the world away. I know you feel dirty. It's something soul-deep you know will never completely disappear. The phantom pains and demons will linger in some ways. But right now, just you and me, a bath, what about I read you your new book?"

Her only answer had been a head nod, and he'd helped her to her feet, sent me a silent sorry about our night extending, but I waved him off. I settled onto the couch. If anyone needed us, they could call or text. I doubted the lab was going to do much more over the weekend. They already worked at a snail's pace on a regular day.

I frowned as a man only introduced as Boss, a squat guy with a thick neck and shaved head motioned me to get up and follow him. For all his lack of height, he was terrifying. He placed his index finger to his lips and leaned back against the wall outside the bathroom. He smiled as he listened to the conversation coming through the crack in the door.

Remy was reading one of the novels he'd picked up for Shine as I heard the soft whisper of water against the side of the tub.

"Do you think the romance is about the meet or the chemistry?" Shine asked and interrupted Remy.

"The story is all about the meet-cute, Shine. It's the pinnacle moment of any romance."

"No, no, yes, the meet is important, but it's about the chemistry. I mean, you can want to jump some dude you just met out of lust, a quick one-off for the fun of it, but some people you have to get to know first before the attraction hits. Fiction runs parallel to reality. They don't always intersect, even when the story is based in some element of reality. Fiction is all about escapism, especially romance."

Remy let out a heavy sigh. "So, we're supposed to suspend our belief to think that love at first sight actually happens?"

"Pretty, don't tell me you haven't fallen in love at first sight. Because I call bullshit. You're the romantic type. You've talked about nothing else but finding a man, settling down, and having babies."

There was a long pause in the conversation, and for some reason, I held my breath. I'd seen him interact with my kids and grandkids, saw the gentle way he treated them. His full focus on the grandkids was as if he wanted to make sure they were safe and happy. Yet, I'd noticed a bit of hurt in his gaze when he talked about his ex-boyfriend having children.

"Okay, I admit to fond feelings for someone, but I don't know if I'd classify that as love at first sight. I did date Harry for almost two years."

"You're skewing the proof, and Harry was not going to settle down with you."

"Thank you so much, you paragon of positivity."

I covered a snort at his snarky reply and heard her soft laughter.

"You know that's not what I meant. Harry was that thing you used not to be bored. Sex was routine. There was never a moment of ripping your clothes off in passion. He wouldn't even move in when you asked him to."

"He liked his space."

"A man who wants to be with you doesn't care about space, especially when there's dirty, sweaty sex involved. Which you told me Harry was as vanilla as they came."

"Life isn't a romance novel. It's not walking into a room and spotting someone, and it hits you that they're your soulmate. Reality doesn't work that way, and also, sex isn't everything."

"Who says?"

"You're frustrating."

"Read me the damn book." I could picture Shine's signature eye roll. She used it a lot around Remy.

He started reading again, and I was once again motioned to follow Boss to the other room.

"Those two and their conversations."

"Have they always been like that?"

"Yeah. I've been around these streets longer than I want to admit. I knew Remy when he was this twinky pretty boy that had all the men and some women lusting over jailbait."

"Remy isn't a pretty boy."

"I beg to differ." He pointed to a picture on the wall, and as I approached, he pointed to a thin, beautiful young man in the front. "He'd just turned eighteen that night. We had a big party for him."

"He's been around here that long?"

"Longer. But not my story to tell. He's a good kid, still is, even if he doesn't believe it. The kids around here trust him, and that doesn't happen, especially between homeless kids and cops. He's known, so he gets a free pass, and you, too, I think. You're safe by association."

"How is Shine doing?" I asked as he opened the fridge and grabbed a beer. I shook my head as he offered me one.

"She's okay. She's tough. It'll just take a while to get back to her old self. She was about to leave the game. Found a good job with benefits. Seeing some guy who worked in finance. She hasn't made contact since the gang rape. Got this thought in her head that this was life's way of telling her what her place is in the world. Called bullshit, but she has to work it out for herself. I can just give her a place to heal."

"Nice of you to let her stay."

"Oh, honey, this is what I do. I own this building. I have five apartments blocked off for this purpose. They come to me hurt, junk sick, sometimes just simply in trouble. I take care of them. Clean up their vomit. Change their clothes when they piss or shit on themselves. They're my babies while they're here with me. Get them back on their feet, and I give them a choice...back to the streets or something safe. They choose that something safe, Remy and I use our contacts to get jobs, pool our money for a few new interview outfits."

"What about the ones who go back out onto the streets?"

"They have our numbers. They come running when they need to. Sometimes you have to go beyond rock bottom to find your way out."

"He doesn't talk much about his past. We've been partners for almost—"

"Two years. He talked about you and your kids, especially the grandkids. You'd think they were his."

I smiled to myself at a memory of Christmas. That was the last time we were all together, but in my gut, I knew he'd seen my children since. Something had come up at the last few family dinners. Emergency calls he never gave me details about. I sensed he wanted to keep me away from his past.

"The partner before you was a massive asshole. Took him forever to get reassigned. He was sad the day they moved him out of Special Victims."

"He's passionate no matter what unit he's working."

"He's like a dog with a fucking bone. Sometimes to the detriment of his safety."

"You talking about shit you shouldn't, Boss?"

I spun at the harsh sound of Remy's voice. In the years I'd known him, I hadn't heard that tone from him.

"Ain't my place to tell...him your business, now is it?"

"There's takeout coming for her. She's going to try to sleep after she eats. Call me if she needs me."

17

"You'll be the first one. Let me talk to you for a minute." Boss glanced at me. "Alone."

"I'll wait outside, Remy. Take your time." I told Boss it was nice to meet him and said a quick goodbye to Shine when I passed her on my way to the door.

As soon as I pulled the door closed and heard the lock click, angry voices rose on the other side. Instead of leaving, I leaned against the wall across from the door in case I needed to knock it down. The voices slowly died down, but I didn't relax until Remy appeared.

"You okay?"

"Yeah, you ready to go home?"

I could tell he didn't want to talk about what happened, and again, I didn't want to push. We all had shit that we didn't want to relive, but it didn't sit right with me that he wouldn't tell me what was going on with him. I knew he was stressed about Shine's case, and the lack of urgency on getting the guys put away. Not to mention our own stalled homicide. "Way past this old man's bedtime."

"You're so decrepit."

"You want me to take you home and pick you up in the morning or take you to get your vehicle?"

"Picking me up in the morning is fine. I gotta get home to Romeo. My neighbor's grandson puts him out when he gets home from school and plays with him a bit, but he doesn't like being home alone so long."

"No problem. You know I'm always up super early."

I motioned him toward the front exit and followed behind the bigger man. I bit my tongue on demanding answers; that wasn't my place. He was a grown man taking care of himself long before we'd become friends. Although, on the way to his house, his quietness was out of character for him, which made me worry that something was going on. He'd tell me if he needed my help; I'd just needed to deal with that.

4

REMY

COLD CASE
UNIT

I pathetically succumbed to my post-orgasm sob-fest as I stared at the ceiling with my legs still pulled back to my chest. The big dildo partially buried in my ass and my shame covering the hairy curve of my belly. How the fuck could you feel full and empty at the same time? I removed my toy, wiped the lube from between my cheeks, and wrapped my dildo in the towel under my ass. I tossed the bundle over the edge of my bed and heard it land with a muffled thump.

My throat was still sore from screaming his name, *Robert*, begging him to tell me he loved me. At the thought, more tears flowed from the corners of my eyes and into my silver-streaked hair. Why the hell did I do this to myself? Fall in love with the straight ones or the unattainable. The men who'd date me and then find the loves of their life after leaving me. I'd even introduced Harry to Tim, and it was love at first sight.

It had taken a bit to get over that one, especially when Harry called to tell me they were having their first child a few years previously. I'd been the one who wanted kids. Harry hadn't wanted the responsibility. I'd congratulated him, and even after a while, his happiness when showing off his first eased the pain.

Pain was something I was used to. My earliest memory in life was learning not to scream. I silently endured because it was the only way it stopped. My silent suffering didn't feed their sadistic need to break me. My first memory was the crack of a whip or belt, the displacement of air only a whisper of warning before it met my back, bottom, and thighs.

Eighteen years of unending torture soothed a bit by me not becoming them. I wasn't an angry person. I'd never lifted my hand to another creature in my life except for the lab director, but the sanctimonious bastard had deserved to be called out on his bullshit. I volunteered. I made people happy. Yet, I didn't know if I was. Normally, I controlled myself better, but the situation with Shine frayed the edges of my calm.

My argument with Boss hadn't helped any. The nosy old Queen knew better than to talk about my business. Very few people knew about my secret obsession—my love for my straight partner. I'd cried into my beer more than once when talking with my old friend. I knew the older man meant well. He'd tried to talk me into confessing to Robert, but I couldn't do that.

The minute I'd met Robert, my first day in homicide, the beautiful older man caught my attention even before we were introduced. His hair was the perfect blend of salt and pepper, he had laugh lines beside his dark eyes, and even with his neatly trimmed beard, you could see the deep dimples in his cheeks. I'd fallen in love at first sight, and then it all came crashing down when he was introduced as my partner.

I'd kept myself under control. I'd never been in the closet, but the ring on his finger said he was taken. I'd asked how long he'd been married, and he'd told me he was divorced almost a year. My heart broke because he had to love her to still wear his ring, but one day it had disappeared. I didn't mention it.

Another reason I had kept my feelings and sexuality to myself was his family had become mine. Children and grandchildren, and sadly that had made me want him more. Watching the loving way he cared for them. He never raised his voice and always praised them. I'd even been there when Becca was born. One of the first to hold her, and she'd been perfect. My happiness was tempered by the pain of what I'd never have.

We had a friendship I wouldn't ruin. I'd nearly panicked when RJ had told me to get myself a boyfriend at Christmas. Awaited the awkwardness that would come from the revelation, but while he'd looked shocked, our relationship hadn't changed. He even took my flirting with a teasing smile. We still had a beer after work and had a standing *date* night for Chinese. I still came to family dinner a few times a month. I saw his kids more than he did.

I groaned as my alarm went off and I rolled from bed, picked up the towel with my toy inside. On the way to my bathroom, I took a deep breath. I knew I was pathetic, but I still wanted him to love me. I just had to remind myself that he wasn't mine to want.

Romeo barreled into my room at hearing my alarm and sprawled his massive, long-legged body out on my bedroom floor. He lived by his routine. My alarm brought him to my room. He'd lie outside the bathroom while I showered. While I fixed his breakfast, he'd run around the backyard. Afterward, he'd go take up the entire sofa to wait for his playtime with the neighbor's grandson. He knew when I got home from work we'd go for an hour-long run or walk, depending on what he felt like.

We both were attached to our schedules, and we rarely varied unless I was on a case and I had a long list of people who'd walk him for me. Romeo huffed hard enough his jowls vibrated, and he stared at me with sad eyes.

"Don't huff at me, I know, but I'm only a few minutes late." I removed the dildo from the towel, cleaned and stored it in one of the drawers.

Thankfully I wasn't high maintenance. I was showered,

dressed, fed the dog, and was out the door within an hour. My phone beeped as I slid into the driver's seat of my SUV.

Robert: *You on your way? Lab results are due any minute.*

Remy: *Pulling out now.*

Robert: *Get off the damn phone, Remy!*

I'd grinned as I threw my phone aside after reading his text in his voice. All sexy and stern, that voice of his would get me in trouble one of those days. The drive across the city had taken a bit longer as I hit the early morning rush hour. That's what I got for buying a house on the edge of the city with good schools and a park; not that I needed either except for taking my dog for his run.

I drove around to the back of the building and pulled into the underground authorized parking. I parked next to Robert's assigned vehicle. Once I pulled the handle and pushed the door open, I slid out and strode toward the elevator. I rode up to the fifth floor, and Robert was waiting.

"What did I do now?" I asked as I took in his irritated expression.

"What did I tell you about your phone?"

"Um, *get off the damn phone, Remy,* do I need to—"

"Don't be a smartass."

"I wasn't even moving. Hell, I hadn't started it yet." I batted my lashes.

"Cute isn't getting you out of being bitched at."

I let out a huff as I walked around him to walk to my desk. He was right on my heels. "What did the report say?"

"We got a hit on one of the samples. The other wasn't in the system. Lance Marstrell. Two-time felon, got off on a technicality for his third about a year ago." He handed me the file, and I took it to flip through the pages. "His last known address is in there. I already called his Parole Officer. He said Marstrell is living with his girlfriend. Problem is, him and our vic are known associates. The DNA could've been left in the apartment at any time."

"Do I get to be bad cop this time when we go to talk to them?"

"What happened last time you did that?"

"The suspect gave me his phone number."

"It was the set-up for a bad porn."

"Now, now." I leaned in close. "Watch a lot of porn, Daddy? No, no, I don't think my innocent ears could take it."

"You're a pain in the ass." I opened my mouth to make a comment, and he arched a thick brow, and I snapped my teeth closed so quickly they clicked. "I thought so. No bad cop for you."

"Shame, I've seen you play the bad cop."

"Get your shit together, and let's go. And no hitting on the bad boys. It's probably why you're single."

I gasped and pouted, let my lip start quivering.

"One damn tear and I'm going alone."

"Fine. When did you get so mean?" He rolled his eyes and spun me back toward the elevator. As much as I worried about Robert finding out, I felt more relaxed, but didn't want to let my guard down too much. He was too smart not to notice the way I looked at him—how I craved his presence.

We silently took the elevator back to the garage and got in the car. Joking around was normal for us. It relieved the stresses of the job, but we were going into the interview with no information other than knowing the man was a two-time felon. While most of the suspect's charges were drug-related, we knew that could change if he got high on his own supply. Would he be alone? Unlike some of my former partners, Robert had my back, and I felt safe. And safety meant everything to me.

5

ROBERT

COLD CASE
UNIT

We stood at the trunk of the car, removed our jackets, and slipped on our vests. We were just going in for information, but we never took that lightly. As homicide detectives, we sometimes came up against the worst of the worst. Most of them were looking at capital murder charges. Things could go wrong at any moment, especially when they felt they were backed against the ropes. The few times we'd come into contact with Marstrell, he had an attitude but nothing crazy for a felon dealing with the cops.

"You ready?" I asked as I checked to make sure his vest was tight enough. I didn't understand this overwhelming need to watch over him—to protect him.

"Yeah, we're just here to talk. That's your area, that pretty face of yours." I batted his hands away as he attempted to pinch my cheeks.

"Get your ass inside," I ordered and waited until he turned away from me to smile. The man was a pain in the ass, but he'd become my best friend. Other than Gladys, I didn't think I'd ever had a best friend.

I followed him up the stone steps and through the squeaky

front double doors and took in the broken lock. We checked the bank of mailboxes, and the girlfriend's last name was on the plate for 4B.

"Hope you got your cardio done this morning, old man. Walk-up."

"I was already at the gym this morning while you were probably still in bed."

"You saying I'm getting fat?" He glanced over his shoulder at me and arched a thick, dark brow.

"We're not arguing." I pointed toward the stairs, and we slowly jogged up to the fourth floor. We'd done this a hundred times, so we worked as a seamless unit. Everything was natural and easy. That didn't mean the nerves didn't start building in my gut, and Remy's joking manner disappeared as we ascended the stairs. There was a faint aroma of food cooking, the pungent scent of weed, and it grew stronger as we stepped onto the fourth-floor landing.

We stopped in front of the door with crooked numbers, the B held on by a prayer, and I raised my hand to knock. We were just there to talk and feel out the situation. No one answered, and I didn't hear any movement inside.

"Robert."

I glanced at him as he said my name and motioned to the door behind us with a nod, and I turned to find apartment C's door ajar. "Want to check it out?"

"I'll take point," he said as he reached for his holster and removed his sidearm. I followed suit, and he took the two steps. He knocked, and the door opened a few more inches. "Police. Is there anyone in there?"

After I called in our location, he looked toward me, I nodded, and he entered. I stayed close as we moved through the apartment clearing rooms.

"Did you hear that?" he asked as he made his way toward the last room, which I assumed was a second bedroom.

"I didn't hear anything," I whispered as we paused outside the door.

I trusted Remy and prepared to clear the last room. His chest expanded with one last deep breath, and I used my fingers to countdown from three. We entered a cluttered room. It carried the stench of body odor and piss so badly my nose wrinkled, but the room was empty. I froze as there was a rustling sound from the closet. He aimed as he reached for handle, and as he turned the knob in slow motion, I moved to the side.

I held my breath, I forced my hands not to clench around my weapon, and he threw open the door. All I heard was a gasp at whatever my partner found in the closet. I opened my mouth to ask what he'd found when the door banged back against the wall. I saw frightened eyes staring back at me from a large pile of laundry, and Remy started to fall to his knees as I sensed we weren't alone and spun to find two men with weapons storming into the apartment.

I slammed the door as I yelled for him to get down and then identified ourselves. The automatic fire shredded the cheap door, and I returned fire. There was nowhere to hide, and all I could think was to protect my partner. For a second, our eyes met as he dove to protect the child, and I tried to buy us time.

Everything slowed down until I could see the bright flashes of muzzle fire. I spared one more glance as I saw him take one round to the center of his back. After that, everything was fiery pain and then suffocating darkness as if the assailants piled onto me. There was a call for officers down as I tried to fight my way out from under the weight. Yet the more I fought, the more intense the pain grew. How much harder it took to draw in more air into my lungs. I swore I felt lips surrounded by a soft beard brush my temple.

Police bellowed as a firefight sounded as if it came from underwater. I tried to call Remy's name, but my mouth wouldn't form the word. Panic took over, and I tried again to open my mouth. Remy, my kids, and grandkids filled my mind—someone needs to watch them for me.

"Detective Kauffman, can you hear me? Squeeze Remy's hand if you can."

I tried to answer. I couldn't feel a hand in mine. Someone repeatedly yelled at me, and then I heard and felt nothing but the pain slowly dragging me under.

6

REMY

COLD CASE
UNIT

Hours ago, I'd called in the code for officers down, and at that moment, the world had slowed down. Blood dried on my skin, and panic had long set in as I kept staring at the entrance to the emergency room. Robert had covered me as I cleared the apartment with the suspiciously open door. The whimpering from a closet had distracted me. I'd heard the shot seconds before fire exploded across my upper back, and adrenaline had made me spin. I could still see the momentary shock on Robert's face as the automatic rifle and muzzle fire filled the apartment we'd made entry into. His vest had been shredded by the armor-piercing rounds. The shooter wasn't even the suspect we came to interview.

The last thing I'd remembered was covering his body with mine as I tried to protect him and the toddler I'd found locked in the closet. As soon as I became their shield, I hadn't cared about me. No one would've mourned me more than to place flowers on a grave. Robert and the baby had shit to live for.

"Remy!" Carol yelling my name brought me out of my stupor. I caught her in my arms, and then RJ was right there, too.

"What happened?" RJ demanded.

"Two shooters. One had armor-piercing rounds. He's in surgery. That's all they'll tell me, but with a promise to update me when they know more."

"Are you okay?"

I didn't get a chance to answer Carol. "Detective Bosley, will you let us check you out now?" A nurse barreled across the waiting room. I'd put her off until her irritation with me showed clearly on her face.

"You didn't get checked out?" RJ stared at me, and that's the moment I realized he noticed the blood. Most of it was Robert's, but some mine. I was spun, and I knew what they saw, my shredded dress shirt. The shooters were so tweaked out they hadn't aimed well enough. A few inches higher, I would've been dead.

"I've had wo—"

Carol and RJ, with the nurse, dragged me through the automated doors to an exam room. I closed my eyes to wait for the reaction as they removed my shirt and undershirt. The gasps were all I needed to hear as they took in my body littered with scars. I never went shirtless, not even with my past lovers, and if I did, I never gave them my back. My heavily inked body hid a lot of the damage—some if it was self-inflicted from decades of self-harm.

"Remy." My name broke off in a sob.

"Carol." I reached out and grabbed her by the back of her neck to pull her close. "I'm a survivor. Don't worry about me." I kissed her temple as she shook her head. I sent RJ a pleading look, and he dragged Carol off to find information about Robert.

I was barely conscious of them getting x-rays and clearing me. I sat alone in the exam room waiting for the discharge papers and had made calls about the little girl we'd found. At some point, I'd answered some questions from Captain Tyson and internal affairs. Nurses and doctors pled with me to stay overnight for observation, but I told them no, that I'd sign whatever I needed. If they were so concerned, they'd find me somewhere in the hospital with my partner.

"Detective Bosley?" A pretty middle-aged woman entered as I pulled a scrub top over my head.

"Yes, ma'am."

"I'm Fran Grier with Child Protective Services."

"How's the little girl?"

"Alive because of you, but she has some...it's one of the worse cases of neglect and abuse I've had to deal with. I was told you made a call about taking her in. Seems you have some pretty powerful friends."

I ignored the comment about powerful friends because I didn't want to explain why I'd had them in the first place. A lot of my past was easily searchable. Yet I preferred some things remained secret.

"Yes, ma'am. I'm registered as an emergency foster parent who specializes in children with trauma. I want her, Ms. Grier." It had been almost two years since I'd taken in a foster. It just became too hard to let them go to homes or reuniting with biological families. I wanted the little girl, not to just heal her but for keeps. When I'd looked into her eyes, I'd seen me at four, ten, fifteen, broken and damaged, unwanted, and I never wanted her to feel that way again.

"She'll be here a while, detective. They're estimating her age at about four, but she's extremely emaciated and nonverbal. We have to do home visits and your job—"

"My neighbor has a home daycare. Her late husband was a cop, and we have a deal—"

"We can take care of all that after you rest. What's your damage?"

I waved off her concern. The pain I felt right then didn't compare to my past. "Deep bruising. I took about six to the back as I laid over her and my partner." Tears stung my eyes, but I turned away to gather up my ruined shirts and threw them in the trash.

"I have all your contact information. Carmen, that's the girl's name. Her mother arrived at the apartment after a friend in the building let her know the cops had taped off her place. She was put into custody for alleged child neglect and abuse. Carmen's doctor said she'll be here for at least a week. We have to do—"

"I want to be there for her exam. She won't understand, but I will." My expression must have shown I wasn't going to back down.

"Very well. We're moving her up to the pediatric floor. I'll meet you there. I'm sure you want to check on your partner."

I nodded as she left me alone, and I shoved my phone, wallet, and badge into my pockets. After I was sure everyone was okay, I'd head home for at least a few things and fresh clothes. First I had more important things to attend to.

TWO HOURS LATER, Robert was still in surgery to repair damage to his shoulder and to remove bullets and check for internal damage. I tried to keep my shit together as I sat beside Carmen's bed and pushed her silky curls back from her face. Focusing on her kept me from thinking my partner could be dying a few floors away.

"Remy?" I glanced over my shoulder to find Carol in the doorway.

"Is he out of surgery?"

"Yeah, he'll be fine. The damage wasn't as bad as they thought, but they still have to check for nerve damage when he wakes up. He'll be in recovery for a bit and moved to a room. Is that her?"

"Yeah, this is Carmen. I wanted to be with her during her sexual assault exam and have her see a friendly face when she woke up. I've been through the exam, so I wanted to be able to help explain, but at this age, they don't really understand. It's just scary."

"Was she?"

"There was some bruising but doesn't appear there was long-term abuse or penetration. There was no internal scarring which would typically be present in a rape/molestation victim of this age."

"God, is she—"

"We'll be going home in a week or so."

"You're taking her in?"

"I'm certified for fostering children with severe trauma. Mine is a specialized home. I'll be taking some leave to get her settled and ease her into daycare, which I've already set up. Her social worker is pushing through the paperwork and home visits to make sure it's all ready by the time she's discharged."

"Remy, your—" Her voice broke, and I knew what she wanted to know.

"It's okay. It was a long time ago. You'd be surprised how much a person can take and still survive. Don't mention this to Robert, okay?"

"He won't judge you."

"But I don't want pity either. I'm always careful to keep my past to myself. I speak at support groups. I mentor and sponsor, but when I'm in my safe spaces, my home, with Robert or y'all, I need to be able to pretend I'm normal."

"I won't say a word to Dad. Do you want me to text you with his room number?"

I turned away and put my attention fully on Carmen. She was beautiful in a fragile way. Too small for her age. "Yeah, that would be great. They're giving her a light sedative and will ease her off them tomorrow. They said the best thing for her right now was to get plenty of rest. They're pushing a third bag of fluids, and they put in a feeding tube through her nose. She has a lot of growing to do."

My eyes slammed closed as arms wrapped around my neck from behind. "Thank you, Remy, but don't do it again. Me and my children would've missed you."

Before the tears started, her presence disappeared, and I breathed deep and even. I'd break down later when I had the time, alone where no one could see me. As long as Robert and Carmen were okay, everything else didn't matter.

7

ROBERT

COLD CASE
UNIT

My throat felt tight and dry, and everything I had hurt. I opened my eyes and was thankful to find the lights low. Dizziness made my vision blurry as I turned my head to find Carol and RJ curled up on a few cots. Remy was in a far corner with a tiny body draped over his chest. He held the child protectively even in his sleep.

"Hey." I turned my head to find Gladys in a chair beside the bed.

"Hey, what—" My voice cracked painfully, and a straw pressed to my lips. My memory was so fuzzy. The one thing I did remember was the impact of the bullet taking Remy down. He'd fallen forward and then nothing.

"You and your partner were clearing the apartment across the hall from your murder suspect. You two found the door open, identified yourselves, and then went inside to make sure everything was okay. Remy heard crying or something from a closet, you covered him, and then all hell broke loose apparently. He covered you and the child with his own body, a few inches higher, and one of the rounds would've severed his spinal cord."

"Is he?"

"His vest took most of the impact, a few flesh wounds. The shooter was high, and his aim wasn't what it would've been. The guy who fired on you had armor-piercing rounds. You'll be fine, but you're out of commission for a bit."

"Who's the baby?"

"That's Carmen. She was in the closet. She's supposed to be on the pediatric floor, but she won't sleep without Remy, and I think it's mutual because he's run himself ragged for three days between you and her. The Peds nurses know him, so one of them comes down every hour to check her. He completely covered you and her. I heard him tell one of the nurses when she fussed at him that no one would've mourned him if he died. No one should think that, but he was laughing when he said it. Carol and RJ were there when he was examined...he was covered in scars. It looked like someone put cigars out on his back. Whip marks. They think a lot more are hidden under all that ink he has."

I was about to talk when a terrified scream had everyone jumping up. Carmen was fighting Remy.

"Hey, it's just me. Look at me, sweetie. Listen to my voice." He had her face cupped in his huge hands. "There's my girl. It's okay to cry, but no one will ever touch you again." Too thin arms wrapped around his neck, and he was on his feet, pacing as he whispered to her as her whimpers died down.

"Remy, does she need a sedative?" A nurse popped in and then came up to them. She didn't touch the girl but turned her head to see Carmen's face.

"We're fine. Just a nightmare. We're becoming champions at kicking the night terror's asses."

"Watch the language. Your girl will sound like a drunken sailor. Took long enough for us to break you."

"I was only twenty. I've matured."

"Not much, though. Still a brat." She patted Remy's scruffy cheek, and then her attention was on me. "Robert, glad to see you're awake."

I groaned as everyone surrounded the bed. I soothed my children and asked where the kids were.

"They're being watched by Mrs. Walton, Remy's neighbor. And they're watching Romeo for Remy. They feel they're doing a very important job, but I need to go nurse Becca soon."

"Your temperature is normal, and your wounds look good." The nurse spoke, but I had my eyes locked on Remy who was standing well back from the crowd.

He looked lost and broken. I thought he was taking as much comfort from the child in his arms as she received from him.

"Remy, you want me to pick you up some clothes?" Carol asked.

"Yeah, thanks. There's a basket of laundry on the end of my bed. You should be able to find everything I need in there."

My eyes grew heavy, but I tried to keep them open. I wanted to know more. I wanted to demand answers from Remy. Yet my body had other plans.

NEXT TIME I opened my eyes the pain in my head was gone, and no one was in the room except Remy, who had Carmen laid on another bed they must have brought in. He was changing her diaper, and she was staring up at him. I smiled at the one-sided conversation as he spoke and paused as if she were answering him. He didn't baby talk to her.

"I know, I know, you're not a baby, but you're my baby. Once we're home, we'll get you a potty. You'll be a big girl in no time." She was wearing a shirt that looked to be one of Remy's t-shirts. "I haven't lost my diapering touch. Becca made sure of that." The tiny girl made grabby hands motion. "Yes, you can hold her again next time she visits. We have a big puppy at home. He's going to love you."

That's when I realized he was shirtless, and I saw what Gladys and Carol talked about. There was barely an inch of skin that didn't contain a scar. Some were highlighted more by the dark bruises. I counted the center of each one—seven rounds had struck his vest as he'd protected us. My tall, slender body would've been hidden completely by his bulk.

No one to mourn. My heart broke for him. He did so much for the people around him without expecting anything in return. He would've given up his life for me and a girl he'd seen for a matter of seconds. He straightened and turned to the side to expose a hair-covered torso and the paunch of his stomach that hadn't reached potbelly yet. He had her cuddled against his chest as she seemed to melt into him.

"Skin-to-skin contact is good for her. Helps the bonding process." He didn't look at me as he spoke. "First day or two was kinda rough. She's so touch starved, she's been a clingy little thing since yesterday. I don't mind."

"You should've taken her and ran."

"If you think I could've done that then you don't know me very well."

"Where is everyone?"

"I sent Gladys home to get some sleep. Carol and John are at my place with Teddy and Becca keeping Romeo company. RJ went home to see Leona and Sammie. They moved a bed in here for us to take naps on. Romeo gets me special treatment around here."

"Any idea when I'll get out of here?"

"A week or two as long as you don't spike a fever and you can take a walk around the floor. Once your shoulder is healed up enough, you'll have to start some physical therapy. Your guess is as good as mine about when they'll let you come back. I'm sure you'll be on desk duty for a bit."

He chuckled as I groaned. I'd broken my arm a year earlier, and being on a desk for a month nearly drove me insane.

"What about you?"

"I'll be taking some leave to get Carmen set up at my place and get a routine going before I try to introduce Mrs. Walton."

"You're fostering her?" I knew he mentioned he'd fostered a few times in the past but hadn't in a few years, I think, at least not since we became partners.

"Yes, with the intention of adopting. With her trauma, she'll be harder to place in a permanent home. That'll work in my favor, especially since I'm certified as a special needs parent. I have a degree in early childhood development and psychology. Did you want some water or juice? They keep the good shit in the nurse's lounge."

"I'd love some ice water."

"If you have any pain, you can push the button. I think they're allowing you a small dose every four hours to manage your pain."

I nodded as I stared at him and realized he still wasn't looking at me. I wanted to demand his attention. An explanation for his scars, his joke about not having anyone, I was his goddamn partner. Losing him would kill me not just because of that, but also as my friend. He put his life on the line for me. Would've sacrificed, almost had, for me and Carmen. I needed to know his story. His past. What had made him the man he was who cared for everyone to the detriment of himself?

He pushed the call button for the nurse and asked for some ice. The friendly voice said she'd be right there. I looked down to find his fingertips drawing up and down the sheet beside my hand. I caught two of his fingers and squeezed. When I brought my gaze up to his face, I saw his eyes were glassy with tears caught on his thick lower lashes. Then he was pulling away as someone knocked at the door, and a nurse in her twenties entered with a cup of ice.

She didn't stay long, just poured some water from a pitcher on the bedside table and handed me the cup. I took a careful sip and then turned my head to find Remy lying on the other bed.

The beautiful sleeping girl was sprawled over his chest. He had a blanket tucked around her, and he was just staring at the ceiling.

I wondered what he was thinking. Had the reality set in yet? The crash from the adrenaline hitting or did caring for her and me keep those at bay. When would the sweet, strong man break?

8

REMY

COLD CASE
UNIT

R obert had only been home a week after being in the
hospital for two. I'd seen an entirely different side to my
partner since getting him home. I massaged the little feet at my
hips as I jogged down the steps. No one else wanted to deal with
his temper. They'd ordered me to go ask him what he wanted for
dinner. He'd growled about throwing soup if we dared serve him
another bowl.

"Jesus Christ, that man is cranky." I stomped into the kitchen
with Carmen strapped to my back in a sari for her afternoon nap.

Gladys snorted where she was standing at the stove heating
up the soup she'd made for lunch that Robert had refused to eat.
She laughed and glanced over her shoulder at me. "I was married
to the man for over thirty years. Sick, hurt, or mildly
inconvenienced, he's a thorn in your side. I'm just glad he's your
problem now."

I tried to ignore the way she said that he was my problem
gave me a forbidden thrill. "I gotta go home. Romeo has probably
torn the house up by now. He's not used to being alone so much."

"Bring him here. Backyard is fenced in, but you're in charge of
the backyard messes."

"I couldn't do that. It'll be—"

She turned down the flames under the pot and turned to me, her arms crossed over her chest. "If you can leave the little koala here, we'll find some cartoons. I'm sure you and her need more stuff."

"As much as I appreciate it, she'll have to come with me. She still won't let anyone else hold her. I brought everything I got for her here, but I need clothes and to check my mail."

I didn't know how it happened, but everyone had moved into Robert's house. Everyone was sleeping on air mattresses in guest rooms, and I was staying in Carol's old room with Carmen. Romeo was going to my neighbor's or home with her son, but I couldn't keep doing that. Either I was going to have to go home or bring Romeo there.

"Well, the offer is open. If you want, I can run to your place."

"I don't want to be a bother, Gladys." At Christmas, I sensed she wasn't a fan of mine. She'd broken through the conversation of me finding a boyfriend.

"It's not a bother, Remy. Although, you probably need a bit of time out of this house."

"It's not that bad. I used to live in communal housing," A bit of a stretch of the truth but not by much. After I left home, I'd crashed in an abandoned house with a bunch of other homeless kids. We learned to co-exist. "I may have lived on my own for decades, but you never forget how to adapt."

"You've been good for Robert. You know that, right?"

"I don't know about that."

"I do. After the divorce, I know he was lost, and then our kids started mentioning that his partner was coming for Sunday dinners and you two were hanging out. He never did that with a partner before. Work and home were completely separate for him."

"Is that why you two divorced? It's hard being married to a cop, or at least that's what I've seen."

"No, I loved the man, still do, but more as a friend now. We got married way too young. Then after college and law school for me, the kids started coming. He joined the academy. Being a cop was always his dream. As the years passed and he made detective, we turned into roommates. It wasn't clear to what extent until the kids moved out. I had no complaints about our marriage except we went days without seeing each other. We didn't fight. He was faithful. We both deserved more than complacency and routine."

"Have you dated since the divorce?"

"A few times. The new guy I was seeing didn't really understand why I raced off to the hospital. He said it wasn't like I was married anymore. It's not like we were dating all that long, a few months. I thought this starting over thing would be easier than it was."

"What an asshole," I muttered, and I heard a little giggle behind me.

"You're going to have to watch that."

"If her first word is a cuss, at least she said something."

She shook her head at me. "You're doing a good thing. Carol and RJ always go on and on about all the things you do. I remember over Christmas."

"You didn't seem to like me very much."

"That wasn't it at all."

"You cleared your throat when it was brought up I was gay."

"I grew up in a very traditional and conservative home. Strict was an understatement. It took me a little by surprise. It was an involuntary reaction."

"I don't have my sights set on your ex."

"I doubt that, but whatever." I jerked my gaze to hers to find her smiling. "Robert is a very handsome man. Anyone would get a crush. Don't get so tense about it. Go do what you have to do. I'll stay here until one of the kids shows up, or you get back. But after that, I need to go home for a bit. My leave of absence ends tomorrow, and I need to get some work clothes and my work bag."

"I'll be back with Romeo in a few hours."

"Take your time. He'll be grumpy whether you're back in two hours or twelve."

I nodded and jogged back upstairs to grab my phone where I'd plugged it in that morning. I kept my phone, wallet, and keys in my hand as I peeked into Robert's room. He was reclined against the headboard and a pile of pillows. The arm was healing, but his shoulder was useless until he started working with the outpatient physical therapist.

"Hey." I leaned into his room.

"What's up?" He barely looked at me, but I didn't have the same inclination. He was shirtless, his chest covered with neatly trimmed black hair, and his subtly carved abs. Damn, a man his age shouldn't be rocking a six-pack and look so good with his thick salt and pepper hair.

"I'm going home."

He finally jerked his gaze to me. "For how long?"

"I don't think you need me here."

"Be quiet. You can't leave me here alone with *them*."

His expression said the thought of being left alone without a buffer with his family was horrifying in nature. All I could do was shake my head. It had to be weird to have your ex-wife move in along with your grown kids, daughter-in-law and son-in-law, and the grandkids. Not to mention your partner taking up residence with my foster daughter. He was probably more than a little overwhelmed.

"You're going to get Romeo and coming back, right?"

"If you don't mind, he's not used to being moved around so much."

"That's fine. You want me to keep Roo?"

"If that name sticks, we're gonna have issues!" I rolled my eyes at him as I tickled the bottom of Carmen's feet, loving the sound of her giggles. We still had a long way to go, but she'd started to feel safe and happy; that's all I wanted for her.

"She's always in her pouch like a baby kangaroo. It's a good name. Also, if you leave her, you have to come back."

"So, holding my daughter hostage is your plan?"

"Whatever works."

"No, I'm taking her with me." I nearly laughed at his irritated huff. "I'll be back. I just can't keep having a rotation of people in and out of my house to take care of my dog."

"Fine, you have an hour, not a minute more."

A grin tugged at the corners of my mouth and I entered his room. I slowly walked toward his bed and leaned over. I crawled up the mattress, and his narrowed eyes amused me. I straddled his legs. "You going to miss me, Daddy?"

"If I had the full use of my left arm right now…"

"You're cute when you're all grumpy and threatening to spank me."

"Go pick up Romeo and get your ass back home."

My chest tightened at what he said, but I shook it off since it was just a figure of speech. I should stay at my house when I got there. Constantly being in his space made everything worse with my attraction to him. I stiffened as he leaned forward and lifted his right arm. His breath then beard teased my scruffy cheek as he stroked Carmen's head through the makeshift sling.

As I turned my head away to avoid contact, I asked. "Want anything while I'm out?"

"My house back," he whispered.

"Let them have their time, Robert. This is your first major injury in the line of duty. They were scared."

He eased back with a grimace. His pain levels were manageable, but I had a feeling he pretended that he was better than he was. Most of the time, I'd call him on that. Yet, I also knew he was at the edge of his patience. I'd gotten adept at reading him during our partnership.

"I know, I do, and I appreciate all of it, but it's all just too much."

"It'll be fine. Give it another week, and they'll be back to their own lives. And then you'll be complaining they don't come around enough."

"Get out."

"Your mood swings make me dizzy." I slipped my right leg off the bed and straightened to swing my left over his legs.

"An hour, not a minute longer. Timer is running."

"Yeah, yeah, Daddy," I muttered as I walked out of his bedroom and toward the stairs.

All the way during the drive to my house, carrying on a one-sided conversation with Carmen, I debated the option of not returning. I'd never seen myself as much of a masochist, pain and humiliation weren't my kinks, but I couldn't stay away. Since almost losing him, my attraction, my stupid unrequited love, all of it was inflated. If Gladys noticed, did anyone else? And could I survive the inevitable revelation?

We'd go back to our regular lives soon; I could hold out for that long. I'd already done it for two years.

9

ROBERT

COLD CASE
UNIT

With my good hand, I rubbed Roo's soft hair as the sadist parading as a physical therapist rotated my shoulder to check my range of motion. Her tiny hands had a death grip on the sides of my t-shirt. Romeo was in the corner in protect mode, and I didn't know if it was for Carmen or me. Remy had a home visit planned for that afternoon and wanted to get everything set up, at least get a basic room ready for Carmen. Ms. Grier knew he'd been at my place helping me out, so she wasn't expecting miracles. She'd even stopped by a few times to check in. I hadn't reminded him I had a physical therapy appointment because he needed to focus on what he needed to do, and me and Roo were fine. I was the only other person she allowed to keep her.

"This would work better if you laid her down elsewhere?"

"I didn't ask you." My voice deepened as she held a bit tighter at the thought of being separated. She was getting better, but she usually relaxed when she knew Remy and I were in the house together. The little girl attached herself to me as soon as Remy had said goodbye, promising to be back and to be good for me. I wondered what would happen when Remy took her to her real home.

We were both keeping each other calm. Outside of Remy and family, I wasn't much on people touching me. I enjoyed my space. Every time the guy had me move or work my shoulder in a certain way, and I had to shift Carmen, I heard his annoyed huff. He'd learn quickly that Roo and my grandkids always came first in this house. And no amount of passive-aggressive tantrums were going to change that.

Not soon enough, my hour was up and I stayed sprawled on the floor and didn't bother saying goodbye. He couldn't get away fast enough. Quiet had been scarce recently. As much as I appreciated my kids and Gladys helping around the house, I couldn't remember the last time we'd all been together for that long. All of it made me miss when my kids were little and teenagers, chaos soothed me, but it also reminded me of how alone I'd become without Remy since my divorce.

I smiled as Roo completely relaxed on my chest, but I didn't stop rubbing her soft curls. Having her there was like when Carol and RJ were growing up. I missed my marriage, maybe not my marriage, but the having someone all mine. There'd even been a few dates, but they were just blind setups that I had no urge to repeat for a second. Remy was the only reason I didn't come straight home every night. We shared dinners or a beer after work.

"Was that your physical therapist I passed?"

I opened my eyes to find Remy looming over me with his hands on his hips. He had dark circles and bags under his eyes. I doubted he was getting much sleep between Roo and me, but he never complained.

"No, I was having an afternoon hookup." I grinned up at Remy as he glared at me.

"So the blond lean athletic look is your thing, huh?"

"Who knows? I might have developed a type."

"P.T. doesn't improve your mood. I'll make a note of that, too."

"You snitching on me to somebody?"

"Would I do that? Would I give all your secrets away?"

"If it was my kids or Gladys, yes, yes, you would." I wouldn't admit the truth to anyone, but I loved how he and Roo fit into my family, even with Gladys. He'd naturally became part of the group. And I didn't know what this compulsion I'd developed about keeping him was about.

"Ouch, you're just mean today. You want me to take her?" He crouched down, and I wrapped my good arm around her, and I lifted my head to see her peeking at him through the hair covering her face.

"No, we're good. How did everything go?"

"Good. I was able to get the new bed, mattress, and dresser in my vehicle after I folded the back seats forward. Got those put together, but everything else is supposed to be delivered tomorrow. Mrs. Walton is going to let the delivery people in, and I told her which room was Carmen's. Maybe after she goes to bed tomorrow, I'll head back to the house and arrange everything. We'll be going home soon."

"Why?"

"Robert, we've been living with you for weeks. It's way past time for us to go home."

"Why? This way, you have help with Roo."

"She's going to be stuck with that name the rest of her life."

"It's a good name." She lifted her head and rested her pointy chin on my chest to grin at me.

"I'm going to start dinner. Don't let her take a nap this late. She won't go to bed."

"Yes, sir. Poor, little Roo can't even have a short nap." I made a face at her, and she giggled. I couldn't explain why I loved that sound so much. She hadn't said a word yet, but I was hoping soon.

"She won't sleep tonight, do as I say." He dropped to his knees to kiss the top of her head, and she cuddled back to my chest.

She rested her ear over my heart, and I just stayed still. It would kill me when Remy took her away. I'd gotten used to them in my home. Sharing meals and watching cartoons after her bath for an hour before Remy took her to the guest room for her bedtime story. He didn't come back to talk to me afterward. As close as we were, I sensed he pulled away over the time since I'd gotten hurt, but mostly the distance grew the longer he was there with me.

I knew he was stressed with getting everything set up for Roo at his place. The time off work. Me getting hurt. But there was something else going on. I wanted to demand that he tell me what was bothering him. We were never alone long enough for me to bring it up.

I hugged Roo to my chest and tightened my stomach muscles to sit up. I grimaced as my shoulder pulled and struggled a bit to my feet, and then I took a seat on the couch. The remote was in the coffee table we'd pushed aside. I turned on her cartoons, and she turned to watch, her tiny fingers, swirling the hair on my forearm.

The front door opened, and I barely concealed a groan as Gladys breezed in with a smile.

"How's Aunt Gladys's girl?" She didn't even bother greeting me, and then she was off to the kitchen.

Remy and her voices carried from the kitchen, they laughed about something, and then I watched her head upstairs to change. Couldn't I have one night just me, Remy, and our girl... alone? I was a stoic man but had never leaned toward grumpy until recently. Leaning my head forward, I pressed my nose into Roo's hair. She smelled of baby shampoo.

I didn't know what was going on with me lately. I'd felt off the last few months, but I couldn't put my finger on what it was. It had started well before the shooting. I wasn't discontent with my life. I had a job I was successful at. I was close to my kids and grandkids. My partner became my best friend, and I adored his soon-to-be daughter. Yes, I got lonely. I'd been a part of a couple for over half my life. Rebuilding my existence as a single man hadn't been easy, and I didn't think I succeeded.

I was the type of man who loved having someone to come home to. My kids excited to see me. Being a cop's family wasn't easy, and there were a lot of sacrifices. Hence one of the big reasons I was single. I'd grown far too old to start over, and I'd do well to remember that.

10

REMY

COLD CASE
UNIT

The day was finally over, and I ended it as I had since we'd temporarily moved in. I blocked another well-aimed kick to the crotch, but just barely. "I'm going to have to invest in a cup if she keeps falling asleep with me," I complained as I watched her sprawled between Robert and I on his bed. He was rubbing her head as he read his book. She'd made me so proud in how she'd progressed since coming home, well, to Robert's home with me.

"She does have a tendency to take up the entire bed," he whispered without looking away from his book.

"You know you're a natural at all this."

I'd spent weeks watching how he catered to her. His patience during her meltdowns and her tendency to cling. I'd learned a lot about Robert since he got hurt. I'd loved him before, but it would kill me when we went back to business as usual. Living with him had ruined me. Earlier that day, I'd experienced my first instance of jealousy. I'd arrived back from the home visit and found a gorgeous, fit younger man leaving, and he'd been alone with my damn man. Then Robert had joked about developing a type, and that annoyed me. I'd known it was stupid, and I'd pushed it aside, yet that didn't change the fact that the hurt had hit me in the center of my chest.

He set his open book face down on his thigh. "With our job, well, I missed a lot with the kids. I learned about most of the milestones secondhand. It's the only thing about the job I regret."

"You're close to your kids. You weren't absent. You love them, and they knew that."

"I know, doesn't help the regret, though. How are you doing?"

I grinned as Romeo huffed from his spot stretched fully across the foot of the bed. "Okay. I miss work. I need more sleep. I'm impatient to hear that Carmen is officially mine, but that could take years to happen."

"It'll happen. She was born to be your daughter." He glanced at me and then back down on her. "She's come a long way in a short time."

"I just wish she'd try to talk."

"She'll do it when she's ready. They said she'd learned to be invisible. It'll just take time, Remy."

"Yeah."

"I love her giggle and her little smiles. The sound of her running through the house. I don't know what I'm going to do when you two go home."

"You'll do a happy dance." I tried to joke, but when he looked up, I earned a glare.

"I'd never be happy to see you two gone."

My heart kicked into high gear when our gazes locked, and I dropped my attention back to her. I had to leave no matter what. It was selfish of me that I'd stayed that long. I couldn't keep playing house with Robert. He wasn't mine to claim, no matter how much I wanted him.

"Remy, are you okay? You've been acting distant lately."

"I'm fine, I promise. I'm just a little stressed, but you have to worry about yourself. We just have to move back home soon, let you get back to your life. With the kids and Gladys spending less time here, I'm sure you're ready to have the house back to yourself."

"I love having you two here. There's no rush." He went back to reading his book, and I studied his profile.

I wondered if he knew what he was doing to me. Did he know how I felt? I turned my attention back to the TV to the movie that was almost over. Carmen hadn't made it through the first fifteen minutes before she'd curled up between us. That old part of me, the one with all the dreams of a man to love—a husband— and the family that I'd always wanted, resurfaced.

Being there with him made me see the future if my partner was gay and saw me the way I did him. To be able to kiss and touch him, cuddle up to him at night. If we were together, I'd go tuck Carmen into her bed and come back to crawl into ours. My chest tightened, and I pretended my heart wasn't breaking. Back in the day, I hadn't dared think about being anything other than a homeless sex worker. I'd had my friends who became family. People I'd trusted completely to have my back and to understand, all our futures were precarious.

Some of us, when we'd had a good night with a little too much drink or drugs, we'd sit around and play a game of what-if. We'd never admit it the next day when we were sober. Yet, we'd told stories of our perfect lives. I hadn't shared my past with anyone I hadn't known back in the day.

Would Robert still look at me the same? He'd already seen my scars, and I knew he was curious, but he hadn't asked…yet. He was my friend and partner, and I couldn't lose that. I just needed to keep my past where it belonged. Boss had told me I should come clean; that maybe Robert would feel betrayed that I didn't share. He would look at me differently. Maybe he wouldn't want me around his kids or grandkids, wouldn't feel I was right to raise Carmen, and all that would kill me.

"I'm going to take her to bed. I'll see you tomorrow."

"Okay, goodnight, Remy." I tried to fuss at him as he picked up

Carmen and hugged her, whispered goodnight to her even though she was fast asleep.

I got off the bed and walked around to his side, and scooped Carmen up, exiting the bedroom before I tried something stupid like kissing him.

"THIS IS A SURPRISE." Harry's voice was full of affection, and I was grateful we'd remained friends. That had turned out to be an easy transition. We'd both had issues to work out before we'd reconnected. I closed the back door behind me as Romeo sniffed around the backyard for his last potty break of the night.

"I didn't wake you or the kids, did I?"

"No, and you know even if we're asleep, we'll always answer. Are you okay? Nightmares?"

I chuckled softly. I knew what he'd ask. He'd been there through a few of my night terrors, but we'd never breached the line where he asked me to talk about them.

"I'm okay. I'm fostering to adopt."

"You'll be amazing, Remy. It's something you always wanted." The happiness in his tone was plain to hear, and I knew he was excited for me.

"Why didn't you ever want that with me?"

"Remy, it wasn't that I didn't want it with you. As much as I loved you, I don't think it was that all-consuming romantic love you needed. I found that with Tim, and I know that hurt you."

"Hate to burst your ego-bubble, but to be honest, I wasn't hurt. When you told me about the baby, now, that hurt."

"I'm sorry."

"Don't be. We remained friends, and part of me thinks if we'd carried on with our relationship, we wouldn't have had that."

"You still carrying a torch for that sexy partner of yours?"

"Why did I ever show you those pictures?" I groaned as I listened to his deep chuckle.

"Well, you were showing off the adorable kids you adore so much. It just happened the sexy man was in the background."

"Sexy straight man." My little bubble of happiness exploded, and I fell back onto one of the patio chairs.

"That is an obstacle. How's he handling you being gay?" I'd told him what had happened at Christmas when RJ unknowingly outed me.

"It's good. Nothing changed, really. We had an incident, he got hurt so Carmen, that's the girl I'm hoping to adopt, and I have been staying at his place to help take care of him."

"How's close quarters going?"

"Well, let's just say it's torture."

"Give the man a kiss and a grope."

I rolled my eyes in the dark. "Sexual harassment, my friend."

"Some things are worth a risk."

"Of course you'd say that."

"Honey, you gotta take a chance some time." He laughed. "Tim agrees with me."

"He would. You've corrupted my perfectly rational friend."

"I totally did. Shit, babies are calling. Call more than once every few months, and I expect a visit soon, or we'll be coming."

"Getting awful bossy."

"Yeah, yeah, listen to me." We said our goodbyes and passed on my love to Tim and the kids. I disconnected the call and yelled for Romeo. It was already late, and I was already extremely low on sleep, and it wasn't all about taking care of Carmen or Robert. Being in his home filled my head with shit I shouldn't have even contemplated.

"Romeo, bedtime." I'd only stay another week and then I was going home, no matter what.

11

ROBERT

COLD CASE
UNIT

I was tired of being stuck in my bed or my recliner. Sitting around didn't make me a happy man, didn't help that I had a shadow in the form of a massive Great Dane and a little girl that made herself comfortable in my bed to play or color. It's as if they ordered her to be my guard, and because I quickly fell in love, I'd do anything when she batted her lashes at me.

She cried when anyone else tried to pick her up. We'd made progress only for her to take a few steps back. Every day we just had to adapt. Whatever made Roo happy and safe we did, but every day was rife with landmines of what would trigger her, and she only wanted Remy or me for comfort.

"Hey, you doing okay with her?" I looked away from her to the door of my bedroom to find Remy there in nothing but a towel around his hips. The fabric was tucked under the lower curve of his belly. Since he'd moved in, I'd learned his tattoos were a lot more extensive than I'd first thought.

"We're good. She's coloring another picture."

"We're running out of room on the fridge. Gladys has taken to displaying her art with the other kids. I'll take them down when I leave."

"They can stay, Remy. They belong there just like with my other kids." I didn't miss the darkening of his eyes before he dropped his gaze so I couldn't see.

"Every time I come by, you're half-naked." An amused feminine voice made me smile.

"Hi, Fran. Didn't know we were due for a visit today. I'm getting ready to go get dressed. Robert was watching Carmen for me."

I waved as the social worker stopped outside my room and smiled at Carmen.

"She doing okay, Remy?"

"Nightmares aren't much better, but we're making it. I'd prefer to be at home to get her on a regular schedule but leave him to his own devices, and he'd be back at work."

"I'm a grown man. I can take care of myself. Now, go get dressed." I complained about him being there just to hide the fact of how much I loved him in my house. Every time we had a disagreement and I told him to leave, I fussed at him when he tried to pack them up.

Remy rolled his eyes, and he disappeared down the hall.

"May I enter?"

"Sure, my room has become meeting central around here."

"How's Remy really doing?"

"Short on sleep, but as sweet as ever. Between me and Carmen, he's going to need a good weeks' worth of sleep when this is all over. Why are you asking? Something up?"

"No, his home is a special place for traumatized children and young adults who need safety. He only ever takes in one at a time, but he removed his name from the list when Carmen became his foster. Do you think he'd make a good parent?"

"He'll make the best. She's only been with him three weeks, but he loves her already."

"He's petitioned the court for adoption. The parental rights were severed so she's available as of three this afternoon. It's still a process, he's a single man, but references came from some powerful names in this city. They are considering his past, though."

"His—"

"I'm a product of an incestuous home, my mother and her father had a sexual relationship. She *cheated* on him, and I was the result. I suffered severe physical, psychological, and sexual abuse from birth until I was eighteen, then I was a sex worker and drug addict until someone got me into recovery. Afterward, I joined the academy. They want to know if I'm crazy or not or if I'll continue the cycle of abuse."

"Remy!" My tone was too sharp, making Carmen jump. "I'm sorry, honey, it's okay. I didn't mean to yell at Remy." I didn't try to reach for her out of comfort because I knew she wouldn't react well. And I was suddenly too on edge from his easily spoken revelation of his childhood.

He crossed to the bed and lowered onto the edge. Carmen immediately crawled onto his lap and buried her face against his chest. "Hey, you know what I told you. No one would ever hurt you again. Uncle Robert wouldn't hurt either of us. He's just a grumpy man."

I watched him hold her head and brush her curls back from her beautiful face. She was silent unless she awoke screaming from her nightmares. A kid shouldn't have to pretend they didn't exist, and that's what she did. She remained silent and small so she wouldn't be noticed. I handed over the sari, and with mind-boggling speed, he had her safely ensconced in her pouch against his chest. Her little feet the only thing you could see.

"That's not it at all, Remy. You went through all of this to become a foster, but this is adoption, and the process is a bit more in-depth and lengthy. Your reputation in the community is of the highest standard. You're a well-respect law enforcement officer. You have no criminal background, no matter if you worked the streets or not. Carmen is perfect in your home, well, your care."

Dog nails scraping on hardwood floors announced the arrival of Romeo. He went instantly to Remy and nosed the lump inside the sari until he heard giggles, and then he jumped on the bed to make himself at home. How the hell was I going to deal with my house when it was quiet and Remy and my little family was gone again? It wouldn't be the same as going back to friends and partners.

I wanted to gather them both into my arms because I noticed the minute he pulled into himself. Very much like when I'd awakened in the hospital. His emotional distance killed me, and I didn't know how to fix that when I didn't know what I'd done. The scars I'd refused to ask about were explained, but how much pain had the sweet man endured to survive?

"Did you stop seeing your therapist, Remy?"

"Twenty years of shit on repeat, contrary to popular opinion, time doesn't heal all wounds, Fran, especially when scars only fade so much. The ink may cover most of them, but they're still there."

"I know. Got a time frame when you're moving home."

"I'm giving the grumpy one another week to detach from me, and then I'm going home."

I grumbled and glared at him when he shot a glance at me, and his mischievous expression was back. The change was almost shocking in its complete turnaround.

"You don't have to stay if you don't want to. I'm not holding you hostage."

"Really? You batting those pretty lashes at me and telling me to unpack isn't—"

"Give me my Roo. I need to make up." Without question, he removed our girl from her pouch and passed her to me.

"Hey, Roo." I cuddled her to my chest. "I'm sorry I yelled. You know I would never do anything to hurt you or Remy. I love you, and you are one of the most important people in my life. As precious to me as Teddy, Sammie, and Becca. Do you forgive me for yelling, Roo?" She squeezed me tight and then relaxed, her little ear directly over my heart. The sound must comfort her because she tended to do that when she was anxious. "Thank you, honey."

"I have to get home. You two behave and quit fighting. You're like an old married couple. Give me a call when you either go home or move in, whichever comes first."

"Smartassery doesn't look good on you, Fran."

"You're gonna break my heart, Remy."

I hid my smile at the wink she sent him, and then she disappeared out of my room.

"Remy."

"Yeah."

"Come here." I removed my right arm from around Roo and held out my hand for Remy. All I could do was wait him out, and then he crawled up the bed and laid against me. His head on my shoulder, and then he wrapped his arm around Roo.

"I don't want to talk about it, Robert."

"You don't have to. We're fine. I think all three of us need a nap, especially you."

"I won't deny it. I'm dead on my feet."

"Then just close your eyes and I'll wake you and Roo up for dinner."

He nodded, rubbing his cheek on my bare chest, and his breathing evened out quickly. I smiled as I watched them sleep. I stroked the long slashes of scar tissue along his lower back exposed by his hiked-up tank top and felt him cuddle closer.

"You starting cuddle sessions now?" I jerked my gaze to the doorway to find Gladys leaning against the frame.

"We had some stress."

"Want me to take Roo and tuck her in?"

"No, they're fine. I said I'd wake them up for dinner."

"I'll make dinner and head out so you can have some family time."

"You saying you're not family?"

"I think you're getting a second chance, so don't fuck it up. I love the newest members of our family. And because I do love them so much, I arranged for you to have solo time with Remy and Roo. You can thank me later, and it'll cost you."

"I'm almost afraid."

She turned and walked away. There was something to be said for having my family around, including my ex-wife. We'd finally gotten over the tension we'd lived with since the divorce. I liked having my friend back, and I'd like her even more when she moved back to her place full-time.

I needed to work on Remy's trust. I didn't want to demand he tell me about his past, but I needed to earn his complete trust. That afternoon I'd learned that as much as we depended on each other, we had some work to do. He was my best friend. He'd put his life on the line for me and the girl we cuddled. He'd saved me, and maybe I wanted to return the favor, but it was more than that. There was something between him and I, and I had to figure out what that was.

REMY

COLD CASE UNIT

"**P**apa. Dad."

Those words still played over and over in my head hours later. Of course, my daughter would say Papa first, and Robert wouldn't refrain from being smug about it. We'd left her on the couch to nap while we had a beer and figured out something for dinner. She'd come running, calling our names with her canine protector right on her heels. It had shocked me.

I tucked the covers around Carmen as she completely covered herself with the quilt. I freaked out about how she slept the first few nights, but she liked enclosed, small spaces. I jogged down the stairs and walked into the living room. Robert was seated on the couch with his head rested on his raised hand.

"Need anything?" I stood in the entryway and waited for him to look away from the TV.

"No, just sit your ass down and relax." He patted the spot on the cushion beside him. "You're going to be too wrung out when it's time to go back to work."

"Too late." I fell back carefully onto the couch to avoid hitting his shoulder.

He crossed his right arm over his chest, and his index finger stroked along the dark bag under my left eye. "Maybe you and Roo need a vacation? A long weekend."

"Probably, but too many changes at once will make her insecure. It's the reason I need to move her home so she can get settled." Sitting down on the couch was probably a bad idea because I'd never been so tired in my life. Also, for the first time in my life, I was extremely sexually frustrated. I loved sex which had taken a lot of work for me not to see intimacy as nothing more than an act of degradation.

"I know, but I'm kinda attached to Roo."

"You're wrapped around her finger, *Papa*."

"Still irritated she ran to me first?"

"No."

"You're cute when you pout." I glared at him as he tapped the end of my nose and draped his arm across my thighs.

"You've been an asshole. I thought you were nice." He needed to stop touching me so much. Every one of those casual touches tortured me. The urge to kiss and hold him; to have him reach for me in something other than friendship. What terrified me the most was that I wanted to feel his chest against my back—his hips cradling my oversized ass. Fuck, before he broke me, I needed to get away from him.

"Stop. Our girl said her first words. We've waited weeks for that to happen."

"We have."

"What's going on in your head? Talk to me."

"It's like everything is falling into place. When I was with Harry, he'd asked about my thoughts on kids. I said I wanted them...that I was a foster parent. He said he didn't want any."

"But you said he and his husband have two."

"Yeah, but we never had a strong commitment. I'd thought we did. We never lived together, though. He said with my schedule, there didn't seem to be a reason to move into my place or his."

"You deserve someone who wants to be with you all the time when you're home."

"Gladys divorced you for lack of time together."

"She did, and we grew apart. I regret the end of my marriage. You spend almost four decades with someone and you think that's it, you've met your one, and then one day you come home from work and your person is waiting there with signed divorce papers. I'm a fifty-five-year-old cop, and divorced father of two with grandchildren."

"Do you think about finding someone else?"

"I tried a few blind dates. I had one girlfriend before I dated and married Gladys. Starting over, I don't know. Maybe I'd thought it would be easier, but there was no connection with them—never felt right."

"No chance of you, Gladys, and a second chance?"

"Maybe if it happened during the year after the judge finalized our divorce, but I'd slowly learned that as much as I loved her..." I turned my head as he paused so I could look at him. "...it wasn't the same. We were friends before we married. I think Roo and reconnecting with my friend were the great things that came out of getting shot."

"I did notice a certain tension between the two of you at Christmas."

"One of the things we agreed on was we'd share holidays. Either at my place or hers, mostly we came here since there's more room than her apartment."

"Did you get the house before or after the divorce?"

"Before, this was the house we bought together. I loved it, but she wanted something smaller, so I bought out her half of the house. She decorated, so I let her have all the bedroom furniture and the stuff in the living room. It was amicable."

"I get the tension, though. It took a while for me to get comfortable with Harry and Tim after they'd gotten together. I wasn't hurt or not as hurt as I should've been about my boyfriend of two years going away for a short vacation and come back hopelessly in love."

"You've never been in love before?"

I tensed at the question.

"Tell me why you got uncomfortable."

"I never thought I was capable of love. Too much damage from the time I don't want to talk about."

"Never thought, did you fall or are you currently in love?"

"I am, was, I don't know, but it's impossible to do anything about it. There are things I can't allow, but I want more than anything."

"Why can't you allow it?"

"There's parts of me I can't share. It's too painful, and to have them turn away from me, well, it would shatter me."

"If you love someone and they could love you back, wouldn't you want to share the pleasure and the pain? Someone who loves you wouldn't mind shouldering some of the burden, at least for a little while to let you recharge. How about we watch a movie and eat popcorn since our girl is passed out."

"Blood and guts?"

"Whatever you want."

Those were dangerous words, and I forced myself off the couch. I had to leave and soon. I loved our routine. Shared meals. A bed shared at night to watch cartoons with Carmen. Us on the couch after she went to bed to watch TV. I didn't know if I could resist much longer.

I sighed as I pulled out a bag of popcorn and popped it into the microwave. I hit the power button and left it to start as I grabbed a few beers from the fridge and a bowl from one of the lower cabinets. I should've been able to ignore my attraction the busier I made myself. Yet, it didn't help stop the thoughts that ran through my head.

Since I'd moved in, it was my dream come true. The only thing that would make it better would be the freedom to touch

Robert. To cuddle up next to him after I put our girl to bed, but that wasn't meant to be, and I had to remind myself of that multiple times a day. Time would pass and we'd return to our jobs, and everything would be back to normal. It had to be because I couldn't live like this. Always loving and never loved.

I lost track of time and almost burned the popcorn, but I'd saved it just in time. I dumped it into a bowl, grabbed the two beers in one hand, and returned to the living room.

"I found your blood and guts, baby. Come get comfortable." He patted the spot beside him again.

I almost took the spot as far away from him as I could get; yet I was weak and returned to my seat beside him. I stretched my legs out to prop my feet on the table and placed the bowl on my lap. I handed him his beer as he pushed play on the remote, and I settled in to enjoy every second of being near him until it came time for me to force myself and Roo to our real home.

13

ROBERT

COLD CASE
UNIT

I knew Roo was with Mrs. Walton as he normally took her to the babysitter before getting ready. He didn't like leaving her alone even long enough for him to shower. I unlocked the door with my key and was greeted by Romeo. I scratched his floppy ears, and he went back to his bed in the corner of the living room.

The house was too quiet. I made my way upstairs, and as I stepped off onto the landing, I heard water running. I would not be late to work my first day back. As I neared his bedroom, I heard different sounds, louder than those of the shower.

Something in me ignored my brain screaming for me to go wait for him in the kitchen. I entered his room. The door to his bathroom was open and as I drew closer, the sight in the mirror stopped me. The doors of the huge shower stall were open. Remy was fucking himself onto a dildo suctioned to the wall.

That alone should've had me running, but it was the tears streaming down his cheeks and the sobbing. His cock was hard and thick, slapping between his belly and thighs, but bodies reacted to touch, to stimulation that didn't mean he was enjoying it.

I didn't know what made me do it, but I rushed to him. I turned off the water and stepped into the stall. I took his face in my hands. His beard was like wet, raw silk against my palms and fingers, and I stroked his lower lip with the pads of my thumbs as I took in the misery on his face. The sadness and desperation in his eyes as he stared at me.

"Baby, what's wrong?" I asked as I eased him forward, and his breathing hitched letting me know the toy was no longer inside him. I stroked my thumbs across his wet lashes. "Let's get you dried off and dressed, okay?" He'd taken care of me, so it was beyond time that I returned the favor.

I jerked a towel off a hook beside the stall and dried his face. He stood there with his eyes closed and not saying a word when I ran the thick cloth between his cheeks. He fisted his hands in the lapels of my jacket and arched into my touch.

"Please don't touch me there." His voice broke, and he pressed his chest to mine. He tucked his face against the side of my neck, and I groaned at the light suction at my skin. He was warm and solid where he pressed his bigger and softer frame to mine, and I didn't care that my clothes were damp from his wet body hair. Fuck, he felt good. Why did he feel just right?

I dropped the towel, and my fingers circled the swollen rim of his hole. He was slick from whatever lube he used. Two of my fingers easily slipped inside. He was hot and wet, tight and my own breathing picked up the pace. I'd spent weeks with him in my space; sometimes in my bed. The days since he'd moved out, I'd started to crave his presence. Those couple things we'd done; the time spent together, fuck, how I missed them.

"S'good. Please make me feel good. I won't ask you to kiss me or do it again—I'll beg if you want me to." My free hand grabbed his hairy ass cheek and spread him wider as I slammed my fingers inside him at a punishing pace as he cried out. It was a high keening cry. My cock was tenting the front of my slacks. I spun him until I pressed him to the wall as I abused his already stretched hole. I brushed my lips across the thick layers of scar tissue. His gasps were loud as I repeated the caresses to every imperfection I could reach without breaking contact with him.

He fucked himself onto my fingers, as he whimpered and moaned, cutting each one off when he seemed to catch himself. As if the smallest sound of pleasure would bring me to my senses, but I had no intention of stopping unless he told me to. I twisted and shifted my hand until my fingers found his prostate. I tortured his gland until he shook and begged.

"Fuck yes." He clamped down so hard on my fingers I had to push past the resistance as his body bowed and trembled. I reached for my belt then he thanked me. I was pissed and horny, and I left him there to clean up.

HOURS later as our shift came to an end, I dropped him off. He hadn't spoken to or looked at me since he'd come down to his kitchen dressed that morning. He was my partner. He'd come hard on my fingers, and he treated me like a stranger. I watched him for long minutes until he disappeared into the babysitter's house to pick up Roo.

I'd never touched a man like that in my life. Had never thought about it until him. The weeks he spent at the hospital and in my home, I'd loved him being there. Liked him in my kitchen, playing with Roo on the other side of the bed as we watched TV before he took her to read her a story and tuck her into Carol's old room.

First, I thought I was pissed because of the thank you. As the day progressed, I realized I was angry because he'd demanded a release and nothing else. He was going to beg me to touch him. Said I didn't have to kiss him. I finger fucked him like someone I'd pick up in a goddamn bar when I wanted to love on him. I just didn't know how to do that.

Gladys had been my high school girlfriend, only the second woman I'd had sex with, and we'd married the summer after we graduated and had been together ever since.

I sat in my car and watched as Remy and Roo appeared. She was holding onto his hand, and it killed me he didn't bring her over to me. I pulled out my phone and scrolled to Gladys's number to connect the call. The tension between us had faded since the shooting. We were friends again like we'd been in high school before we'd started dating. I'd realized slowly over the last year that what we'd had, while we loved each other, was more about familiarity and expectation than a romantic love. Yet it still felt odd to no longer wear my wedding ring. It had been there for thirty-seven years.

"Hey, how are you? Good first day back?"

"Not really. They moved us to the Cold Case Unit until I'm deemed cleared for the street. I still have dust in my nose."

"Aw, no more excitement for you for a while. You said us, did Remy go with you?"

"Yeah, he asked for the temporary transfer. The hours are better for him right now with getting Roo settled. Once she's more secure, we'll see about going back to homicide. Can I ask you something and it stay between us?"

"Of course."

"Was I good lover?"

"What?"

"Was I good? Did I make it pleasurable for you? Was I selfish?"

"No, you weren't selfish in any way. If sex could've kept us going, I don't think we'd be divorced. For a man your age, you have a scarily high sex drive. I loved you, Robert, but when the kids moved out and it was just us. There was nothing there anymore except companionship. I didn't want that for either of us."

"I know, and I get that. But I'm in my fifties. Why am I even thinking about dating?"

"You're not thinking about dating, my old friend. You're thinking about a certain hot single dad."

"Shit, can people tell?" I wasn't ashamed of it. Hell, I'd been thinking about a repeat of that morning all day, but doing it right this time.

"Remy is clueless. Me and your kids, not so much. Loving someone doesn't have anything to do with the gender of the person. He loves you, ya know? We saw it those three days you were unconscious and the way he catered to you after you came home. I used to catch him watching you sleep, and I swear he wanted to curl up with you so badly. So maybe I thought I'd see you bring a woman home some day for a family dinner or whatever, but you could definitely do worse than Remy. That man is almost too sweet to be real."

"I just don't know if I can give him what he wants. He's on his way to being a single dad any day now. He's my partner. I don't want to lose him in any way."

"Let me ask you one thing."

"Okay."

"Would you rather take the chance on something that's going to make the rest of your life happy or pretend that you're not falling in love with him? I didn't miss that you took your ring off a few months after he became your partner. You may not have been conscious of your feelings, but part of you knew. I just want you happy. We'd had close calls before, but seeing you in that bed, I realized I'd put so much distance between us that I'd lost sight that you were my friend first." She paused. "I love Remy. He's a sweetheart who does everything for everyone else. He deserves something for himself, and so do you. Yeah, it'll be hard to start over. A dad again, but don't tell me you don't want it."

"I do."

"Then maybe the koala will let me watch her so you can take Remy out. She's rather fond of her Aunt Gladys."

I chuckled and shook my head. "I think the feeling is mutual." Carmen had easily become a part of my family, just as Remy had.

"You can do this. I have all the faith in you. Seduce your prospective boyfriend."

"You know, you telling me to seduce some man is weird, right?"

"No it's not. I love Remy. I trust him with you in every way. Unlike the past, I never have to worry that he'll make sure you come home."

We ended the call after I told her I'd let her know my plans. I started the car, checked the street, and pulled away from the curb to head home. *Date.* Shit, I never dated in my life. What the hell was I going to do? Maybe start simple, beers and conversation, maybe a talk about what happened in the bathroom. This wouldn't work if that specter was between us, and I couldn't have him uncomfortable around me. He had never been before, and I missed his smile—his snarky attitude. I wanted my Remy back; I just had to figure out how to do that.

14

REMY

COLD CASE
UNIT

I threw myself onto my bed and grabbed a pillow to cover my face, and screamed. I'd behaved for two years, kept my attraction to myself, and what the fuck did I do? A week passed since the incident, and I wasn't handling it well.

"What's with the nine-one-one text?" Shine's voice had me tossing the pillow aside. "Do you have any idea what a bitch it was to ditch Boss? That nosy Queen sniffs out potential gossip like a dog scenting a bitch in heat."

"I did a bad, bad thing."

"Pretty, have you broken your abstinence stretch?" she asked as I watched her approach the bed and stretched out beside me with her head on my bicep. "Are you the bitch in heat of this story?"

Why the hell did I do that myself? I shouldn't have thought I'd get any sympathy or a caring shoulder to cry on.

"Robert walked in on a private moment in the shower, and in my lust-addled brain, I asked him to get me off...told him I'd beg and that he didn't have to kiss me."

"Were you having fun or causing yourself pain? Because if you were punishing yourself for something you can't change, then the sexy man walking in ended the logical way. I love you, Pretty. We've been friends longer than either of us want to admit to, but wanting love isn't a reason to hurt yourself. We've discussed this before."

"I'd sell what's left of my soul for a kiss. How pathetic is that?"

"It's not pathetic, Pretty. It's human. You've been working toward sainthood most of your life. It's time to be selfish. It's time to get what Remington Alistair Bosley wants. And how white is that name?"

"My host had delusions of grandeur. I just want to make the world better, Shine."

"It's not your responsibility to make up for anything. You lived through hell. Most people wouldn't have survived to accomplish even half of what you have. Talk it out."

"After Harry left, I thought a complete cleanse. No dating. Just me time."

"And your right fist time and your very expensive, and scarily large toy time. There's not enough lube in the world."

"Moving on." I rolled my eyes at her giggle. "And I did good with me time. I volunteered more. I bought the house. I didn't even look twice at a guy after the breakup. And then I walked into homicide and everything imploded. I fell in lust and then love with my very straight, divorced partner. Years I've been doing great, calm and cool..." She laughed. "Okay, maybe not calm, but you don't have to bring it to my attention."

"You remember the night we met? We sat on an abandoned couch underneath the overpass. We smoked a joint and played what-if. At sixteen and forty-six, you still want the same thing. A husband and kids, that nuclear family that none of us saw outside sit-coms on fuzzy TVs in cheap motel rooms."

"I know, y'all always made fun of me."

"We didn't make fun, because we knew out of all of us you'd be the one to make the what-ifs come true."

"I gave him my back."

She jumped up and straddled my stomach. "You let him come up behind you?"

"He even kissed my scars while he had his fingers up my ass."

"I'm gonna sound so white right now, but wow, just wow. That shows a lot of trust in someone. You didn't let Harry touch your back or finger you. That's a huge thing. So what's wrong?" She held up her hands. "And before you bring up the *he's my partner* excuse. You've done nothing but talk about him like a teenage girl with her first crush. If your baritone wasn't as deep as it is, there would've been squealing."

"Why do I put up with you and the rest of our family?"

"Because we're all each other had and there's strength in numbers who share the same experiences as you. There's no judging or pity. Do you think that's something Robert would do?"

"In my gut, no. During one of the home visits, Fran brought up my past, but Robert and I haven't talked about it again since."

"Did he treat you differently after the revelation?"

"No, that's not something he does. But after that morning in the bathroom, I've put distance between us. No shared car rides. No shared meals. He saw how needy I am. I've never let anyone see that. You get me, Shine, you know, the first time I had sex after I got off the streets and started therapy, as soon as I felt him start to push inside, I freaked out and pushed him off me."

"We have trauma, Pretty. We're conditioned by said abuse to react at a primitive level. We learned to survive by any means necessary, and the right man will understand that. Unfortunately, I haven't found that yet."

"What about Mr. Finance-three-piece-suit-guy?"

"His niceness and attraction only went so far. I confessed what happened, and he did that man-bullshit and started questioning me. Like you said, we know each other. You washed me when I couldn't bear to do it myself. So here I am telling you that you're ruining your friendship with Robert."

"But tell me how to fix it."

"You have to talk to him and explain. Ignoring the elephant in the room isn't helping. Just think, he didn't push you away or tell you to go to hell."

"He's a nice guy."

"Pretty, I've met nice guys, and I don't know any of them who would finger fuck a friend, a male friend no less, just because they're nice. Has he asked for a partner change? Stopped being respectful?"

"No, but I did say I put distance between us since last week."

"And that's your mistake to fix. You're happier than I've seen you before. You have an adorable daughter and a really, fuck-worthy potential boyfriend."

"Aren't you being a little too optimistic?"

"Nah, think about it. I'm liking this switch in pace where I'm the positive and cheery one, and you're a miserable bastard."

"I am not feeling the love here." She smacked my chest.

"You know I love you, but sometimes you need tough love, and an epic fuck to knock you out of your funk. So, what's it going to be? Make up with your old man or drown your dairy-intolerant ass in ice cream?"

"I'm calling Vicki next time."

"You would bring up her right now? That's how we're going to play this? She is *not* your friend. She fucked your first boyfriend. I am not hearing this."

"Have you always been this dramatic?"

"Yes, yes I have. We're a match made in Drama Queen Hell."

I sat up and caught her before she tipped backward. "I am not a drama queen! I am the calmest one."

"No, Griff is the calmest one. He's so Zen he makes Buddha look like he's on amphetamines."

"Good thing Buddhism is a philosophy and not a religion because we're already going to Hell in all the religions."

"At least we can say we were never boring." I grinned as she rested her arms over my shoulders.

"Are you like completely committed to this gay thing?"

"In our formative years, we already worked out my tab A does *not* go into your slot B."

She heavy sighed and rested her forehead on mine. "I know, that was a night we shall never speak of again."

"Thanks for this, Shine. I just don't...I'm lost."

"Of course you're lost, Pretty. Think about it. Every other commitment you've made in your forty-six years ended in infidelity or with the strength of wet fireworks. This one matters, Robert matters, and you know that if you step out of your comfort zone, he has the ultimate power to destroy you."

"Don't worry about my fragile ego or anything."

"It's the truth. I knew it the first time I met him. You do know that you two are never out of touching range. Which for you is shocking. Why not just take a leap?"

"I'm terrified he won't be there to catch me when I do."

"I get that. I took the leap, but what happened when no one was there to catch me?" She smiled at me. "You and our family were. You were there to pick up the pieces to make it right. Even when I shattered into a million pieces, you carefully picked up even the splinters. And if Robert isn't there, me and Boss, and everyone else will be."

"I'll try."

"That's all I ask."

"You want to sleep with me tonight?"

"I think we could both use some major cuddles. I'm going to steal a t-shirt."

"I'll go lock up and grab us some water." I hugged her waist and flipped until she was under me. "You're doing amazing, Shine. And when the time is right, the perfect person will come along."

"You, too. But I think your perfect person is already here. I just need you to be brave."

I dropped a kiss on her lips, easing off the bed, and left her laying there staring at the ceiling. "Shine."

"Yeah, Pretty."

"I love you. You know that, right?"

"I love you, too, and I'll always be there when you fall."

I nodded and rushed to take care of locking up the house and checking all the doors and windows. Even years later, I still needed to make sure I was safe. Even though, intellectually, I knew locks wouldn't keep anyone out that wanted to get to me, but I needed the routine. When I stayed at Robert's, I never once worried about mine or Roo's safety because we were there with him.

If I took Shine's advice and I leapt, would I survive? I'd experienced the worst atrocities that could be inflicted on another human, but losing my safety net of two years...it really would destroy me, and I was more terrified than I'd ever been in my life. And that I didn't know how to handle.

ROBERT

COLD CASE
UNIT

I checked my phone and another day without messages from Remy. He'd completely cut me off except for work and cases were all we talked about; I wasn't even getting check-ups on Roo. I was getting tired of him freezing me out. That hadn't happened in all the time we'd known each other.

The memories of that morning still stuck with me. It also hadn't skipped my notice that the more I was around him, the more my curiosity grew about what his lips felt like. I already knew what he felt like in my arms. The way he moved closer in his sleep. I was confused yet so sure of what I wanted, and I wanted a certain stubborn man.

That was the problem, though. I didn't know how to claim him. It wasn't like my kids and Gladys didn't know who I wanted. And I wasn't having an issue because the person I wanted was a man. No, I was losing it over the fact I was completely out of my element. Even if my sexual history had more than two people, I didn't know how to bridge the void he'd opened between us.

I hadn't fully realized the amount of time we'd spent together until we'd become strangers again. I couldn't call my ex-wife again for advice. I was desperate but didn't want her to know to what extent.

I slouched into my chair and reached for my phone. I searched through my contacts and found my daughter's number, and I hit the call icon and listened to it ring.

"What's wrong?"

"Hello to you, too, my favorite daughter."

"That is so clichéd, such a dad thing. And you know Roo is your favorite because she's still adorable."

"Then help me."

"What did you do to my soon-to-be stepfather?"

"I didn't do anything." I wasn't explaining to my daughter what had happened. It was bad enough when I asked Gladys about my skills as a lover. That had to be my lowest point in my life so far. "We may have had a slight...disagreement, and he's given me the cold shoulder."

"That doesn't sound like Remy, so spill it. You know I'm an adult. If you fumbled sex, maybe you can redeem yourself."

"I didn't fumble sex. There was no...okay, we may have crossed a line, and now I have no idea how to get him to talk to me."

"Dad, you do know you're a divorced fifty-five-year-old grown-ass man, right? Are we entering the mid-life puberty? Because I have no interest in talking you through your first post-divorce hook-up."

"I am not looking to hook-up. I wouldn't even know how to start. I just want my Remy and Roo back. He's withholding visitation."

She hissed. "Oh, you fucked up. I know it's been a long, long time since..."

"We're not going there, there was no sex, we just crossed a barrier in the heat of the moment, and I think he's embarrassed, and I don't want him to feel as if he can't be around me. I already called your mother once to ask for advice. I couldn't do it twice."

"Okay, this is what we're going to do. We're going to arrange for my baby sister to come visit. Mom will pick her up to spend the night. You will buy Remy his favorite food, and you will talk, and you will act like a grownup."

"Maybe I don't wanna."

"Too damn bad. Dad, you've been happy these last few years. You're making friends because of Remy, and you're not as stressed. He's been good for you, and we love him."

"You're not freaked out that your middle-aged dad wants to date a man?"

"No, not in the least. Besides, it's Remy, and to be honest, you're already very couple-y. I'm surprised you didn't share a bed after you got hurt. You kinda jumped the gun, Dad. You already have a kid. Usually sex and commitment come before the adoption of mini human lifeforms."

"But did you see how adorable my youngest daughter is?"

"You're a lost cause, and she's going to be spoiled rotten. You do know that Remy and Roo bat their lashes at you, and you cave."

"No, I don't. I'm very strict with Roo and Remy." I couldn't even say that with a straight face, and from her loud laughter, she hadn't bought it either.

"They get away with everything. Friday you will be at Remy's at seven PM, and you'll have alone time with your man. Fix whatever the hell you did. And before you try the *what if I fuck this up* argument, would you rather have Remy for the long-term or let whatever this disagreement was make you lose even your friend."

"That's what I'm worried about, honey."

"It'll work out. I know it will."

"Thanks."

"Be ready to claim your man on Friday."

I thanked her again and disconnected the call. That was fixed for the time being, and I just had to make it until Friday. Work wouldn't allow us to have the privacy to talk like we needed. I closed my eyes, and as it had recently, the image of Remy naked in the shower formed in my mind.

He was soft with the cutest, furry belly, and he'd desperately wanted to be touched and loved on, and I wanted nothing else than to give him what he needed. The texture of his scars was still burned into a sensory memory on my lips. I needed to know what his softness felt like cushioning my harder leaner frame. I didn't think either of us were ready to jump into sex. Yet, it was time I fostered a sense of intimacy.

That didn't mean I hadn't pictured what it would be like to fuck him. His thick thighs squeezing my sides as I sank into him. I knew he had sexual trauma, and I didn't know how that still affected him. He needed a softer touch. He needed to be seduced and shown that his safety and boundaries were important to me.

I didn't like how quiet he was when I got him off. Was he ashamed of what we did? If he was, that would kill me. Nothing we did together should embarrass him, especially when we loved on each other. I palmed my thickening length beneath the cotton of my pajama pants and moaned as I raised my fingers to my lips and stroked the firm curves. In my head, he was there, straddling my thighs as we wound down before I'd lead him to our bedroom.

In the last few weeks, I'd become reacquainted with my dick. I loved sex and the intimacy of being with someone. While masturbation eased the ache, it wasn't my favorite pastime. I was frustrated, and I missed Remy, and it wasn't simply because my friend was ignoring me. No, I craved the man. His sweetness and vulnerability. The way he blushed when he was praised for all the good he'd done.

I didn't know when it had happened, but I'd fallen for the beautiful person Remy was. And I wanted everything a relationship between us would entail. The night breeze ruffled the trimmed hair on my chest, and I slipped my hand beneath the waistband of my pants. My fingertips moved through the trimmed bush at the base of my cock.

My muscles tensed as I fisted my thick length and slowly stroked from the base upward, squeezed my thumb and index fingers just below the sensitive tip.

"Daddy, is this all for me?" Remy's voice filled my head as I pictured my man drawing a single fingertip along the underside of my cock. I mirrored the movement with my own touch. I shifted my hips as I started a slow, easy rhythm, focusing on the pleasure and not the end. Sex, making love, whatever people wanted to call the act, for me, it was all about the buildup.

I craved the tension and the retreat before it crested, hours of touching and kissing; a tease that drove me and my lover insane. A car door closing in the distance warned me I was outside in my backyard. Fenced yard or not, I was too old to be caught dick out while jerking off.

I savored the pleasurable ache of my erection. I stood up and grabbed my phone, dropping it into my pocket. Plans needed to be made. I had my man to claim. Remy was worth fighting for, and we deserved to see where a relationship would go.

16

REMY

COLD CASE
UNIT

Gladys had called to say she was having a girls' day with Carol and Becca, and wanted to take Carmen with them. I'd started to protest until I'd arrived at Mrs. Walton's to find her dancing excitedly as Gladys asked did she want to spend the evening with them. She needed some female role models, and Carol and Gladys had taken that on without hesitation.

We'd walked next door to my home, and I went up to her room to pack her a bag.

"I'll drop her off with Mrs. Walton tomorrow if you're not home from work yet, or I can just keep her until you are." I glanced over my shoulder to find her in the doorway with my girl on her hip.

"If she gets scared or—"

"You'll be the first one I call or Papa. Because other than you, he's the only one who can calm her down."

My face heated. Carmen's first words were Dad and Papa, which was what Teddy and Sammie called Robert. He hadn't said anything, so I didn't protest. We were the people she'd spent the most time around. She tended to stick to us like glue, and my shame was that I loved sharing her with him. He read her stories.

Picked her up from daycare. We all shared meals, and it was too painfully like a family. The one I'd never have.

I'd kept a distance between us since he'd caught me punishing myself in the shower a few weeks before. I'd never come that quick or hard from just a man's fingers in my ass. My neediness scared me. Almost losing him, spending twenty-four hours a day in his presence while he healed, I'd started to crave him more. I hadn't bottomed in over twenty years, and the only penetration was with my toys. I was a big masculine man, so people assumed I was a top. But while I enjoyed it, that wasn't my favorite thing.

Since his slim, strong body had pressed to mine, I wanted it all. A kiss. To have the right to cuddle up to him in bed. I wanted to be able to straddle his hips and ride him as he stared at me, while he loved me.

"Remy?"

I turned as I placed Carmen's sari and favorite book into her bag. "Yes?"

"Are you okay? You've been a little off lately. We're getting worried."

"I'm fine. It's just hard being away from her. I think the stress of the last few months has been getting to me a bit. I think I just need a lazy night and early to bed."

"Well, she's going to be just fine. Tonight it's just us, chicken nuggets and mac-and-cheese, and then tomorrow we have a whole day planned. Breakfast. Shopping. Afternoon tea and dinner after the park to let her play."

"Thank you, Gladys."

"Oh, honey, you don't have to thank me. We've become friends, or at least I hope so."

"We have."

"Okay, come say bye to your girl, and you need to check the car seat for me. I swiped the one from Robert's car he bought to keep for her. It's been awhile since I did the whole car seat thing.

With Becca and her nursing, Sammie completely attached to Leona, and Teddy being out of a booster for years, I'm hopeless."

"Come on, let me get you set up." She handed Carmen over so I could say goodbye, and I handed her the kid's phone I'd bought her. "Do you remember one and two?"

"Dad one. Papa two. Red button nine-one-one."

"Good girl." I nearly cried as soon as I got her secured in the seat. She'd become a beautiful chunky little girl. Still scared on occasion, but she was becoming secure with me. I was getting impatient for the judge to sign the papers to make her legally mine, but until then, she was in my home as a foster child and would be until she aged out. She'd never have to leave me.

I kissed her cheeks until she was giggling and fighting against my scruff tickling her.

"Remember consent."

"Yes. We are to ask her for consent for hugs to bath time. We have this, Remy. She's safe."

"I know, but we have to teach her yes and no, also no euphemisms for her vagina and all, okay?"

"Yes. You even have Carol and RJ using anatomical terms now."

"It's just my first night away from her."

"And I know it's hard, but being a dad doesn't mean you can't have a night to yourself for a little self-care and catching up on sleep."

"My phone will be next to me all night. If she wants to see me, just video call."

I told my girl I loved her, and after pushing her curls back from her face, it took everything in me to straighten and close the door. My eyes were locked on the taillights of her car until she disappeared around the corner. My feet were still rooted to the sidewalk, and I looked at my house.

I'd take a run with Romeo at the park and then come home, maybe have takeout. I tried not to get it as I preferred if she had a home-cooked meal. With just me, it didn't matter. Fuck, I was already missing her, and she hadn't been gone five minutes yet.

DAMN, I was out of shape. My usual five-mile run was down to three, and I was huffing as I slowed near the steps that led up to the house. When I opened the gate and let Romeo off his leash, he started barking and I lifted my head to find Robert sitting on the top step with a six-pack and takeout bags between his feet.

"What are you doing sitting out here? You have a key." I asked as I approached slowly.

"Didn't know if I was still welcome to just come in."

"You're always welcome."

"Hasn't been that way recently. You barely look at me." His tone wasn't judgmental or harsh. He stood and picked up the beer and food as I passed him.

"I shouldn't have asked you to do what you did. I'm sorry."

"Gladys said she was taking Carmen tonight. I thought it would be a good time to talk, work out whatever that was in the bathroom."

"Okay." I unlocked the door and entered with him close behind. Romeo took off around us to the kitchen where his water bowl was. "I'm just going to take a quick shower and change. You know where everything is."

He didn't say anything as he headed to the back of the house, and I detoured to the steps. I jogged upstairs, stripped out of my clothes, and jumped into the shower. Usually, I liked long showers. Let the hot water loosen my muscles, but I didn't linger.

By the time I was clean, dressed in jeans and a t-shirt, and joined him in the kitchen, he had everything laid out. Our favorites from the local Chinese place we used to get dinner from every Friday night. He had beers and plates, chopsticks already set out, and I lowered onto one of the barstools. He took the seat beside me. His arms brushed mine, and he leaned into me to reach a container.

Every grazing touch caused my body to react and my throat started to close up.

"So, what was that in the bathroom? You weren't enjoying it. You were crying, Remy."

"It didn't feel right, but I wanted to feel something. I've been single a long time."

"Why?"

"Why am I single?"

"Yeah, you're gorgeous, sweet. You treat everyone with respect and care. Why single?"

"My last was Harry. We'd been together a few years. As I told you, we weren't living together or anything. We'd talked about it. I wanted all that silly shit, ya know, marriage and a family. He didn't want the responsibility of a kid messing up his life. He was thirty-six, loved his life as is. Being able to go and do as he pleased. Spur of the moment vacations."

"Not really suited for a cop's husband."

"No. He'd planned this big trip, and I couldn't go. He already had the tickets and everything was set. I told him I had a friend from the crisis center where I man the suicide hotline. Tim had just lost someone during a call, and I thought he could use the time away. When they returned from the two-week trip, well, they were in love. Other than a kiss, they hadn't acted on anything, but I saw how happy they were."

"And you broke it off."

"Yeah. Then three years later, I'm getting a call that they want me to be a godparent to their son."

"You told me that hurt."

"It did. Years of hearing it wasn't possible, or maybe one day. And in a few short years, he'd gotten my dream. I felt selfish."

"You weren't selfish. Still doesn't tell me why you were doing something you obviously didn't like."

"I'm a big masculine guy. People look at me and see top. You know—"

"I know what a top and bottom are, also vers." I glanced at him to find him smiling.

"Well, I always swore that I wouldn't bottom again until I found my one. My childhood and being a sex worker, it ruined sex for me. Me and my psychologist have worked through my intimacy and sex issues. I know what happened to me doesn't define me. It's okay to be scared sometimes. I'm terrified to give anyone my back, let them see the scars or take me from behind. Back then, men just bent me over. My parents pimped me out for almost three years when I got too old for them." I pushed my plate away that I'd barely touched.

"Remy."

"I know it was wrong, but it's all I ever knew. It took forever to learn what healthy sex and intimacy were. I spent a year testing every three months. Sweating for days until the clinic called. I never went without condoms, but they never prepared me or used lube. Condoms aren't a hundred percent effective. They break. After a few years and I was finally clean and sober, I'd applied and graduated from the academy. I wanted to make a difference, and I wanted to be on the frontline where people weren't just case numbers."

"And you've done an amazing job."

"Thanks. Sometimes I still don't think I do enough."

"Remy, you go to the hospital every chance you get with Romeo to cheer up sick kids. You hand out lube and condoms and your card to any kid you see with the promise of a no-judgment ear. You spent a fortune in donations at the shelters and in food cards. You work the mobile clinic every month to make sure the sex workers and homeless kids get tested. What more can you do?"

I shrugged. I always felt like it wasn't enough. I could always save one more from becoming me or the version of myself I'd have been if I hadn't escaped.

"You done eating?"

"Yeah, I'm not so hungry right now."

I tried to tell him I'd clean everything up later, but he gave me that stern look I loved so much. Why did everything about him have to be so sexy?

"We can heat everything up later."

I nodded and just studied him. "Are we okay?"

He answered me as he opened the fridge and put everything inside. "Of course, but there is something that bothered me."

"What?" I asked as the door closed. As he approached me, I counted each step he took until he was standing beside me. He turned the stool until I faced him.

"This." When his rough, warm hands cupped my cheeks, I froze and fisted my hands in the sides of his t-shirt. He nudged my thighs apart with his hips, and as he pressed his body to me, his lips brushed mine.

I'd fantasized for almost two years what his mouth would feel like. His full lips were firm and surprisingly soft. I almost pulled away until I felt the slight hardness of his cock lined up with mine. He didn't rush or force the kiss. The passes of his lips on mine were light and teasing. My hands slipped under his shirt and he broke the kiss, his forehead coming to rest on mine. His stomach and chest were warm and silky, and the trimmed hair on his chest teased my palms.

"I'm not in my twenties or thirties anymore. Fifty-five may not be attractive to you."

"You were shirtless a lot. And that's the only thing you're complaining about? Not kissing a man."

"I've thought about it a lot these last few weeks. Even called Gladys to make sure I wasn't a selfish lover."

"You talked to her about—" I didn't know how to finish that.

"Us, not specifically, but her and my kids, well, I think they figured it out. I think her words were hot single dad. I hated you told me I didn't have to kiss you. Even though I had no right, it pissed me off that you ignored me afterward. But I can't forget the way you tightened around my fingers or how hot and slick you were. Now, I have a very important question for you."

My chest tightened until I felt his smile against my mouth, and he pulled me closer to the edge of the stool. "And what might that be?"

"What are we going to do with a completely child-free night, or can we go pick her up? You kept her away from me, Remy, and I can't have that. No matter what goes on in that head of yours, you two are my family."

"I'm sorry. I was scared."

"You never have to be scared of me, baby. What do we have planned for tonight?"

"I'd planned to just stretch out on the couch and catch up on sleep. I still haven't caught up."

"Then that's what we'll do. Come on, I missed my Remy cuddles."

I pouted. "You started it."

"I did, and I'm not going to complain."

"Robert, I…" I dropped my attention to his chest.

"Hey, what's wrong?"

"We…I can't lose you as a friend or partner."

"You won't. We're going to take this slow. I'll even break out my rusty dating skills and take you out for more than Chinese and pay for dessert without expecting sex." I rolled my eyes. "Listen, this is new for me. I'm fifty-five with grown children and grandchildren, and this is like starting over completely. I'm very much out of my element here, and as scared as I am, I want this, Remy. You and Roo and everything that comes with that. The good days and especially the bad ones."

"It's too much."

"For you two, no such thing. So am I getting my cuddles or not, baby?"

I let out a long, annoyed sigh. "I guess."

With his hands on my sides, he urged me to stand and then backed up to lead me into the living room. He released me to throw the back cushions to the floor and then stretched out on his side. He patted the spot in front of him, and I took a deep breath as I laid down with his chest to my back. My head rested on his bicep, and against my better judgment, I let all the built-up stress disappear. I grabbed the remote and handed it to him. I doubted I'd be awake long enough to choose something to watch.

Two years of daydreams and fantasies coalesced into that moment. Wrapped in the arms of the man I'd started falling in love with from the second I'd spotted him across a squad room. I trusted him; more than even Harry, but I didn't know if I was ready to trust myself. There wasn't much I was positive about in life, but his power to destroy me was a certainty, especially after my talk with Shine.

17

ROBERT

COLD CASE
UNIT

I peeked at Remy over the top of the file I pretended to read. Our two desks were tucked to one side of the dark, dusty room that housed the small Cold Case Unit. He had his dark brown hair pulled back into a half ponytail. I remembered how soft the strands were between my fingers. With every kiss we shared, I hadn't resisted the urge to tangle it around my hands. I didn't know why but I couldn't remember this compulsion to touch anyone as much as I did him. Work was a nightmare as I tried to control those new urges.

When we'd awakened on the couch that morning, his body was completely wrapped around mine, breath teasing the side of my neck. I loved sharing space with him.

"Are you going to do any work today?"

"I am."

He leaned his upper body over his desk and arched a thick brow. "Okay, and what does that file say, Daddy?"

"It says can we take off early today."

He rolled his eyes. "No. Be serious."

I let out a heavy sigh as I closed and tossed the file aside to join the stack of thirty others. He'd been bored the first few days of our new assignment and had randomly gone through several homicide cases. Each one dealt with a bunch of missing person reports that had been assigned to homicide when bodies turned up. Something about them intrigued Remy, and the more he showed me, I'd started to notice the pattern as well. Although, since they were reported as runaways—troubled kids—the original investigators had thrown them aside as just another addict and hustler disappearing.

"How many are we up to?"

"Fourteen I'm sure of, sixteen that vaguely follow the pattern. I know some of these cases because they came through when I worked Sex Crimes."

"How far back do the cases go?"

"The oldest file so far is eight years. It looks like they did the minimum work on it before they tossed it aside."

"What do you want to do about it? I'll go with whatever decision you make."

"Even if people think I'm overreacting to some homeless kids dying that no one cared about?"

"Baby, you care, and I trust you. And they weren't just homeless kids. They were humans that deserve respect, and families need closure. Why don't we box up the files and take them home? We can work on them after we tuck Roo into bed."

"You've never doubted my gut once, not since we started working together."

"Because I may have a lot more experience being a cop, but you're a cop and a former street kid, you know them and what they go through firsthand. Knowledge I'll never come close to having. So, when it comes to this, I trust you to know what needs to be done. If you think there's a predator out there killing kids they see as disposable, then the bastard needs to be stopped. I know when we go down there, they will tell you everything you want to know."

"Thanks."

"No need to thank me. What we can do is figure out if these cases are close enough to move them to one investigation. Do some legwork of our own and then see if someone will move it to an active case. Have any similar cases come in during the last two years?"

"Nothing across our desks. I don't have a lot of friends but..." He batted his thick lashes at me.

"I'll see what Stevenson has to say. His nosy ass knows everything. I'll call Coleman at the lab and see what was run and what wasn't. If we have DNA, at least we can compare between our potential serial."

"You're so good to me."

"Just behave for the time it takes me to get the information I need, please, baby."

"I won't even look in Coleman's direction. I'll even smile and be polite."

"I'll believe that when I see it."

"So little faith."

"You stand up for what you believe in, and I respect that. Yet sometimes we have to be nice even if we don't particularly like it."

"That's never been my strong suit."

"No, it hasn't, but that's what you have me for."

"Having a mature, a lot older boyfriend has to be good for something."

"Ouch, baby. That was unnecessary."

He rolled his eyes, pushing up from his chair and disappearing into the many rows of shelves. I relaxed back in my chair to tip my head back to stare up at the water-stained ceiling. As much as I adored my man, I wasn't looking forward to talking to Stevenson, and especially not Coleman. I didn't know what the lab supervisor had against Remy other than the one punch. Maybe he was just an asshole.

I lifted my head and got up and went to find my man. I checked each row from left to right until I caught sight of him in the very back. He was looking at a clipboard with a frown. I eased in behind him, and I caged his body with my hands flat on the shelf in front of him. I rested my forehead on his nape.

"You okay?" I asked.

"Yeah. A lot of these cases I've seen before. There are people who care, I know that, I do, but these cold cases are filled with victims that no one cared about. Until I was twenty-six, I was always one mistake away from being right here with them."

"But you're not. What are you doing right now?" I paused, but all I heard was his heavy sigh. I dropped my hands to his sides and turned him to face me. "You're giving these people a voice, one that a lot of cops failed to do. Maybe we won't figure it out. It's possible that a suspect or conviction never comes around, but we gave them time. We cared that their files were sitting here doing nothing but collecting dust."

"I get it."

"Baby, listen to me. You can only do so much. You put so much pressure on yourself to make amends or pay for some sin you won't tell me or don't want to talk about. You're an amazing, compassionate man, and it hasn't escaped my notice or that of others everything you do. We'll do what we can. I'll support you in every way because that's what you need from me."

I smiled as he set the board aside and draped his arms over my shoulders.

"Now, Detective Bosley, what do you think you're doing?"

"Harassing my very hot Daddy."

"Is that right?"

"Oh yeah, it's been five hours since I was able to get my hands on you."

"I think I suggested going home early." I lifted my chin until my lips almost brushed his, and I didn't miss the way his gaze dropped to my mouth.

"You did, but we have to be responsible adults and do the right thing."

"Doesn't mean I have to like it. I've missed you these past few weeks you pulled away from me." I stroked my hand up his back until I could fist my fingers in his hair. I brought his lips to mine and groaned as the softness of the curves conformed to my firmer ones. I tasted his little whimper as I lost myself to the kiss. At that moment, I didn't care if we had the entire precinct as an audience.

His soft belly conformed to my flatter one as he pushed closer. I slipped my free hand under the back of his t-shirt, letting my fingertips dance over the raised scars. I didn't hesitate, but I also didn't linger. I loved the warmth and weight of him in my arms. His tongue teased mine, and I went from half-hard to wanting to slam him back against the closest wall.

I eased the kiss, but smiled as he pouted and tried to follow my retreat.

"Not the place, baby. But as soon as we get home, you can have all the kisses you want."

"You're a tease, Detective Kaufmann."

"I know, I shouldn't have started anything. So that we behave, I'm going to go talk to Stevenson and give Coleman a call at the lab. You keep looking."

"Thank you."

"For what?"

"Not thinking I'm overreacting to all this."

"You're passionate but also logical. If you're seeing something, then it's there. We just have to figure out a way to get everyone else to see the same thing."

I gave him one last quick kiss as I heard the squeaky wheels of one of the desk chairs, and patted his rounded, lush bottom, then slipped out of the storage shelves. I barely acknowledged the other old-timer. I think he'd been down there twenty years. I exited to the hallways and took a right toward the elevator.

On the trip up to my old squad, I tried to put on my friendliest expression. I'd do anything for Remy, but my diplomacy only went so far. I had to admit Remy and I were about the most anti-social partners in the city. Dalton, my last partner, only spent enough time together to work and went our separate ways.

"Look who it is. You getting bored down there in the dungeon?"

"Graves, not if it keeps me from seeing your face, I'm quite happy down there."

"At least we don't have to deal with that partner of yours."

"You got something to say about Remy? You might want to keep it to yourself. They can't demote me any lower than Cold Case, which means popping you one won't hurt my feelings or career aspirations." I looked away from Graves to find Stevenson coming from the Captain's office. "Stevenson, can I buy you a cup of coffee?"

"Thought cuddly Bears named Remy were more your type?"

I smirked as I crossed the room to perch on the corner of his desk. "He is, but I have a favor to ask which keeps me in his good graces."

"And off the couch, but let me tell you, Kaufmann, I ain't a cheap date." Stevenson steepled his fingers.

"I'll even buy you a large coffee *and* a donut."

"I don't put out on the first date even for the stereotypical donut."

"My man would protest anyway. Remy started going through some of the cold cases and found a pretty obvious pattern. I was wondering if any cases had come through here in the last few years that fit the profile."

"Give me the profile."

"Fourteen to Twenty-one. Runaways or ones with a history of solicitation. Reported missing a week or two before bodies were found posed in new clothes. All had signs of sexual assault."

"Have you called the ME and Coleman yet?"

"ME, I have no issues with…Coleman, let's just say I may have issues."

"What you really have is a Remy problem and Coleman's homophobia and racism, and that tooth he lost at Christmas."

"Remy promised to be on his best behavior."

"It's Remy, Kaufmann, and"—he leaned forward—"what I heard is you two have gotten really close. How much ink does he have? This is info I need to know."

"Leave my man out of your fantasies and gossip. I can handle Remy. I'll give him a very nice reward for being good. Are you going to help us?"

"I like Remy, and I tolerate you. He's got that hot cuddly thing, but I would kill to see his skill with a pair of handcuffs. You think you can give him my number? One date, and I'll give you whatever intel you want, and I mean all of the intel."

"You want to end up a cold case?"

"So possessive. Fine, give me a few days and I'll email you any case numbers I come across. But since I can't have Remy, you still owe me a coffee and donut. I expect the payment on my desk in the morning."

"Tyrant."

"I haven't had a date in a year, and you got the hottest, out detective to come through this precinct in years, so, sue me, I'm a little jealous."

"How do you know we're not just friends and I don't think you're good enough for him?"

"Please, you do know you two are pretty touchy. You two are your own little clique around here. It was only a matter of time."

"We going to have issues?"

"Graves might be a little jealous."

"He better not even be looking."

"You've got it bad."

"I do, so, no flirting. I know you, well, I didn't know you wanted my man and his handcuffs until today."

"We can't help our fantasies. It's all harmless."

"Don't even look at him," I threatened as the asshole laughed. Then I went to find a quiet place to call the ME and Coleman, without Remy around. I couldn't do a face-to-face with the lab supervisor. I may have talked big, but Coleman pissed me off as much as he did Remy. If my man hadn't hit him first, I would've done it. The shit I would do to make Remy happy should scare me, yet nothing was too much for him.

18

REMY

COLD CASE
UNIT

Working the Cold Case Unit was like living in a tomb all day, every day, which was appropriate since most of my cases were in dust-covered boxes. We only worked with two other detectives, and I could tell they were all burned out from sometimes chasing a lost cause. Testing on older cases was rare unless new information came to light. And you had to get someone to pay attention to the new information. Good thing Robert was in my corner.

There was also Vega Carlyle, who was a forensic genealogist I knew from back in the day. The department had received a grant to have all the cases analyzed for possible review. She was one of my closest friends, and I could get her to help with the long and growing list of connected sexual assaults and murders getting retested or at least tested. I pulled the forensic logs, and a lot of them said the post-mortem rape kits hadn't even been tested against the national DNA database.

The strong hand stroking along my lower back brought me out of my thoughts. Normally, I made the trips to my old stomping grounds without him. Not that I had an issue with him mingling with my past. We hadn't had a repeat of the revelation when Fran came to Robert's house or the heart to heart when we discussed the bathroom incident.

"Relax, baby. You're tense."

"We just...this is the first time you've been down here knowing my history."

"There isn't anything wrong with your history. It made you the man I adore, okay?"

"Okay, thanks." He hugged me to his side and released me as we turned the corner.

"Hey, Pretty, slumming again?" I rolled my eyes and elbowed my partner as he laughed at the fifth person to call me Pretty that night. I couldn't help back in my day I was the quintessential twink that could be mistaken for a girl in the right light. Back then, I was sought after because the closeted tricks could bend me over and pretend they weren't having sex with a man and intensifying their already overinflated internal homophobia.

"Davian, you been to see Boss yet?" I asked as I leaned against the brick wall, and our shoulders touched.

"No, but I got it on my full dance card for next week. What are you doing down here? And who's your friend?"

"Davian, meet Robert. Robert, meet the ever-beautiful Davian."

"Nice to meet you, Davian." Robert held out his hand, and I didn't miss the double-take between the offered shake and me.

Paranoia was second nature around there. I still lived with some decades later, and Robert had his badge clipped onto the waistband of his jeans. Law enforcement and us were never friends. I was shocked when they hadn't turned their backs on me like I was a traitor the first time they saw me on patrol in my uniform.

Robert, with his usual patience, waited until Davian took his hand and gave it an unsure shake.

"What do I owe for the pleasure of two handsome men gracing me with their presence?"

"I have some pictures I want you to look at, and I just want to know if you recognize any of them."

"Sure. This have to do with a case?" He reached out to take the stack of photos I pulled out of the inside pocket of my jacket.

"Sort of. Robert got hurt some months back, and they transferred us to the Cold Case unit for a bit while he healed up. I was going through some files, and recognized a few names from when I worked the Special Victims squad. There was forensics and DNA, but no suspects."

"You know they don't care about us down here. No offense, Robert."

"None taken. My baby here does, and you're *all* important to him. We're kinda doing this off the books until we get some more solid information to take to our superiors."

"Your baby, huh?" Davian asked with a grin, and I rolled my eyes as he started checking out my Daddy with a little more interest than I was comfortable with.

"Yeah, mine."

"Well, well, well, Pretty is coming up in the world, getting all respectable with a man…"

"And a kid," I said and watched Davian's eyes widen.

"Congratulations, Pretty, that's great. You always wanted babies of your own." He enveloped me in a big, exuberant hug. "You'll have to bring the family to one of our dinners. You haven't been around in months."

"Like I said, Robert got hurt, and I nursed him back to health and getting used to taking care of my daughter…it's just been kinda crazy. I've missed y'all, though, so I'll definitely make plans for the next one."

When you're on the streets, you develop crews or found families. My old crew kept growing. And even when we left that life behind, we still got together for dinners. Reunions of sorts to catch up and share community with people who understood what you went through or were still going through. Being part of a unit was sometimes integral to survival. When I'd worked as a hustler, I was part of a team. We checked in with each other before and after a date, and if we didn't show up, we had license plates and descriptions.

"So, what am I looking at?" Davian asked as he retook his place beside me and started thumbing through the photos, each boy looking younger than the last. "Sylvan." He tapped the picture of a pretty brunet boy. His file said he was twenty-five, but he definitely looked younger. "He worked the streets for about a year, got himself into a very exclusive stable. His Pimp treated his boys and girls like royalty. What the fuck was his name..." Davian cursed under his breath. "Eugene Forester, nice enough for a pimp, real respectful, too. A few of the faces in these I think belonged to him. He runs a club about five blocks from here. Hide the badges, though. You know how things work down here, Pretty."

"We just got off work and waited for our kid to go to bed before coming out. We're still dressed for the day gig. Know any of the others?" He recited names as he kept going through the stacks.

"Most of them were independents or fresh meat. There was this big Italian strutting around, throwing around cash and promises of being treated well if you're under his protection. Yet you know that's normally just talk until they snare you. Us old-timers, well, we can see through the bullshit. Sometimes even we ignore it when it's cold, and your belly is eating itself. You've been there, Pretty, these kids..." Davian tsked as he shook his head.

"I know, but if we have a predator on the streets, then we need to find him before any of our kids turn into a case number in a storage room."

"You can't save us all."

"Not that I don't try."

"True. And quit being such a stranger. You can still hang out with us. We never judge you for that badge of yours."

I laughed as I took the pictures back and returned them to my pocket. I pushed away from the wall. As soon as I was back at Robert's side, his arm went around my waist. I loved his affection, and he didn't push for anything I wasn't ready to give.

"Do you have any info on the Italian guy that was around?" Robert asked.

"No, but I can ask around for a name. He's not a regular, but enough that he's recognizable. When we have breakfast before going home, I'll ask and send you a text."

"I appreciate it."

"Anything for you, Pretty. And no matter what anyone says, you're still as pretty as you were back in the day. You ever want to come back…"

"I'll keep that as my retirement plan." I kissed his cheek, and we were headed off down the block.

"You know, I'm going to have to up the perks of staying with all the offers you keep getting."

"Aw, would you miss me, Daddy?"

"You know I would. Where are we off to now because I want you all to myself."

"You have me all to yourself." I shot him a bratty grin and batted my lashes.

"Yes, but some place where I can preferably get you naked."

Fuck, I wanted naked, really badly, but I was still nervous about the sex part of our relationship. My man was gorgeous, and I was a hairy, overweight bottom. Not that he didn't know about that after having his fingers buried in my ass.

"Oh, now, I see, you just want me for all the fluffy sexiness. Just to have your sweaty, nasty way with me. You cheapen me. Maybe I'm waiting for marriage?"

"Is there a jewelry store or one of those machines with the plastic bubbles so I can buy you a ring?"

I laughed loudly as I shot him a glance to find him grinning. "Wow, the romance died before it even started."

"I lived with you for months. I've seen you in the morning. You drool on my chest in your sleep. And the snoring, so much snoring."

"I want a new boyfriend." I quickened my steps as he chuckled behind me, and then I felt his hands on my hips.

"Too damn late, we're practically cohabitating. We have a kid and a dog. We're the old married couple. Get used to it."

"And like an old married couple, you're not going to be getting any."

"How long can you resist me?"

"I've had years of abstinence. I can hold out for a long, long time."

I waved as someone else called my name and was thankful for the distraction. I hated being scared because I trusted Robert. But even though I'd worked through my intimacy problems, there was still that scared kid in the back of my mind. He'd never go away, and I knew that. But Robert made me want different experiences—the things I'd denied myself because being vulnerable was dangerous.

19

ROBERT

"What's with your friend?" Gladys asked as she peeked around my shoulder as I stood there studying Shine and Remy. A few weeks had passed since Remy and I talked about giving a relationship a go. We'd decided to have a big meal at my house, a couple type thing. See how the kids reacted to making the official announcement. They hadn't even blinked an eye.

We'd invited Shine because he said she needed time away from Boss and being around other people. Shine was still too withdrawn, and we'd all worked on getting her out of her shell. He'd set her up with a great therapist, but as much as talking helped, things took time. Yet Shine had to talk for therapy to work.

"She's been through a..." I didn't know how to explain. "She was hired as a dancer for a party and several of the bastards..."

"She needs friends." I knew that hardened tone. Gladys had Mama Bear tendencies, but she still wasn't up there with Remy though. I would admit that Gladys and Remy would make one fearsome duo.

"Remy arranged for her to live with an old friend of theirs, but she's only talking to Remy. We tried to get her to see that psychologist we know. It was a no-go. She's just not ready to talk to a stranger yet."

"She's got us now. How are things with Remy? Seems to be less tension, but there doesn't seem to be the glow of plentiful sex."

"It's not all about sex. We're doing good. We had a talk about his past and decided to take things slow. It's best for both of us." I'd observed Remy for years, and after we'd discussed his past, I knew he was still unsure about moving us into a physical relationship. For me, the kisses and touches, our nights curled up on the couch—I was happy with that. I adored my baby too much to push. I wanted his love and trust, and that took time. I was no longer in my twenties and obsessed with orgasms on an epic scale.

"That's good. Talking is the first step. Does it feel weird?"

"I thought it would, but no. I wasn't expecting"—I looked away from her and to Remy—"him and Roo to be my second chance. Hell, you know I wasn't even looking for a second chance at all."

She turned to lean against the door frame and smiled at me. "I know you weren't. And yeah, the package is a bit different than I thought of the person I'd have to share my best friend with, but that's not a bad thing."

"Papa." I glanced down to find Roo staring up at me. She was getting so happy and chunky, and we were proud of how far she'd come in such a short time. She saw a therapist twice a week. The nightmares were getting better.

"What, honey?"

"Hungry." I chuckled as I scooped her up and carried her instantly into the kitchen with Gladys following us.

"Again? We just ate. Do you want a snack or do you want a plate?"

"Plate, please."

I sat her on the counter and went to start digging out leftovers. "I don't know where she puts all the food."

"She has a lot of growing to do. Don't you, Roo?"

I caught her nodding her head. I couldn't imagine anything better than spending time with her, Remy, Gladys, and the kids.

"How's work going? Still doing okay in the new unit?"

"It's not homicide, but I like the Cold Case Squad. Remy and I are alternating nights working late so one of us is always home with Roo, but Mrs. Walton doesn't mind letting her spend the night if we both needed be MIA."

"You're so cute with the new boyfriend."

"Ha, ha, ha."

"Quit. You know if you ever need a babysitter, me or the kids would jump at the chance. You have to make time for dates and alone time."

"But I like spending time with Remy and our Roo." I dropped a kiss on top of the little girl's head as she giggled, and I heated up her plate. "Is there something wrong with that?"

"No, there's nothing wrong with wanting to spend time with your family. I also know you don't want a repeat of the guilt you felt for missing out on Carol and RJ growing up. It's different with Remy. You two are partners at work, you spend every day together, and Roo needs more time so she feels secure. Once everything settles, you'll find a routine."

Yes, I felt bad about missing a lot of my older kids' milestones, but I made up for it with Roo and my grandkids. I loved the routine we had, work and then home, dinner for the three of us, and putting Roo to bed before we had a quiet evening just Remy and me. We still had work to do. I knew he trusted me, but we had a ways to go before he let go enough to let me love on him. I loved sex, and I wanted to have a lot of sweaty, alone time with him, but I was honestly happy with the cuddles and kisses.

I jumped as the microwave beeped. I opened it and removed her plate as I saw Gladys put Roo at the table on her booster seat.

I served Roo, and she instantly dug in. She was doing better about how quickly she ate as she learned that when she was hungry, she'd get to eat, and no one would ever take her food away.

The more I learned about Roo's life before we found her, the angrier I became. How they could've treated the sweet girl worse than a hated pet astounded me.

"Okay, I'm headed out. I have a meeting with my client in the morning. Why didn't you ever talk me out of this lawyer career?"

"Um, you're the one who thought being a lawyer would change the world."

"Such bullshit."

Roo giggled, and I shook my head. Our Roo was going to have a potty mouth at some point. Gladys kissed my cheek and then the top of Roo's head. Quickly, my kids and grandkids came to say goodbye, and Gladys yelled she was driving Shine home.

"They abandoned us. What did you say?" Remy asked as he filled the doorway of the kitchen.

"I didn't say anything. They probably think we need alone time."

"Do they know we're together almost twenty-four hours a day?"

"Are you complaining?"

"Of course not." He stepped into the room and leaned down to kiss Roo's soft hair. "Was our girl hungry again? I'm going to need a second job. Should we clear out so you can have quiet time? House to yourself?"

"Why? I already got Roo's room ready. Her pajamas and bubble bath are ready for bedtime."

"I think you're just dating me so you can share custody of my kid."

"Yes, yes I am." He rolled his eyes and crossed his arms over his chest, and I chuckled. "Have you seen her little face? She's so adorable."

"I can already see where I stand in this relationship."

"Aw, don't be jealous, baby. Go get our kid ready for bed while I finish cleaning up and lock the house down."

"I'll yell when it's time to tell her goodnight."

I stood back as I watched him ask her if he could pick her up, and when she said yes, he scooped her up and left the kitchen. My phone beeped from where I'd plugged it in. I picked it up and stroked my thumb up the screen to see the email notification from Stevenson. I opened up the attachment with ten possible matches with case numbers. I replied with a thanks, and then sent one to our old Captain to get copies of the files. I hoped none of them belonged to Graves; I didn't want to deal with the bastard.

I didn't like Graves. His ego was out of control. I put my phone to sleep and placed it back on the counter. Family time meant no phones. Roo yelling my name had me jogging through the house and up the stairs behind Romeo. The dog knew when it was bedtime for his favorite kid. We went through the bedtime routine, five stories because I couldn't tell Roo no when she batted her lashes. I swore Remy taught her that, and it was an unfair advantage. I didn't stand a chance with any of them. Roo and my grandkids knew it, too.

Then it was goodnights and hugs, and I was leading Remy from the room.

"Now, I have you all to myself." I nudged him into my bedroom and circled him to look up at his gorgeous face framed by his thick, dark hair.

"And what are you doing to do with me, Daddy?" The corner of his mouth ticked upward.

"I can think of a lot of things, but we have something important to talk about." I backed up until I sat on the end of the bed and patted my thighs.

I didn't take my focus off him as he crossed the room until he placed his hands on my shoulders and straddled my lap. His thighs and calves squeezed my hips and sides. I laced my fingers at the small of his back and leaned up to brush our mouths together.

"What's on your mind?"

"I want to know what you're scared of."

"I'm not..." I kissed him to cut off his denial.

"Baby, we have to be honest, and I'm nervous about sex, too. I've had two partners in my life. What if I completely suck at it? I'm also old. What if I suddenly get ED? Jerking off doesn't require peer review...that's all about the end and then the snooze. There's no grading on a curve."

"Is there a curve? Because I really want to expand on this line of questioning. Is there show and tell? Please, tell me there's show."

"Serious, baby, serious. I want you to trust me, Remy, with everything...even the things that you think are embarrassing."

"Robert, I trust you, I do, but I'm—" He tipped his head back and groaned.

"Just say it, baby. I want to know everything remember, good or bad." I nipped at the front of his throat and kissed the small sting away.

"I'm not exactly in my twenties anymore." He dropped his chin to his chest, and I rested my forehead on the top of his head. "I'm a hairy, chunky, middle-aged man, and you're...perfect."

"I'm halfway through my fifties. I have gray in my pubes, for fuck's sake." He snorted, and I glared at him. "I think you're gorgeous, and you did parade around in a towel a lot while you stayed here. Oh, and let's not forget the shower incident. I saw everything then. And that rounded ass and belly have fueled more than a few fantasies. What else is wrong?"

"I want you to fuck me, and I'm terrified I'm going to freak out because it's new. I haven't had sex since Harry, and we didn't have the busiest bedroom around. It was routine, and I always topped. The one time I tried to bottom with him, my brain went into fight or flight."

"We'll take all the time you need. I want you to feel safe with me. Yes, I want to have sex with you, but that doesn't mean penetration or you giving me your back. I don't care how many times they say time heals all things, that's not true in every case. Time can dull it. Time can be a band-aid, but what happened to you growing up and into your twenties...a lot of people don't survive that. You did, and I respect your strength and everything you made of yourself."

"I feel like such an asshole."

"Baby, you are not an asshole for having boundaries and expecting your lover to respect them."

"Why are you so nice?"

"Nice is usually the mood killer."

"I like nice, Daddy. I haven't had a lot of nice."

"From what you've told me about Harry, he seemed nice."

"Harry fell in love with someone I sent him on vacation with. I don't think you'd do that, so you're a lot nicer and loyal."

"You're making me sound like man's best friend. I just want you to know that bottoming for me isn't required to be in my bed. You just curled up beside me, and I'm happy. I don't believe penetration equals sex."

"But I want it, Daddy, so much. My toys are getting a lot of action lately."

An idea came to me, and I wondered if he'd be open to it. All I could do was ask. "Would you try something for me?" I brought my left hand around to pinch his chin and tugged his short beard to bring his mouth to mine.

"I trust you."

"Why don't we go out on a date? A real one. We get a babysitter, and I pick you up, and we do it the old-fashioned way. Making out. Backseat of the SUV. Couch with an ignored movie in the background. Sneaking upstairs to your room."

"Really?" I loved the adorable smile that curved his mouth, and I wanted to make sure it always stayed there.

"Yeah, because I have a feeling you never did those high school rites of passage."

"Why would you go through all the trouble? Maybe I'm not worth the effort."

"Baby, if you don't want to, I'd bottom for you."

"You'd do that for me?"

"Yes, I can't say I'll enjoy it, but I'll never know if we don't try. Whatever happens between us as long as it's consensual and mutually enjoyable, how can that be wrong?"

"You have to have a toxic trait in there somewhere."

"Do I need to tap into my inner Bro so we don't disrupt the universe?"

"Please don't."

"Want to curl up in bed and watch a movie? We have to get up earlier to go to your place in the morning and get Roo to the babysitter."

"If this isn't working for you, just promise you'll tell me."

He closed his eyes, and I cupped his jaw. "Look at me, baby." I waited for him to open his eyes and noticed they were glassy with unshed tears. "I don't want anything more than I want you and Roo in my life." I stroked my left hand down his chest and over his belly; I wanted warm, hairy skin.

I pushed my hand under his t-shirt. My free hand went to the back of his neck.

"Daddy." His lips brushed against mine, and I groaned as he shifted on my lap.

"Fuck, baby, you're driving me crazy." I fell back, bringing him with me. He braced his forearms on either side of my head. "I want skin," I growled as I worked his shirt off, only breaking the contact of our lips to strip him.

"I thought we were taking this slow." He whimpered as I pinched his hard little nipples.

"We are, making out, baby, nothing more than this. You'll have to tell me yes every step of the way." I tugged at the thick hair on his chest. "You're fucking beautiful." I sunk my teeth into his lower lip and sucked at the generous curve. He shook and writhed on top of me, and as much as I wanted him naked, I refrained.

My heart was kicking a frantic pace in my chest, and my cock strained against my zipper. His hard length rubbed against mine as I kissed him. Each time I started to retreat, I couldn't bring myself to break contact.

"I've wanted you since the minute I spotted you talking to the captain," he whispered between brushes of our lips. "He introduced us, and my heart broke that you were my partner... that you had a ring on." He laced our fingers and pinned my hands above my head.

"But, baby, I told you I was divorced."

"But, Daddy, you still wore it. The next morning"—he rolled his hips, and I tightened my fingers through his—"I fucked myself with my favorite toy and screamed your name."

"Don't tease, love, especially when you're in our bed." I protested as he sat up and released my hands, then he rutted his lush ass on my cock. "Don't be mean to Daddy."

"You like when I call you that, don't you?"

"Only you, baby." As soon as the words were out, he removed my shirt and tossed it over the edge of the bed. "Fuck." I arched into the drag of his hands over my stomach to my chest. He was so sexy straddling my hips and his beautiful belly on display; everything about him was irresistible. He lowered his upper body until his weight rested on me.

"Where are you taking me on our first date, Daddy?"

"Some place where I can have you naked the entire time."

"Find all this fluffiness sexy?" He smirked against my mouth and my fingers sunk into soft rolls along his ribs.

"You know I do. You're gorgeous from the top of your silky

hair to the tips of your toes. If you haven't noticed, I can barely keep my hands off you."

"And I do love your hands on me."

"I want you to sleep with me tonight. You know Daddy gives good cuddles."

"You really do."

"Then say yes, baby."

"Yes."

I stroked the tip of my tongue along his bottom lip until he opened for me. I hugged him to me, loving the feel of his thick body hair on my smooth stomach and trimmed chest. I braced my left arm along his lower back and flipped us until I rested heavily between his strong thighs.

"You're always safe with me."

"I know. You've always made everything alright. The day of the shooting, I'd never been so scared. I couldn't imagine losing you."

"You'll never lose me because I always have you watching my back. I'm going to lock up, get ready for bed, and after I put Romeo out and check on Roo, I'll be right back." I made myself give him one last kiss, and then I lifted off him and headed for the door.

I was going to make our first night together perfect. Make it everything he ever wanted. His happiness meant so much to me. I wanted a life with him with all the good things and to be there to support him through the bad. I knew he still had some issues and insecurities he needed to work through. When it came time, I wanted it all. I just hadn't anticipated how much my life would change with the arrival of one bratty man. There was no way I was going to complain. Remy was all mine, and I was keeping him.

REMY

COLD CASE
UNIT

"**P**apa, why is dad in your bed?" Those were the first words I'd heard that morning, and I'd held my breath as I'd waited for Robert to answer. He'd told her that I was his boyfriend and that I would be sleeping with him whenever we'd spend the night.

I'd wanted to be irritated that he didn't talk to me first, but I'd rolled over with a stupid grin on my face. He'd kissed me and picked up Roo to carry her downstairs to make breakfast. That wasn't the first time she'd seen us together or cuddling, so the situation probably didn't even register.

"Baby, stop." He grabbed my knee to stop me from swinging my legs and kicking the metal drawer with the heels of my boots.

I was going cross-eyed looking at the new files we'd received for the list Stevenson had sent us. How this slipped past anyone's notice shouldn't have shocked me as much as it had. I knew how expendable we were. Yet when I looked at each photo from their missing person reports and then the autopsy images, I saw myself and my chosen family. This could've been us, and had been for far too many of my friends. I'd tried to convince myself they just went home, and they were safe and happy. That they'd made a clean break to start life over.

"These kids never had a chance of getting justice." I held up the thick stack of folders.

"Yes, they do because you know about them now."

"Quit being so damn positive. I want to sulk."

"Sulk away, baby. I won't interrupt."

I glared as he went back to work and tried to hide his smile at my expense. "You get no more cuddles from me."

"Now, now, baby, don't be mean. I'm respecting your boundaries on your right to sulk."

"I think you need to find your inner-bro because I'm annoyed right now and I'd rather be mad at you for being a Cro-Magnon, knuckle-dragging bro than whatever this is." I motioned towards his patient and understanding boyfriend/Daddy act.

"Have you had enough caffeine?"

"I don't need caffeine."

"Trouble in paradise. Does that mean I can get his number?" Stevenson's voice came from the direction of the door, and we both jerked our attention to find him leaned against the frame.

Robert was instantly on his feet. "And I told you, you could end up as a file down here."

"He's a big boy. I'm sure he can make up his mind about the better option offered. Obviously me. I'm younger. Hotter."

"Hello, Stevenson." My lips slowly stretched into a smile as Robert cursed under his breath. "What brings you to the dungeon?"

"That's a loaded question if I ever heard one, but I'll behave for now. I come bearing unwanted presents."

My stomach sunk as he held up a file. "Another one?"

"Came in last night. I offered to take it before the Captain had time to assign it. Same MO, and the autopsy hasn't been performed yet, but I sense they're going to find the same thing.

It's scheduled for this afternoon. I wanted to know if you two wanted to take a ride?"

"Yeah." I placed the file I was holding on top of the others and slid off the desk, then I took the folder Stevenson held out to me. "What are our chances of getting this to be an open serial homicide case?"

"I'd like to be positive about it, but to be honest, I don't know if it has a chance. What's current will get investigated but probably still make it down here to where a lot of cases go to die."

"And I'm not disagreeing with you, but there's got to be something." I leaned into Robert's side when he stepped up beside me and wrapped his arm around my waist.

"We'll figure it out, and if nothing else, we can work the cases we have, and Stevenson can help us from Homicide."

"I'll do what I can. I already put out feelers to get the other newer cases. If I can get them to acknowledge we may have a serial offender, then maybe I can get the cold ones moved upstairs. When's my scenery returning because I know he's only down here because of you?" Stevenson glared at Robert, and I snorted.

"I should be cleared soon, but I may ask to stay down here longer to give our combined cases a chance. Baby, you have to have to call Mrs. Walton if we're not home in time to get Roo."

"Who's Roo? Did you get another giant dog?"

"No, Carmen. He"—I pointed at Robert with my thumb —"thought nicknaming our girl Roo was cute, and now it will never be anything else."

"Hey, our daughter is perfect and special, and likes to hide in her sari slings, hence, Roo. I don't know why you keep complaining. Unless you're still mad she said Papa first?"

I hid a chuckle as Robert stormed away toward his desk. I already saw I was going to be the bad dad in this co-parenting relationship.

"Um, how long have you two been dating?"

I choked on a laugh. "A few weeks officially."

"Quick to pop out some kids, man."

"You remember the shooting?"

"Yeah."

"Carmen was the little girl in the closet. I'm fostering to adopt. I transferred down here because the hours put in are more workable for the both of us. And one of us can always be home with her in the evening. If not, our babysitter lives next door. Things kinda shifted a bit with him and I in close quarters while I helped him get better."

"Don't tell him because I don't want to give up the pleasure of annoying him when I flirt, but you two are good together. I'm a perpetual bachelor. When did one-night-stands get so damn tiring?"

"You've become an adult, Stevenson, it was bound to happen." I patted his smooth cheek and rolled my eyes as I heard Robert muttering. "So possessive."

"He is, but he always has been. You just didn't notice. I'll meet you in the motor pool, and we'll head over to the Medical Examiner's Office. He's waiting on me before he starts."

"Thanks for this."

"I may be a bitter bastard where this job is concerned, but that doesn't change the fact I know too much shit gets lost in the cracks. I don't care what people think of what those kids allegedly did. They deserved as much effort as anyone else."

He didn't wait for me to answer before he disappeared, and I crossed the room to stand beside Robert's desk. "You have nothing to be worried about."

"Doesn't change the fact I'm suddenly terribly insecure."

"I know, and you're not the only one. So, let's get to work, and then we can go home. While I take my run with Romeo, you can spend time with Roo and figure out dinner."

"Yes, dear."

"I kinda like the sound of that."

"Don't start, baby. You already bat your lashes, and I apparently give you whatever you want."

"You do, Daddy," I whispered as I leaned in. "I learned that early. Also, Daddy makes you drop your gaze to my lips."

"Shit, I have no upper hand in this relationship."

"You don't, and it's always been that way. How did you not notice I was training you to be Daddy from day one?"

"Was that what you were doing with your bratty behavior? Preparing me to give spankings?"

I gasped. "Success!" I shouted. "My job here is done." I grabbed my jacket off the back of my chair and headed for the door with Robert laughing behind me.

I loved the sound of his happiness. The first few months as partners, I'd dealt with the closed-off man who didn't want to get too close to me. I'd worked hard to become his friend, and then he'd included me in his family. After that, I was lost, but two years ago, I hadn't seen myself in the position to say that my best friend was mine. We shared a daughter. The transition from friends to more happened easily except for those few weeks I'd pulled away from him. You didn't ask your straight best friend to get you off. Yet that one moment of weakness had brought us to that point. I wasn't going to deny what I needed to myself or him.

He was all in, and I just had to work through decades of fears. That was even harder than it sounded.

21

ROBERT

No one wanted to sit through an autopsy, and it was even harder when it was a victim like that one. He was fourteen and so small and delicate. Unfortunately, the end he met on the street was just as violent as the one he escaped. The ME pointed out old and badly healed breaks on the x-rays. The boy's entire right hand looked to have been crushed at some point.

"You okay?" I glanced over my shoulder at Remy as I looked away from the light box with the films displayed. "Home or run away, it really wasn't much of a choice, was it?"

"Hate to say it, from my experience, the streets were a helluva lot kinder. My host had men lined up outside my room. I'd see her take the cash before she left me alone with one or a group if they paid enough."

"Remy."

"You don't have to say anything. Sad to say, my story isn't a once in a lifetime one. Some parents use their kids as a commodity. Some are just more depraved about it. I wasn't brave enough to run away, though."

I was about to say something, but his warmth disappeared and moved to the table. "Do the cases match?"

Dr. Warner sighed. "The clothes were so new I found the plastic tag holders still on them. He's had repeated sexual trauma, but I can't tell from when. I took swabs and sent them to the lab. The scarring of his rectum is about the worst I've seen. He had more care shown to him after death than he had before."

"I have several cases that match this one," Remy spoke up.

"Wouldn't surprise me. I have at least a decade of similar homicides come across my table. He had a meal at least a few hours before death. It had just started to break down. Whoever he is, he treats them like angels when he's done defiling them."

"No one is taking the idea of a serial serious," Stevenson said.

"Again, not surprised. The investigators assigned barely stay to listen to my findings whenever the prints don't match a homecoming queen or a quarterback. If you get together all the cases and I did the autopsies, I'll swear you have a serial killer to whoever will listen."

"Can you say if the suspect keeps them for any length of time?" I asked as I moved close enough for my arm to touch Remy's. His eyes darkened the longer we were there, and he was doing everything he could not to stare.

"I can't be sure. Any wounds they had were well before they were found. This young man had several bruises that had turned yellow, at least a week or more. They're clean. Nails manicured. Hair done. There is some irritation of the skin as if they were waxed, but I found no residue to test."

"The files show someone came to report the victims missing anywhere from a week to two weeks before they were found. So we can say it's possible he could've kept them for a week?"

"Could be, but I'll go back through my files and pull the cases if you have numbers for me." Warner covered the body and walked around the steel table, and took a seat at his desk. Remy perched on the corner, and I stood beside Stevenson.

"I can get those for you," Stevenson offered.

"If I could put in my opinion?"

"Go ahead, Warner," I answered.

"Every one of these cases I remember was one every four to six months. If he actually kept them for at least a week, then he cared for them. They were clean, and except for the sexual assault, they arrived without obvious trauma. I've seen a lot of cases in my thirty years here. I'd say he's playing out some fantasy with these kids. And, Remy, you know they're street smart enough to follow along. I don't think killing them is his ultimate plan. They rebelled and ruined his fantasy."

"These kids know how to make it out of every situation. I've seen the autopsies and their medical reports. They were survivors. We kinda know what happened to them. We just don't know what they did to piss the guy off. What's his trigger?"

"Won't know that until he's caught. You going to make some calls, Remy?"

I turned my attention to Warner and then to Remy. "What's going on here?"

"I occasionally run a free, unauthorized clinic for Remy when hospitals ask too many questions."

"Half my scars he stitched. I'll give the crews a call to spread the word to travel in packs or pairs for a bit. Davian is going to keep me updated with information as it comes in."

"Davian still as pretty as I remember? If I wasn't old enough to be his daddy…"

"I'll let him know you were asking about him, Doc, and I don't think daddy is really an issue."

"What the fuck is going on here?" Stevenson demanded.

Remy turned his attention to the other detective. "I was these kids. I've been there, so, this is personal. I can get info that none of y'all can. Maybe Robert is a step ahead of you, Stevenson, because he's safe by association."

"No wonder everyone just hands us your card when we try to question them." Stevenson shook his head.

"Loyalty and trust are a huge thing, and outsiders, especially ones with badges, are not to be trusted."

"Doc, I'm taking my man home. I'll email you the case numbers." I placed my hand on Remy's lower back and nudged him off the desk. We needed to get home, and my baby needed some air.

"Why wasn't I informed of this? Boss tells me everything."

"Doc, you and Boss hanging out is scary." Remy rolled his eyes and leaned down to kiss Warner's thick, silver hair that was flattened a bit by the cap he'd worn.

"Get out. I'll do my research and get back to you with my opinion. Should I call Coleman?"

"You think you can get more cooperation than me?" I asked.

"Definitely. I've met every ex-wife, and he has three. Don't let the adorable face fool you. I can be vicious when I need to be, especially if it gets me a call from Davian."

"I'll see what I can do." Remy and I chuckled as I led him from the chilled room and toward the elevator. Stevenson stayed behind.

"Does Doc really have a thing for Davian?"

"I don't know. He met him at one of my clinics. Davian may have a bit of a crush, but my friend is a bit self-conscious around the cute doctor. It's adorable to watch them flirt. I'll have to arrange for you to have front row seats."

"I'd like that." The doors opened, and I ushered him inside the elevator. "Now, tell me, are you okay?"

"I knew when I took this job that it would be harder for me because a lot of the victims had the same background as me. It's personal, and everyone tells you that you need to keep an emotional distance. Robert, these are kids, maybe they've lived a lifetime in their short lives, but they're still babies."

"I get that. I've never been able to keep an emotional distance. Especially when my kids were the age of some of the people in my cases. There's nothing wrong with caring, baby."

"I still beat myself up, though. I don't know how to do this job any differently."

"No reason to change, but you need to have a few minutes to breathe. Get some cuddles from our adorable daughter."

"I really need that." He leaned back against the wall as the car ascended and the elevator beeped each floor we passed. He looked exhausted and ready to collapse. Maybe I could talk him out of his evening run, but he liked sleeping in and wouldn't run with me in the mornings.

"Then we can go home and ask."

"Thanks for that, too."

"What?" I asked as the door opened, and I grabbed his hand, pulling him out and leading him to the back exit where we parked in the employee lot.

"The asking for consent."

"You act like it's a hardship. She needs to learn boundaries even when it comes to us. I'd rather our daughter and grandchildren know early they have the right to say no."

"Our grandchildren?"

"Not like you didn't claim them already. Let's go home. I want kisses where we won't get walked in on. And it seems everyone finds my man irresistible."

"Not everyone, I mean, Coleman can't stand me or it could be he's so attracted to me he can't stand it."

I rolled my eyes and kept walking. I opened the passenger door and motioned him inside. "Get inside."

"Don't be jealous, Daddy." He dropped a kiss on my lips before sliding into the seat. "Be proud you have such a sexy boyfriend. Revel in the knowledge they only get fantasy, and you get the real thing."

"You have no idea how badly you're asking for your first spanking."

"Oh, I know, I am very well aware." He winked at me, and I slammed the door.

I wouldn't smile, it would just encourage his behavior, but the whole *brat thing* really worked for me. My baby had finally driven me over the edge, and I wasn't going to complain about it. I kept the stern look on my face as I got in the driver's seat and started the drive home with him grinning and batting his lashes the entire way.

22

REMY

COLD CASE
UNIT

I was drinking coffee as I swiped through the files that were scanned and emailed to me earlier that day. My first official date with Robert was due to begin in thirty minutes, and I'd dressed two hours before. I couldn't remember my last date. To be honest, I don't even think I dated Harry. It went from friends hanging out to one night we spent together.

That had been easy, and maybe I'd allowed it to be that way even though I never saw it going anywhere. I tried to talk a big game with Shine about my relationship with my ex. Yet it hadn't hurt when he left. The only thing that had devastated me was that he kind of got the life I'd always dreamed about.

"Baby, you ready?"

"It's a date, Daddy. You couldn't even knock?"

"Sorry. Should I go back out and knock?"

I was about to say yes when he appeared in the entryway of the kitchen, and I froze. He wore an expensive, perfectly tailored charcoal suit with an electric blue shirt and a striped tie in several shades of blue. It emphasized the width of his broad shoulders and chest, his narrow hips, and leanly muscled thighs.

"Damn." My cheeks heated as he chuckled.

"So, I pass muster?" he asked as he circled the island until he could wrap his arms around my thick waist.

"You're gorgeous, and you know it." I smiled as I straightened his tie. He tipped his chin, and I lowered my mouth the few inches to his. At contact, I forgot all about doing anything other than kissing him and curling up on my couch to savor the time for just the two of us.

"I'm glad you approve because this cost me several months of our Chinese budget."

"You're so romantic." I chuckled with his lips still against mine.

"And you're so fucking beautiful." He brought his hand to my cheek, and I leaned into his touch. "I always thought so, even when we were just friends. You were always too good to be true."

"I like you thinking I'm beautiful even though I'm a bear of a man, but I'm just me. My childhood broke me, but it made me build myself back stronger. Even though sometimes I still see myself like that kid."

"You still are in ways, and it made you the incredible man you are. I know how cliché it sounds, but I wish you hadn't gone through it."

"But where would I have been or, for that matter, Carmen? She was meant to be mine, and I wished she'd come to me differently, but that isn't mine or her lot in life."

"But I'm happy to have both of you. So, are you ready to go on our first date? I'm majorly out of practice, so you'll have to be patient with me."

"Well, Daddy, the dates I've been on weren't really *dates,* and let's just say there wasn't much talking involved. Yet, I have to say I haven't really had a date since I stopped waxing and starving myself. Twink me kept me alive."

"Good, low expectations."

I pushed against his chest. "I may have changed my mind."

"Too damn late, we have a kid, we've test cohabitated , next step date and post-date making out. We've been training for this moment."

"Then let's go, you did get all handsome for me, and I want to show off my very sexy Daddy." And just like he always did, he dropped his gaze to my mouth, and I lowered again, brushing our lips together. "You're so easy."

"You've trained Daddy well."

"I so have."

He gave me a squeeze, and then he let me go so I could grab my jacket and stuff. I smiled as he filled up Romeo's food and water bowls and then turned off the lights. We really were an old married couple, and I admitted that I loved the comfort. It's weird when you wait forty-six years to realize, other than your chosen family, you'd found your person. And in this case, persons, Robert and his family, even his ex-wife.

I met him beside the front door, and he opened it. I went out first, and he locked up.

"Where are we going?"

"It's a surprise. Let me have my moment."

"Moment away."

"Baby, your snark is not appreciated by my stomach that's already dancing with nerves." He raised a thick brow and opened the passenger door, motioned me inside with a deep bow.

"You're such a gentleman, kind sir."

"Hm, maybe I haven't lost all my skills. Buckle up, baby, I need you safe."

"Yes, sir, but I'm always safe with you, Daddy." I smirked at the eye drop. There was this intense power in the knowledge that you were desired, especially by a man like Robert. He always made me feel like I was enough.

"Stop. Now you're just being snarky about it."

"No, I'm not because anything that gets kisses from you is not meant in snark." As he closed the door, I pouted at him through the window. He really was too easy, but I added that to the long list of things I loved about him. I forced the corners of my lips not to curl downward. I wasn't ready to reveal or confess how deep my feelings went for him.

I jerked my gaze to him as he rested his arm over the console and laced our fingers. His thumb brushed teasingly over my knuckles. "Tell me something you've never told anyone else?"

"So we're beginning our first date with Q and A?"

"Yes. We've learned a lot about each other, but I wanted to know everything."

"Right before they transferred me to homicide, I was going to quit to join an outreach program as a special therapist for at-risk youth who have complex trauma disorders."

"Really? Why didn't you do it?"

"I still thought I had some good to do as a cop. But honestly, I was scared. I volunteer at the outreach when I can. The thought of completely changing my life made me panic, and I went with the safe option." I paused. "What about you? Tell me something no one knows?"

"I found my birth parents a decade ago."

"Did you ever meet them?"

"Yes." He paused and squeezed my fingers. "I flew them over. I thought there would be like this instant connection. You know, this spiritual thing, but we spent three hours staring at each other, making idle conversation about the weather and all those other silence-filling subjects. Although, I found out I was an only child, and my biological father got sick, and they just couldn't take care of me. According to the records, I was malnourished. They just never had enough food to go around. They made the best decision."

"Did you stay in contact?" I asked as I lifted his hand to my mouth and kissed his knuckles.

"No. They went home, and there were a few letters, but just one day it stopped."

"Did they meet the wife and kids?"

"I just didn't know how to broach the subject. If it turned out bad, I guess I didn't want my kids hurt. Next question, how many degrees do you have?"

I allowed him to change the subject because he'd do the same for anything I didn't want to talk about. I needed to respect his boundaries, too. "Psychology, Early Childhood development, Criminal Justice, and there was also a partial I was working on, behavioral science."

"You wanted to be a profiler?"

"No, but it was something to fill the time as I worked to stay clean and sober."

"What happened to make you change your life like that?"

"One of my regulars was a cop. Old-timer. Extremely closeted with a wife and kids."

"What?" I laughed at his shock.

"Yeah, he was actually a nice guy. He took me out to eat, talked to me like I was a person, and yeah, he fucked me, but he was one of the few who cared if I was okay or not. Too much information?"

"No, I wanted to know everything, good or bad."

"One night, he picked me up for our regular date. I'd been jumped the night before, and I was in terrible shape. He pulled off in a secluded spot, and he asked me what I truly wanted from life. I told him the one thing I never told anyone else outside my chosen family. I wanted to be loved. That night he got me into rehab, gave me options, and helped me study for my GED. And he didn't even try to fuck me again. And that's how I started the third phase of my life."

"Third?"

"First phase was up until I was eighteen, and they put me out because I was too old to make them the money or elicited favors. Eighteen to twenty-six was me finding my chosen family, the one that has stuck with me all the way till today. Third phase was building the life I never thought I was entitled to. I didn't have to starve myself to stay skinny, and I stopped waxing myself from toes to shoulders. And let me tell you, I saved a ton of money."

He snorted, and I noticed him pull into the parking lot of a fancy restaurant that we'd talked about going to but could never justify the money when burgers and fries were fine with us.

"I adore every part of you. And I'm so proud of you," he said as he released my hand and pulled into an empty spot before turning off the engine. "While the pictures of twink Remy were adorable, I prefer this incarnation."

"You're just dating me for my body. I knew it."

"And it's a sexy as fuck body."

"Why isn't this weird for you?"

"Do you want it to be weird? You want some display of toxic masculinity? Hold on," he said as he got out, and I waited as he jogged around the vehicle and opened the door.

I held my breath as he unbuckled my seatbelt and turned me until I was sideways, slipping between my spread thighs. Did I make him mad? Did I push?

"Remy Bosley, I didn't expect you. You barreled into my life and made yourself right at home. I allowed you into my home, and I shared my kids and grandkids with you. You became my best friend, and maybe over our time as partners and friends, I noticed you were handsome. And after the revelation you were gay came out, pun very much intended..." I snorted, and he hugged me. "You were so much more relaxed and happier, and, god, you were so beautiful. I enjoyed the flirting and bratty behavior. Then the shooting happened, and you completely derailed your life to move in, parading around my house looking sexy and confusing the fuck out of me."

"But it wasn't bad? I didn't make you"—I bit my bottom lip —"uncomfortable around me?"

"Baby, I'll remind you, I'm fifty-five, yes, I didn't think I'd find myself attracted to my male partner, but that's what happened.

And the time you pulled away from me, I had a lot of time to think."

"Did the shower incident freak you out?"

"No, I was hard when I left you to get ready. I was pissed I didn't get a kiss, and I wanted a chance at a do-over so I could feel you skin-to-skin. You might not be the package I was expecting, but that in no way means I'm disappointed it's you. Let's go have a nice dinner, and then it's your choice for the next item on our itinerary."

"Baby's choice? I like the sound of that."

"Remy, all I want is for you to be happy. And no matter what happens between us, you're still my best friend. My family is still your family. I don't want you to stress about that."

I nodded as I closed the distance and pressed my mouth to his. His reaction was instantaneous. He gripped my hips in his strong hands and jerked me closer to the edge of the seat. His tongue nudged my lips, and I opened, submitting. A whimper slipped free as he rubbed the ridge of his cock against mine, and I tried to focus.

"It's been so fucking long." I let out an unmanly squeak as he shoved his hand between us, and he cupped my dick. "Shit. I'm not going to make it through dinner."

"You will, baby. You'll sit there like a good boy and let me romance you." He nipped at my lower lip. "And then when we get home, you're all mine."

"Wh-what if I can't?" I humped into his touch like some teenager hoping for his first hand-job.

"Then we go to your limit, and we try to push that limit farther next time."

"That shouldn't sound as sexy as it does."

"Daddy makes it sexy for you."

"You keeping petting my dick and I'm going to be uncomfortable with cum in my pants the entire meal."

He removed his gentle caress from my hard-on, and I pouted even as he did what I asked. "Food first. Petting later."

"Quit being such a gentleman, Daddy."

"But my baby deserves all the romance and gentlemanly overtures. This is me, Remy. I don't know how to be different."

"I didn't mean for that to make you insecure. I swear."

"I know you didn't. I adore every part of you. I need you to do the same for me. Even the parts that most don't find all that attractive."

"You're perfect, always have been." I cupped his bearded cheeks and gave him a quick kiss, making sure to keep it light. I was still aching with the need for him.

I felt the loss as he stepped back to let me out of the SUV. He twined our fingers together as he led me across the parking lot. No subterfuge. No distance between us to make anyone who looked at us assume we were just friends. We entered, and a hostess smiled from behind her podium.

"Good evening, gentleman, just the two of you?"

"Reservation for Kaufmann."

"Yes, Mr. Kaufmann, your table is ready. Please, follow me."

"Fancy. How much Chinese is this costing us?" I whispered in his ear, and he squeezed my hand and then led me along behind him through the maze of tables to a private, half-moon booth. He removed my jacket and then his, draping them over his arm. He motioned me in and followed me until our shoulders touched. He placed our jackets on the bench beside him. We normally didn't do it, but he laid his phone on the table in case Roo needed us.

We ordered drinks, and she gave us our menus and told us our server would be right with us. I pretended to read the menu and not look at prices. Years of struggle still made me anxious over spending money.

"Baby, stop. Order what you want."

"I'm value menu and lunch combos."

"You're worth a helluva lot more than that, so let me spoil you." He leaned to the side and brushed his lips to the side of my neck.

I nodded, and my beard rubbed against his. My breath hitched as he sucked lightly at my skin, and I nearly bent the sides of the menu when my fingers tightened.

"One day, I'm going to mark every inch of you I can," he casually said and then straightened to go back to his menu.

"You're mean, Daddy."

"No, I'm not because one day I'm going to be very, very good to you." I caught his smirk as he placed his left hand on my thigh.

He was trying to kill me. I could already see it. My sexual frustration was going to hit terminal before I got over the mental block of opening myself to him. He was too good, and I was terrified to disappoint him.

23

ROBERT

COLD CASE
UNIT

I placed my yarmulke on my head as I entered the temple. It had been decades since I'd visited the synagogue. I'd never seen myself as a religious man, but respectful of my parents, I'd attended for them. I'd lapsed after their passing, but I'd always found that talking to the Rabbi helped, while Gladys had gone for weekly confessionals at her church.

"Well, strange things happen every day. Robert Kaufmann coming to temple may be the strangest." A tall, thin man approached, and I smiled.

"Eli, finally took over?" I accepted his hug and stepped back with a smile, and he motioned me to sit.

"A few years ago. Father thought it was time. What do I owe for the visit? You look...troubled."

"Not in the sense you're probably assuming. I met someone."

"Congratulations. I know your divorce from Gladys took you by surprise."

"Not surprised it happened. In hindsight, I think I saw it coming, but ignored it."

"Marriages rely on two committed people, and sometimes

that isn't always possible in the long-term. How are the children, grandchildren?"

"Amazing. Carol gave me a granddaughter a year ago. RJ and his wife are quite happy with just the one. And my grandkids are perfect." I shifted slightly and stretched my arm along the back of the pew bench. "Gladys and I have returned to friends, and I love that, too."

"You spend thirty-odd years with someone, grown children or not, people should still have a bond. Does the new someone get along with the family?"

"Immediately taken into the fold. Remy is...I don't even know how to describe him." I glanced at him to see if he reacted to my someone being a man.

"Religion doesn't exactly have a reputation for being accepting, but I foster a sense of inclusivity so that anyone who wants to worship doesn't suffer for who they choose to love. God has gifted us with the ability to love, and why should someone be condemned for loving someone of the same sex. How did you meet?"

"A few years ago, he was reassigned to Homicide and became my partner."

"I sense the relationship is newer than that."

"A matter of months since our partnership shifted."

"Are you having doubts?"

"No," I answered too sharply. "Sorry, no, it feels right, and I have no intention of questioning my feelings for him."

"Then why are you here?"

"I know he trusts me and feels safe with me, but I feel that he needs something more from me that I'm not giving him."

"Have you asked Remy? Communication is essential."

"I know everything about him. He had a horrific childhood. I won't share because it's not my story to tell, but..." I sighed. "He's a survivor. He's forty-six and does anything for everyone but himself. He puts himself last, and as much as I love that about him, I want him to be selfish with me."

"People who feel compelled to be of service to others don't always know when enough is enough. Self-care goes by the wayside. People who long for their soulmate and find them, have to care for that person. Show them they're enough."

"I think...hope I do that for him. He's adopting a little girl, so we have a daughter."

"Your proudest moments in life were about your children. A new one? You must be ecstatic."

"She's a survivor, too. We went to talk to a homicide suspect. When we arrived, we noticed an apartment across from the one we were at had its door ajar. When we entered to do a welfare check, she was hiding in the closet. There was a shootout. I got hurt. Remy covered us both with his body. He was willing to die to save us because he felt there was no one who would've mourned him. Remy and Carmen, we call her Roo, came to stay with me while I recuperated, and while we were in close quarters..." I stopped and scrubbed my hand over my face.

"Robert..."

"Don't say it's gratitude."

"I wasn't going to. You were friends before. You felt something for him but didn't understand what it was, right?"

"Yeah."

"The more time spent together made you examine those emotions you didn't understand. You got married at eighteen Robert. Gladys was your first serious partner. You had no need to debate your sexuality."

"But I don't remember ever being attracted to another man until Remy."

"Because you were in love and hopelessly devoted to your wife. Not to mention an exceptionally demanding and sometimes dangerous career."

I nodded as I looked around and savored the silence of the

temple. Places of worship had always given me a sense of peace. They were made to reflect; to commune with whatever deity you prayed to. I may no longer observe my religion, but I still came for a bit of meditation.

"What really brought you here?"

"Maybe my age. Some sense of insecurity. That I'm so unworthy of a second chance." I pulled out my phone and opened the gallery to the picture I'd taken of Remy and Roo as we'd shared breakfast. He looked happy, and she was curled on his lap eating her fruit salad with her fingers. "I couldn't bear to lose them." I handed him my phone, and I studied his expression as he took in my family. "I lied to him."

"How did you do that?"

"We had our first official date. It wasn't an overt lie, but it was an omission. Us going back to friends if we don't work out romantically will destroy me, and I told him no matter what, he would always be my best friend."

"You're in love, some people aren't lucky enough to find that once, and you, Robert, found it twice. Don't think about the end. In your line of work, you know that our lives aren't guaranteed a definite number of years. You have a beautiful family, and look at your Remy's expression." He turned the phone to me. "That is a man who has found his place of peace. He's found his family. And no matter what happens, you gave him that. That is a gift more precious than anything."

I took my phone and gave my man and our daughter one more look before I tucked it back into my pocket. "I did. I love him and Roo so much. Not to downplay how much I loved my wife, but something about my love for Remy is so much more intense."

"Which is a blessing." He rested his chin in his upraised hand as he gave me a compassionate smile. "We should all be so lucky to find our person. Whether you believe or not, I do, and God has given you a gift, several gifts. He found you worthy of caring for survivors, ones who believe they are broken but became whole when they were sent to you. Because your love mended them... showed them they were worthy just by being even if they don't see it themselves. My logic is flawless."

I chuckled and shook my head. "Your ego hasn't changed."

"It's why Dad refused to retire for so long. Did you find what you needed by coming here?"

"I already knew what I needed. I'm just letting the stereotypical midlife-crisis worry hit me."

"We all have our worries and insecurities. It's human nature. It's not about loving them. It's about accepting our flaws. Those supposed imperfections are what made us. It's our experiences, good or bad. We're a planet of survivors in different degrees. Life doesn't leave us untouched."

"Are you going to tell me how God has a plan?"

"No." He looked around and then leaned in, and when he spoke, he whispered. "God is an individual thing. We create them in our image, some choose to see him as a merciful God, and others, well, you know the others."

"Nice pronoun switch."

"I have Trans and Nonbinary members. If you ever want to come back, you know you would be welcome."

"You know I just come here for the quiet and the great advice."

"That works, too."

"I better get going. I told Remy I had to make a stop before I could come home. He had to get home to get Roo."

"Robert, I'm very happy for you. And I can see that he makes you exceptionally happy. Over the years, when you came in to talk to me and Dad, we could see that you weren't."

"Thanks." I held out my hand, and he took it for a brief shake. Pushing up, I walked back up the aisle and removed my yarmulke as I exited the temple.

I felt better that I'd talked it out, not that I'd doubted Remy was mine, but I needed to talk it out with someone who wasn't already in love with him. For a month, I've been resisting the urge to blurt out the L-word, but I didn't know if either him or I were ready for the revelation.

Also, I was dying to make love to my man. Even after our date, the kisses and touches didn't stray further than he was comfortable. I was going to wait as long as I needed and even if we never got to the point he was comfortable with penetrative sex, I respected him enough to know he'd let me know he was ready.

I pulled out my phone and sent a quick text to let him know I was headed home and did he need anything. When he said he just needed me, I smiled and drove home to my little family.

2 4

REMY

I fell face-first onto my bed. The case was going nowhere. Doc was still working through the cases to help us argue our need to combine them. We'd worked late, and Roo decided she wanted to stay with Carol.

"Papa loves you, too. Let me get Dad." Robert's voice carried, and the floorboards creaked under his feet as he made his way to the bedroom. I rolled over and scooted up to lean back against the headboard. Just like always when my man appeared, I couldn't help the warmth that bloomed in my chest. We hadn't spent a ton of time together this past week as we split our time between work and Roo.

He had his phone held out, and then he was crawling into bed to sit beside me.

"Hey, sweetie. You okay?"

"Yes. Papa had to read my bedtime stories."

"Stories?" I shot a glance at Robert and saw his cheeks darken.

"She said please."

She giggled as I caught his wink in the picture-in-picture on the screen. I'd be worried about her getting spoiled if I hadn't learned that his parenting style was the same with Carol and RJ as it was for Roo. No matter if she was gone or not, there was at least a quick video call for him to read to her. He'd confessed he'd called her before he came to pick me up for our date.

"Bat our lashes, and you cave."

"I do, and I'm not ashamed of that," he said without taking his gaze from Roo.

We went through our usual nightly routine of talking about what we did that day, more her than us. Plus, everything she had planned for the next day. I couldn't stop listening to her sweet voice—a voice I'd thought we'd never hear. We got all her happiness and giggles. Her safety with us at one point had only been a dream. Her therapist told us that she sent her recommendation that there was no home other than mine suited for Roo.

Every day it drew closer to her being mine...ours officially. It wouldn't happen soon enough for me.

"Time for bed, Roo. Papa and Dad are headed to bed, too. We love you."

"Love you. Night." She waved so hard her entire body shook, and we disconnected the call.

He tossed his phone on the nightstand. "How you doing, baby?" he asked as he spread his legs and patted the space he'd made.

I didn't even hesitate to crawl over between his legs with my back resting on his chest. "Frustrated."

"I know."

I closed my eyes as he kissed the side of my neck. His body and arms felt so perfect; strong and lean. "I knew it would be hard, but I thought if we gave them the proof, they'd combine the cases."

"We can only do what we're doing. If they don't take us seriously, what can we do?" I moaned as his fingertips slipped beneath my t-shirt and teased the rounded curve of my lower belly. I'd always had a complicated relationship with my body, what I'd done to it and what others had. I hadn't had a choice in my sex work, but that didn't mean I hated all the memories tied to it.

"What are you thinking about?" He hugged me to his chest, and I felt so comforted—safe, and there was no judgment in his voice.

"My past...sexual past."

He barely released me as I rolled over to my knees, and as he crossed his legs, I sat in the cradle made by them. A groan slipped past his lips as I wrapped my legs around him. I wanted to look into his eyes as we talked. He never hid his emotions from me. I hugged his neck and laid my forehead on his.

"And what are your thoughts on that?" he asked as he pushed his hands under my shirt and flattened them to my back, stroking upward.

I shivered at the small callouses on his strong hands, and the movement brought our bodies into closer contact. There was an uncontrollable compulsion in both of us to connect, even in something as small as our fingers or arms brushing as we worked. There was something about just having that casual intimacy with him that fed my neediness.

"Not all my memories of that time were bad, well, the ones not hazy from drugs and alcohol."

"Are you embarrassed by that?"

"No, not at all. I did what I had to do to survive. When the host and her *husband* kicked me out, it was the first time I had freedom...had a choice of what was done to my body. I had no education. They made me drop out as soon as they could because not letting me attend would draw too much attention. I remember going to school swearing I still smelled like the men they sold me to. I hated everyone then."

"Do you still feel like that?"

"Not so much. After the first night with Harry, we'd been friends for months, and I enjoyed his company, but then I asked myself what did he want from me." I straightened as he started to protest, and I removed my shirt; that sent him into silence. "With you, those thoughts never even threatened to come. Daddy, take off your shirt, please."

I was commando beneath my pajama pants, and my cock was quickly thickening as he removed his shirt. He moved almost too slowly, but I took in every inch of deeply tanned skin exposed as the hem eased upward—the slight fuzz under his belly button that moved upward over his belly to where the trimmed black chest hair urged me to touch. I spread my hands on his belly and followed the fabric.

"I can't get enough of you touching me, baby." He uncovered his silver-streaked hair and beard.

Before I could make a comment, he had his right arm around my back and his left curled around my nape. My gaze dropped to his mouth, then to his eyes, back and forth. I gasped as his hand roughly fisted in my long hair. He teased me with the warmth of his breath and the impression of his mouth almost touching mine. Tightening his grip if I tried to close the distance to take his mouth with mine.

"Why can't I kiss you?" I forced the words through my throat that felt like it started to close. Drawing oxygen into my lungs was a battle I felt as if I were losing.

"Easy, baby, I'll give you just what you want, but we have to come to an agreement first. Red, yellow, and green, safewords. I want something in place that makes sure that your boundaries are respected."

As soon as the words were out, my eyes started to burn, and I closed them, feeling a tear tease my cheek.

"Please, baby, don't do that. I just need you to know you're safe. I want to know at every step what I can and can't do. This is important to me." As he spoke, he'd kissed me between words, just barely there brushes, but his words were their own caress.

What he'd done was make my safety unquestionable. "Pistachio."

"What?"

"Safeword. I've never had one for myself before, and I loathe pistachios. No one has ever thought to ask for one. And I'm kinda surprised."

"I've worked several cases, came across people in the lifestyle. Boundaries needing to be respected, I thought it would work for us."

"Thank you."

"Did I ruin our possible moment?"

"Not at all." I laughed as I got off the bed, opened the drawer for my bottle of lube and a condom just in case. I didn't think I was ready for that step yet. I placed them on the edge of the bed, and then I tucked my thumbs in the sides of my pants. It wasn't like he hadn't seen me in the shower at my worst, but I still hesitated as I took in how perfect he was.

"Take them off, baby. I've missed seeing what's mine." His voice was nearly guttural as he scooted down, removed his pants, and threw them over the side of the bed. He crossed his arms under his head and watched me from under heavy lids.

If I was supposed to have functioning brain cells, that went the way of his pants. His cock was perfect. He was average and thick enough that I knew if he fucked me, he'd make me feel it the next day. Okay, maybe the condom was a good idea.

"Come on, baby, let Daddy see. And remember, safeword, and you have the right to stop at any time. Your pleasure always comes first."

Dammit, okay, I can do this. I pushed the waistband over my hips and down my thighs, but nerves had softened my erection. I swallowed hard as I kicked the fabric aside and crawled back onto the bed, then I stretched out beside him. I stiffened as he rolled to his side. He placed his fingertips under my chin and turned my face to him.

"I want you to relax. Just because you're naked in our bed doesn't mean it has to go farther than this." He lifted to brace his weight on his forearm and lowered his mouth to mine.

The caresses were soft and gentle, teasing and comforting. My breath shuddered past my lips as he spread his hand over the middle of my chest. I jerked as his fingertips teased my nipple.

"Robert." There was an edge of fear in my voice, and I didn't know where it came from.

"It's okay. I'll be gentle." He stroked downward over the hairy softness of my belly, cupped the curve of it before moving to my side. And with a subtle tug, he urged me to roll to face him. I eased my thick thigh over his much leaner one, and he groaned. "Fuck, you feel good." His kisses turned rougher and demanding.

Sweat broke out on our skin as we writhed to get closer, but there was no way to do that without him inside me. My once soft dick pushed hard into his flat stomach. I was too conscious about the way his hardness melded too perfectly with my softness. His hands and fingers were finding a hold in the rolls along my ribs, the subtle curve of my hip, and finally pillowed in the lushness of my thigh.

His tongue roughly fucked past my lips. Ragged breaths sounded too loudly in the almost silence of the room. He thrust his hips forward and ground our cocks together, and I threw my head back. He instantly took advantage of the exposed length of my throat.

I'd had more sex than I wanted to remember, but even when it felt good, it had never reached the limits of what he did to me. I reveled in his care—of being larger yet submissive. I didn't fight as he rolled me to my back until he rested between my legs. The feel of his hips on the inside of my thighs was everything I'd imagined it would be.

"You have no idea how long I've dreamed of being right here," he whispered as if he contained us inside of a bubble that was just us. "How many times I've awakened with you in my arms, always the best way to wake up." I felt his smile, the familiar curve of it, and then I froze as his hand curved around the back of my thigh and lifted it higher on his side.

"I've dreamed of you right here since the morning after I met you."

"What did you imagine, baby? Tell me." He kissed my chin, drew his lips down my throat with gentle sucks until he reached my collarbone. My fingers sunk into the subtle wave of his hair as he latched onto the skin there and sucked hard enough to mark me. He repeated it on every spot he reached. "Tell me."

"You fucking..." My throat closed up as he loved on my belly.

"Keep talking. Stay with me. Did you imagine me doing this?" He licked the sensitive spot where groin met thigh and then placed my leg on his shoulder.

"Oh, fuck." I scooted up the bed when he nuzzled my sac. "Yellow."

"Too much, baby?" He pushed up to his hands and knees and crawled upward until he planted his fists on either side of my hips.

"You're the only one who's played with me in five years."

"How have you stayed untouched for that long?" he asked as he let his gaze move from my lips to my cock rested on the lower curve of my rounded belly.

"I don't have to be Remy the detective, former sex worker, current foster parent, with you...I can just be me."

I panicked as he moved away, and I tried to grab him, but all he did was sit cross-legged in the middle of the mattress and patted his thighs.

"Sit on Daddy's lap and wrap your legs around me." He groaned as I obeyed. "That's so much better." He roughly stroked his hands from my lower back upward to curl around my shoulders. He closed the distance between our mouths. Once again, the kisses started off sweet and gentle, building slowly back to the desperation of tangling tongues and our bodies coming together.

I frantically rubbed my cock against his subtle six-pack. He buried his face against my neck as I hugged him to me. I didn't care about the lumps and bumps, the scars I was sure he could feel under his hands. All that mattered was him and I, the way he held and took care of me. It urged me to be selfish like I'd never done before him.

"That's right, take what you need, baby," he whispered as he gripped my hips and moved me faster against him.

I whined loudly and didn't care how it made me sound. I didn't want to break contact, but I searched for the lube, and finally my fingers touched the bottle.

"I-I don't know, but I need it..." He took the bottle from me.

"And you'll get what you need." I held my breath, and by the time I felt slicked fingers moving between my cheeks, I waited for the panic, but I reminded myself of what it felt like before. The stretch and the burn, the pressure of someone else's fingers...of his fingers.

"I want your cock so bad. Make me need it. Please."

"Like this?" I threw my head back as the tip of a single finger pushed inside. I clenched my ass cheeks. "Relax, it feels so good, doesn't it? The way I'm filling you. Just a little odd, but you can't wait for more." As he spoke the last word against my throat, he pushed all the way in. "Still as hot as I remember. But the finger isn't enough, is it? Only Daddy's cock will do, right?"

It was odd but right, and then I was taking a second slicked finger. He fucked me with a slowness that soothed and frustrated me.

"Show Daddy how you want me to love that beautiful ass."

"Don't be..." I let out a long, deep moan as he buried both fingers inside and held still. The roll of my hips worked me on and off the digits and rutted me against his stomach. I dropped my chin forward until I could reach his lips. Tears slipped free from squeezing my eye shut so tightly.

"It's okay, baby, don't cry, just do what feels good. Do you feel how hard I am?" The words forced my eyelids open to meet his, his gaze locked on to me, and I could see the strain his control cost him.

I nodded as I felt the thick length against my sac, rested along my taint, and instead of fingers, my brain conjured what he'd feel like inside me. "Daddy, let me ride you."

"Are you okay with that?" His voice broke as I increased my speed and slammed down onto his fingers.

"I wanna try."

"Right to say no." I nodded. "No, I need the words. I never want to see the pain and sorrow on your face I did that morning in the bathroom."

"Yes, I want to try."

He shifted his legs until he stretched them out, and I chuckled as he fell back, even as I felt the loss of him filling me. "I'm all yours."

"You better be. I was a good boy for a long time."

"You were."

I twisted my upper body to search for the condom and found it tucked underneath a pillow, then I grabbed the lube. "Can I play with you?"

"Baby, I'm yours. As long as we both enjoy what we do to each other..." His sentence broke off as I leaned down, teasing his lips with mine. "I love kissing you." He whispered against my mouth and growled in warning as I moved lower.

I didn't mark him like he did with me because I hadn't asked permission. But right then, I had better things to do with my mouth, tongue, and teeth. I loved on his chest, bit and sucked at the flat, pebbled points of his nipples. The hair on his chest tickled my nose. He smelled so good, sweat, male musk, and a faded spicy cologne he wore that always reminded me of safety and home. I pressed my face to his abdomen and inhaled.

The head of his cock bumped my chin as I pressed my lips just under his belly button. His hips jerked as I cupped his sac, and when he grabbed my hair, I savored the sting. I circled the base as I lifted to place the broad head to my lips. I met his gaze and licked my lips right before I wrapped them around his cock and sucked him to the back of my throat. I hummed as I easily swallowed around him.

I loved sucking dick. It had always been one of my favorite things, and my Daddy had a perfect one. My heart beat an almost dangerous rhythm in my chest. Every part of me ached to be possessed; to have Robert, my Daddy, own me. It was everything I'd dreamed of for two years.

"That's right, baby, fuck!" He held my head as he thrust all the way in, and I contracted my throat around the tip as he ground against my mouth. The hot, silky length pulsing on my tongue was as close to perfection as I was ever going to get. I watched him with his eyes closed, his teeth sunk into his lower lip, and I loved the look of agonized pleasure on his face.

My dick ached and was leaving smears of pre-cum on my thighs as he lost control and fisted my hair in his hands. He held me off him enough for him to quickly open his eyes to watch his cock disappearing into my mouth. I forgot to relax my throat and he hit the back, pressure built in my face and I gagged. The involuntary action upped the retreat and thrust of his cock, forcing me to gag over and over again.

"My baby looks so good gagging around Daddy's cock, but I'm not coming until I'm buried in your ass." His harsh breathing and grunts broke up the sentence.

As he tried to pull out, I sucked hard to trap him, and his shoulders left the bed, his stomach pulling in tight making the muscles stand out under the sweaty brown skin.

"No, baby, let go." He tenderly stroked my bearded cheek, and then his thumb moved along my lower lip as if trying to get me to unlatch.

I wanted to taste him. To wear his release on my cheeks and chin, my chest. I wanted him to mark me, but a gruffly whispered *please, baby* made me let him go.

"Thank you, baby. I want my lips on yours when I claim you. I've never been harder in my fucking life." He curled his hand around the back of my neck and drew me upward until he kissed me. "I should've gotten shot sooner."

"Don't joke about that," I whined, and I felt the lift of his lips under mine. "Would you try to take me from behind?"

"Are you sure?"

"If it's going to be anyone, it would be you."

"On your hands and knees, baby."

I crawled off him and turned to offer him my ass, and I brought up the memory of the bathroom. The ghost sensation of his lips stroking over my scars pushed some of the anxiety away. My cock still softened, and I was glad I was turned away from him.

I lowered my head to the thick comforter as his beard and lips pressed to the top of my crease. "You're so sexy, bent over and waiting for me to fuck your gorgeous ass." He cupped my plump, hairy cheeks in his hands. "I'm gonna treat that sweet hole right, aren't I, Remy?"

"Yes, Daddy." My back bowed as he licked up the indent of my spine. Thankful he hadn't lingered on the marks that marred my back. I faintly heard the sound of the condom opening, and he tensed with his forehead laying between my shoulder blades.

"I just want you to enjoy and feel, let me do all the work."

I fisted my hands in the bedcovers as he moved until his hips cradled my ass, the tip of his covered dick pushed to my hole. I reminded myself to relax, push out, relax, push out, breathe. Robert would never hurt me. Oh, fuck, the second his thickness breached my hole, my cock went to full attention. My muscles locked up as shudders took over. I shook from head to toe. The pleasure was intense with just the head of him inside.

I felt the circle of his thumb and forefinger against my rim as if barring me from taking him before he was ready.

"Baby, Daddy isn't going to last long." A groan vibrated his chest that rested on my back as the pressure and almost painful burn of my ass stretching to take him. His hand disappeared, and he grabbed my hips as the front of his thighs pressed to the backs of mine. "Are you okay?" His breath teased my ear as he asked, and then he was kissing all of my scars he could reach.

"So okay. I never thought"—he pulled his hips back, and for the first time in my life, I had a man who I loved and wanted moving inside me—"I'd have this. Daddy."

"Yes, baby?" he asked as I turned my head and his lips found mine.

"I want to still feel you tomorrow when I sit down at work."

"Daddy's boy gets what he wants." There was something darker in his tone, and all sense of the past disappeared. Nothing but us in that moment, him buried deep. And he went from protector to predator. I glanced over my shoulder as he straightened, and I watched him as he stared at where he was buried so deep I never wanted him to leave.

He spread my cheeks wide, and I saw the heat in his gaze turn his eyes darker. He shallowly fucked me in a slow, easy rhythm, but I saw the strain in his face—the tightening of his lips. His lean muscles stood out starkly under his dark skin.

"Hold on, boy, Daddy needs to fuck you. I've waited too long."

I almost braced myself too late as the strength of his thrusts took me by surprise and pushed my face into my pillows. He deep-stroked my clenching ass as he too easily found my prostate. I tipped my hips and offered him more as he grunted and praised me. He used me in the best possible ways, and my cock slapped against my belly.

I screamed and cried, and felt no shame in the tears on my

face. I'd waited forty-six years to know what it was like to be loved and used by a man who desired me for me.

"We're getting tested, boy, because I want to breed your ass soon."

I buried my face in the fabric under my face as it became damp with sweat and tears. His hands were bruising vices over my shoulders as he pounded me with all his strength. "Daddy, harder." I didn't even know if he heard my muffled plea, but the stinging slap of skin against skin increased until he rocked me, my legs collapsed, and he didn't even break stride as he blanketed me with his body.

"That's right, boy, you take it." His words were harsh against my ear. "Damn, your fat ass was meant to cushion my fucking you."

The pleasure became agony, and between my Daddy's fucking and the rutting of my cock against the covers, I was going to come. "Daddy, I'm gonna..." A scream escaped as he took me with feral force. I arched my hips, lifted them to meet him thrust for thrust.

"Boy, so greedy, but I don't think you want it enough."

"No," I yelled at the shock of brutal to loving in the span of a single stroke.

"That's right, baby," he whispered as he loved on me. The arch and roll of his hips so gentle it was more torturous than the rough fuck of seconds before. "Daddy wants to love on my boy. You giving me your back makes me so proud. So humbled you trust me. God, Remy, I don't want this to end. I was made to be right here. Loving on you in our bed," he breathlessly whispered, and I turned my head until I found his lips again. "I want you right here the rest of my fucking life. It scares me how much I need you...how you were made to be mine."

And as easily as he'd gentled the pace, he was back to the piston-hard snaps again, and he pushed out embarrassingly high-pitched squeaks. I opened my mouth to ask for permission to come, but it was too late. My head went light as everything faded when the breath locked in my lungs and come spread under me.

"Hold on, baby." He laced our fingers as he thrust his tongue into my mouth and took his pleasure. The pounding rhythm kept on, and his stamina shocked me until several minutes or hours later his movements faltered, and he slammed into me so hard it arched my hips from the bed and bowed my back.

"You"—he cleared his throat—"you okay, baby?"

"Perfect." My voice was hoarse with my sweaty, wet hair stuck to my face, and I tasted the salt of tears and perspiration as he gentled me.

"You were so good for me. So beautiful when you allow me to love you. Let's take a bath. You're gonna be sore tomorrow."

I nodded as I whimpered and pouted as he pulled out. He kissed me repeatedly on my lips and wherever else he could reach. Like him, I never wanted it to end, but reality lived outside our bedroom door, but for tonight I didn't have to share him with anyone, especially not work.

When he helped me off the bed, I laughed as my legs tried to collapse as my feet touched the rug. We were both a mess, and he still had the condom on his soften cock, but he cupped my face and held me still to kiss me with so much tenderness it tightened my chest.

"Thank you, Remy. You won't ever know how much your trust means to me. How unworthy I feel that you trust me to keep you safe. I always want that, baby, and I'll do everything in my power to keep it."

ROBERT

COLD CASE
UNIT

I came awake instantly as my phone rang, and I reached out in the dark in an attempt to find it. The corner of my mouth twitched upward as Remy cuddled back into my side and hugged my arm to his chest. I checked the screen and groaned. I slid my thumb across it to answer. Stevenson. I wasn't expecting good news.

"Kaufmann."

"Hey, man, sorry to call so late or early, whatever. We got another one."

"It's barely been a week."

"Yeah, and this one is a helluva lot more violent than the others, but other than that, it fits. I tried calling Remy, but he didn't answer."

I turned my head and kissed my baby's soft hair, and he groaned.

"Daddy, it's not time to get up."

"Remy, baby, Stevenson is on the phone. We got a crime scene."

"Fine, let me get dressed." Remy was still half asleep as he clumsily rolled over and pressed his lips to mine. I groaned as he crawled over me, his body rubbed over mine, and then he was stumbling toward the bathroom. "I'll get the shower heated. Just join me when you're done."

I willed my cock to behave as the light came on and showed every inch of my gorgeous baby. "We'll see you in a few."

"Of course, just rub it in, man. I texted you the address."

I laughed as he disconnected the call and put my phone back on the nightstand. Luckily I kept clothes there. I got up and went to join Remy in the shower. He was already inside, so I took a piss and then opened the door. The second I stepped inside, he turned to rinse the shampoo from his hair. While he soaped his body, I took his place to wash my hair.

"Kinda quick between body drops."

"Yeah, Stevenson said this one wasn't exactly like the others. Something about more violence."

"Bad for the kids but good for us. He's escalating, and serials usually fuck up. Davian is still on the street at this time. I'll give him a call. They normally know if someone goes missing before the family or cops."

"Are you okay this morning?" I stroked the marks I'd left the night before. I'd put us in the bath just to soak, and afterward, we'd passed out. I'd worried I'd been too rough our first time. He deserved everything I could give him from the trust he'd shown me when he gave me his back. The trust that simple act for anyone else would mean nothing, but for him, he'd made himself vulnerable and open.

"I'm perfect, Robert. You were perfect. I didn't think..." We switched places again. "I'd trust anyone at my back. I won't say I didn't get anxious. You made everything right, don't think anything else, okay?"

"Okay, let's get to work. I'll text Carol to let her know what's going on."

"Doc will probably be at the scene so we can get his opinion.

The Captain has to see this for what it is. I can't keep going to these crime scenes and knowing we won't get any help."

I grabbed him around the back of his neck and pulled him slightly down. I made sure our bodies didn't connect; I couldn't guarantee that we wouldn't arrive late at the scene because of me.

"We'll take care of it. If nothing else, we can play dirty and go to the press. I'd hate to do it."

"Would you be mad if I say I wanted to stay in Cold Case? They're short on detectives, and I think I can do a lot of good."

"Then we stay in our current unit. Where you go, I go. No one else is watching your back."

"Thank you." He kissed me quickly and pushed open the glass door. "I'll get dressed and lay out your clothes."

"You're so good to me."

"Of course I am, Daddy." He winked and left me to finish up my own shower. I went through my routine in half the time, and I was dressed, jogging down the stairs to follow the scent of coffee.

Two travel mugs sat on the island next to two of those frozen breakfast sandwiches. They were horrible, and the microwave got them dry and hard on the edges. The egg, sausage patty, and cheese were still slightly icy and watery. It was better than nothing.

"Let's go, Daddy, been a while since we attended a crime scene, you think you'll still know how?"

"I'm not old and senile yet." Romeo barely paid attention to us from his bed in the kitchen corner. Remy made sure the dog had his collar that would activate the doggy door. Several minutes later, we were headed to my SUV and on our way to the address Stevenson sent.

I STOOD beside the gurney with the body on it. Fuck, he looked like a baby, not even old enough to shave yet. That was from what I could see of his swollen, misshapen face. Doc was looking him over.

"My opinion, it's the same guy. Except for the beating, which we're not sure he did, clothes to the manicure and pedicure. He's only been dead a few hours, still warm."

"Do we have an ID?" Remy asked as he stared down at the kid. His eyes were glassy, but the tears wouldn't fall until he was away from everyone but me.

"No, and I checked missing person reports, but none match him. Our killer didn't keep him long."

Remy turned suddenly and started searching the crowd. He seemed to catch sight of someone he knew and started jogging toward the crowd that had formed. Macabre interest in the police and body. I tracked Remy's every move.

"Remy know something?" Stevenson asked.

"I don't know. Let's wait and see."

A tall, beautiful woman stood beside Remy, and they talked for a few minutes. Whatever they were talking about, it didn't appear pleasant. But I saw the woman's shoulders drop, and Remy led her under the tape and toward them.

"Di, do you know him?" Remy asked and stepped aside.

"He's fresh. Been around the last few weeks. Got a good beat down about a week ago. Don't know his name. Maybe Forester would know."

That's the second time we'd heard Forester's name during that investigation. They definitely needed to make a visit.

"What do you know?" Remy's voice hardened.

"Pretty, you know how it is down here. I'm already fucking up talking to a cop…even you."

"I just want a name, and what you can tell us will give us one."

"Before someone stomped on his face, he was beautiful, tried to say he was sixteen, but he hadn't been around long enough to learn to lie. You know he's a target for every pimp riding around out here. I don't even know if that boy was experienced enough to have a kiss yet. He's been walking around with Cherry and her crew. You warned us to move in groups. Maybe her or one of her girls knows who he took a ride from."

"Thanks, Di. I'll owe you one. You know how to get me to collect."

"You know I will, Pretty." She turned on her toes and walked away like a Queen holding court. Chin up and shoulders back, and I didn't look away from her until I saw her safely in a group of other women.

"If he's losing his cool, then he left something behind." Remy shoved his hands into his pockets and seemed to be fighting off the early morning chill. It was barely four AM. "Could these be from a beating a week ago?"

"Could be, depending on how severe and his overall health, but several of these are still recent, maybe last few days."

I glanced at Doc. "So even with the beat down, this kid got another one from our killer."

"He's new, which means he probably doesn't have a survival instinct. While the others conned him until their luck ran out." Remy crossed his arms as he spoke.

"I got the results of the DNA comparisons after I forced them to upload all the DNA profiles to the database. The ones that were definite all came back to the same contributor. I'll put a rush on our young man's here when I start the autopsy. With this case and the escalation, we really need to force the higher-ups to combine the cases."

"I'll set up a time to sit down with the captain. With the DNA, there's no way they can tell us no." Stevenson stepped away from the gurney as the EMTs loaded it for the trip to the ME's office.

"You'd be surprised. I haven't found any more cases farther back than the decade or so. The ones before the expansion of our database, I entered those in. I ran a search in other states, but the age of the cases, I wouldn't hold out much hope. I didn't think it would hurt. We need to go back to the first case that we know. Killers like this always strike close to home first in their geographic comfort zone." Remy pulled out his phone. "There's a genealogist who's working through all the backlogged cases. She may be able to help, but she's kinda hard to pin down. I'll send her another text message."

"Any other way to get in touch?" I asked.

"We can find Vega hiding in her pit, but it's dangerous to go there. Her extremely butch wife is highly territorial. Stevenson can come with us."

I rolled my lips between my teeth at Remy's amusement and Doc's snort. Apparently, they knew more about Vega than we did. I'd met her a time or two, but nothing more than polite hello and goodbye in passing.

"I'm going to go grab a few hours of sleep. I'd just gotten home when the call came in." Doc grabbed his coat and backpack, and headed for the door after giving Remy a hug.

"You want to go home and get more sleep, or go out for a greasy breakfast and then go see our daughter for a few when she wakes up?" I asked Remy and mentally cheered when I got a smile at the mention of Roo.

"Food and then see our kid. Stevenson, stop by in the morning, and I'll see if I can get Vega to see us."

"Remy, if you can do anything to get us help, I'll brave getting my ass kicked."

"Good sport. Doc, call when you start the post-mortem."

"Will do, Remy. I'd like to stop getting these cases on my table."

We spoke for a few more minutes, then Remy and I walked back to our vehicle. He had dark circles under his eyes, and I wanted to take him home, back to bed to curl up and grab a few more hours of sleep.

"You sure you don't want to sleep? Snuggling all warm in our bed."

"I'd be more willing to take a nap, Daddy, if I get a reward for it."

I knew what he was doing, every person with a high-stress job had a coping mechanism, but with those cases being so close to him, he needed more. He needed me to allow him to forget for a bit that the world is shit and too many people don't care to change that.

"Oh, is that right?" I opened the passenger door and made my way around to the driver's side. "And what would be a sufficient reward for taking a nap?" As I slammed the door and twisted my upper body to face him.

"Blowjob."

"Receiving or giving?" I asked and resisted rubbing my hand against my hardening dick. The sight of him getting face-fucked as he gagged. The moment he panicked as I'd tried to pull out—I could become addicted to being desired that much.

"Definitely giving."

"How is that a reward?"

"I get permission to suck your cock, Daddy. That's better than anything."

"We're going home. I can make you breakfast." I started the SUV, backed it up onto the main road, and headed toward Remy's house. I relaxed as I listened to his carefree laughter. There was no way that I'd ever get tired of hearing that sound or being the cause of it.

REMY

COLD CASE
UNIT

"Vega, Vega, Vega, you haven't gotten rid of Cash yet?" I swung my feet where I was seated on one of the long tables in Vega's basement office. The place really was like a pit. No windows and soundproof. She had an entire basement that was basically a self-contained panic room. Cherry had been able to give up a first name on the new victim, Silas, but that was all she'd had for us. Luckily, his parents had filed a missing person's report. He'd come out to less than stellar reactions and decided to run away. He'd only been on the streets a few weeks before he'd ended up in the morgue.

"You have seen my wife, right? You think five-foot, fat *Velma* wannabes gets the hot, possessive rockstar all the time? No. And she has a tongue with award-winning skills. I have an IQ of one-eighty-five, I sure ain't lacking in a functioning frontal cortex."

"If I wasn't gay, I'd totally fuck you. The whole severe bob and heavy black frames. And please don't get me started on the acid-tripping hippie who dressed you. Irresistible."

"Aw, if you weren't gay, you'd still have, well…" She motioned broadly towards my crotch, and I let out a loud laugh that echoed in the room. "And I am totally not bottom material."

"Is Cash ever going to let my colleagues down here? They showed their badges."

"She knows you. She doesn't know them. Let my babygirl have her fun."

"If my Daddy has one mark on him…"

"Please tell me it's Mr. Salt and Pepper. I knew I sensed something going on when I saw y'all last time."

"You know my type, Vega."

"I do, which surprised me when you dated Harry for so long."

Why did everyone wait until the break-up to tell you how much of a mistake you were making? I'd always preferred if someone was honest instead of the usual platitudes of *we just wanted you happy* even though they assumed you weren't actually in relationship bliss.

"I should've arrested her," Stevenson mumbled, and I chuckled as I turned to find Robert patting him on the back. "Assaulting a police officer."

"Should've just told her about your backup piece." Robert snorted. "Hey, Vega."

"Hey, Kaufmann. Sorry about my babygirl."

"She wants you safe, no problem. I don't think you'll get the same concessions from Stevenson." He left the blond, grumpy man and crossed the room to lift onto the table beside me. "Did you explain why we're here?"

"No, mostly I said I'd fuck her." I grinned as Robert snorted and shook his head.

"I'm just glad she's a Lesbian, and my jealousy is minimal."

I caught Robert's wink from the corner of my eye as Vega giggled.

"Doc sent over the information. Forensic genealogy has some gray areas. We're allowed to use public DNA databases from those ancestry websites that let people build their own family trees. I'm still shocked by how many people don't read terms of service in the age of police states. Offense completely meant."

"Kinda weird you're part of the police state, Vega." Stevenson plopped down in a chair near Vega.

"Do you understand the amount of access I'm granted if I say I need it? It's a goldmine."

"Did you find anything?" I asked.

"I found something, but you're not going to like it."

"Those are not words to say to instill comfort." Robert scooted back to lean against the stone wall.

"Sorry, wish I had better info for you, but I can only work with what I got. So, I got a distant familial match, cousin several times removed. I followed the trail from there." She stood and walked to a large whiteboard with a rough family tree. "So I went backward to the great-grandparents, worked forward from there to children, grandchildren, and great-grandchildren. The male descendants that I found aren't anywhere within this area or geographical profile. There was one daughter who had one child, but that line died out. So most likely this child was born out of wedlock to the line that died out and was given up for adoption."

"So, at the core, how bad is that?" Stevenson asked as he spun in the chair. He was like a kid when he was bored.

"Cash, that is *not* a concealed weapon, although, being short no one expects the equipment." Doc's voice carried from upstairs. "Is it sad the most action I've gotten recently is from a lesbian?" He jogged from upstairs and appeared flustered at the bottom.

"How the fuck are you like all besties?" Stevenson yelled and motioned toward the four of us. "I'm a detective, and I apparently suck at my job."

"Aw, I think Blondie is feeling left out with all the cool kids." She retook her seat.

"Focus, people." Doc hissed as he straightened his clothes and crossed the room to sit on Vega's lap. "Hey, baby."

"I love a man who's just my diminutive size, but that very impressive dick is getting nowhere near me." Vega sighed. "Have y'all seen it? No wonder his growth was stunted."

Stevenson's groaned, and we all chuckled at his obvious frustration being out of the loop. The man was a King of Gossip. He knew everything first. The knowledge he didn't know everything had to be driving him insane. Also, we weren't the sanest crew. Stevenson was adorable in a pout, though.

"So, if there was a child given up for adoption, what are our options?" Robert asked as he slipped his hand under my t-shirt and lovingly stroked the long stripes of scar tissues across my lower back.

"There's two options here. Neither of them is positive. With a legal adoption, we have paper trails to follow even if it was closed. But that's time-consuming to get through the red tape. If this was handled secretly, which this may have been, someone could've taken the baby to the doctor and said it was a home birth and wanted to register the child. I need to do some digging to follow the crumbs. My main issue is if she did give birth, when? We're looking at a huge span of time she could've had the baby."

"While our victims were young and slender, they're not pushovers, Vega. They'd fight out of a corner whether they thought they'd survive or not. We all have a heightened fight response. It's human nature to save ourselves. I went up against men three times my size when I was hundred-thirty pounds and weak from malnourishment. Adrenaline kicks in."

"I get that, Remy, but they'd also cooperate until they were able to make a move."

"Doc and Remy said the same thing. Isn't the key to survival not being taken to a second location?"

"Stevenson, think about it. These kids were on the stroll. Most of their lives were being taken to a second location, or if they worked for a service, then they'd arrive at a location. Most of the guys I know with a service usually send a driver or guard, sometimes both. It's why sex workers are high-risk targets."

"Remy's right. We spread the word about traveling in groups, but once a transaction is in progress, they split up. I've been running plate numbers for days from what Davian has sent me, but him and his crew are only a small fraction of the workers down there. So, Vega, can you narrow it down?" Robert asked.

"Give me a few more days to do some more digging. I may need to keep Doc."

"Is that safe?" I asked.

"He'll be fine. We'll feed him and even put him to bed on time."

"Do I get to be the center of the sandwich? If not, I'm going home." Doc pouted, and I always forgot he's a total *brat*.

Vega stretched up slightly to reach Doc's ear. "Snuggles, all the snuggles."

"Cash, I get to spend the night." Doc jumped up and ran toward the steps and disappeared.

"That man needs a keeper," she said with a smile.

"So, we're no closer to finding our guy?" Stevenson asked, and he let out a heavy sigh and rubbed his hands over his face.

"We're closer than we were an hour ago. We know he belongs to that line." I motioned toward the board. "The adoption is a complication we don't need, but I have all the faith in Vega she'll work it. Right now, what do we know?"

"Our unknown subject is possibly adopted." Stevenson leaned forward to rest his forearms on his knees and laced his fingers.

"Shit!" I threw up my arms. "Attachment disorder."

"What?" Robert asked.

"Well, think about it. We think he's performing some ritual or role. If they played into his fantasy, what happens when that shatters? Let's say he's searching for someone that's just his, playing house, and it's ideal because the kids are playing the role to perfection. He thinks he's finally found the one. Then they do something like try to run or say no. The clothes he dresses them in, they're demure, high-quality, very upper-class, preppy shit." I looked around.

"We need to find the first victim," Stevenson said.

"The oldest file from the DNA matches is a Nino Alvarez." Vega turned to her desk with several monitors, and the keyboard keys clicked along. "Seventeen. Went into foster care at twelve. He was reported missing to his social worker about two weeks after he failed to return after school. In total, he was officially missing a month. They interviewed friends, and everyone said he was a sex worker, trying to make money for when he aged out. This kid was a straight-A student, honors classes. He threw up no red flags until he went missing."

"Who was the foster family?" I asked.

"The...Mitchells. Tom and Evelyn, three biological adult children. File says they signed up to foster after the youngest graduated high school. No red flags. No criminal records. Typical suburbanites, mother stayed home, father worked at a firm that specialized in human rights cases."

"Why the hell did they wait two weeks?" Robert's voice went deep and guttural as he kept absentmindedly drawing circles over my skin. He hadn't stopped since he'd slipped his hand under my shirt. I liked that he took comfort from me as much as I did him.

"Seems they were receiving texts from his phone, but when they tried to track it, the phone would be off. He only left it on for the amount of time it took to send the message. Phone records showed that he was in the city, but without being able to triangulate the signal, we can't see specific towers it pinged off. They claimed they didn't want to get him in trouble, and he was a good kid. He had a history of running away, though. When he didn't text for two days, they called social services."

"Does it give a list of people interviewed, known associates?" I tapped out notes on my phone.

"A few kids at school who were born with the proverbial silver spoon but liked to slum at the clubs with him. There was no real investigation into his missing person report, barely even got started on a homicide investigation. Sex worker equals waste of time."

"Not all of us think finding a killer is a waste of time just because our victim wasn't straight, white, or cisgendered."

"The not all of us argument from the cis, white man, why am I not surprised?"

"Vega, Stevenson, claws sheathed," I warned. "We won't do much good fighting amongst ourselves. If Nino was our first victim, then we have to look at his circle. Vega, can you get me information for all the homeowners in a two-mile radius of the Mitchell home? Serials normally start on their home turf. Why don't we look at the males in that general area thirty-five to forty-five to give us a window and cross-reference birth records and see how close they lived to the familial link? Maybe we can get lucky."

"You're so smart and sexy." Vega let out a longing sigh even as her fingers moved across the keys.

"Robert and I will hit the streets to ask around if anyone remembers Nino. Can you text me one of the pictures from his missing person's report?"

"Done," Vega announced even as my phone pinged.

"Oh, I don't want to throw up any alarms, but could you check out Eugene Forester? Find out what you can. His name's come up a few times. Maybe it's just a coincidence, but never hurts to check." Robert stroked higher on my back, and I leaned into his hand.

"While you're doing that, see if a mention of him has come through on the other cases. Off the record for right now. Forester is a sleazy bastard but seems fair, better safe than sorry," I said as I slipped off the table and Robert followed me. "Stevenson, anything you'd like to add?"

"Can you search and see if you can find where the clothes they found the victims in came from? It can't be normal that the same outfit is bought in pretty much bulk. All tags and brand identifiers were removed, but quality-wise, someone has to know."

"I have a friend who runs an online boutique. Maybe he can recognize the items and give me a brand. If he can do that, I can run a cross-reference on the supplier and any buyers/stores in this area."

"Thanks." Stevenson suddenly looked haggard. His normally perfectly styled blond hair was dull and limp. The bags under his eyes were almost black. I hadn't noticed until he really stopped moving and performing.

"Stevenson, how about dinner at our place? Chinese night." Robert asked, and I turned to find him looking concerned and was sure the same expression was on my face.

"I don't want to be in the way."

I spoke up. "Not in the way. Roo is a pretty laid-back kid and doesn't make a ton of noise. We'll order food and forget about the case for a few hours. Sometimes the best option is just to put it out of your mind and not stress about the details. Normally that's when everything comes together." I caught his nod. "Doc is to be fed and tucked in, don't make him call me."

"Your precious Doc is going to be just fine. Cash is cooking, and he can help me go through some of the medical files. I'm looking for hereditary illnesses that may have been passed on. Doc can help me sort through medical profiles."

"Okay, call or text me when you know something. If I don't answer, call Robert. One of us usually has our phone handy."

"Will do."

We said our goodbyes and climbed the steps. Cash and Doc were nowhere to be found. I didn't hear any noise so maybe they went out. We took a few steps forward, but it always seemed like we were still too far behind where we needed to be. We had a decade-old case and not much hope of finding out more than vague rumors, that's if anyone remembered Nino at all. So many names had faded to black over the years, friends and acquaintances lost to time and short memories.

But someone had to know something because the longer these cases kept going, the more they'd pile up in storage with no hopes of anyone solving them. We had the information to get a task force together, even if that was just the three of us, Doc and Vega. They just had to give a damn about our kids like they did theirs.

ROBERT

COLD CASE
UNIT

The house was quiet. Stevenson was passed out in the guest room, and Roo had gotten her usual five bedtime stories read to her. Romeo was let out and had just slipped into Roo's bedroom for the night. The TV in Remy's room was on mute, but the screen sent flickering lights across the walls. Water ran in the bathroom, and I walked toward the sounds to find Remy. I leaned in the doorway of his bathroom and watched him as he got ready for bed. All night I'd watched him tense up and that haunted look I hadn't seen since the hospital returned.

"Talk to me, baby." I caught his eyes in his reflection.

"Why don't they care about us?"

He didn't have to say who *us* was. I could see it in the tears that filled his eyes and the break in his voice. Intellectually, he understood who got top priority. But in his heart and soul, he hated it, and he must have felt it like a knife to the chest. Young boys, men, who didn't rate the care that the so-called good kids got. The news that ran missing person cases when the person was white. The verdicts that let white kids off because a justice system didn't want to hurt the future star.

"It never changes, Remy. It's the same every year, and no

matter how enlightened we become as a society, there are still the haves and the have-nots. People standing on some moral high ground."

"I get that, fuck, Daddy, how much I get that." He sighed and turned to rest his ass on the edge of the sink counter. "But it's different for me. At twenty-six, twenty years ago, I could've been one of those kids on the steel table. A case number and evidence growing mold before anyone gave a fuck. I don't want that for my kids...the ones like me who have a chance. They're just working it out their way."

"You can't save them all, Remy." I entered the room. And as I stepped in front of him, I placed my hands on the counter beside his hips. "As much as you want to put them all in your pocket and protect them, you can't. I know it kills you that these kids are falling through the cracks. I can see in your eyes every time we went to a crime scene or you read a case file...every autopsy we attended. Save the ones we can and bury the ones we can't with dignity and respect, avenge them if we can. I love you, Remy, and I love how passionate and caring you are. I love how you're unafraid to stand up and tell someone it's bullshit. I love your strength. You do so much for others, but, baby, you're going to break. I hope it never happens, but if it does, I want to be there. I always want to be there to put the pieces back together and love the new scars." I paused and realized my baby had stopped breathing. "Breathe, baby. It's okay." I cupped his face in my hands and leaned up to brush our mouths together.

He released a shuddering sigh against my mouth and gripped my wrists in his large hands. He just stared at me with tears on his cheeks as if he were trying to figure me out. To see if what I said was true. I hadn't meant to confess it in the middle of our case or his crisis, but since I'd seen my Rabbi, I'd wanted to tell him. Falling in love for a second time had never crossed my mind. After Gladys, I figured I'd be a bachelor for the rest of my life.

"Keep breathing, deep and slow," I whispered as I listened to him softly sob, it was like the nights we slept together and he'd awakened me crying in his sleep, almost soundlessly weeping at whatever nightmares played out in his head. I always held him tighter and whispered soothing words until he calmed, but he never awakened.

I wondered how many nights he mentally suffered alone when I could've been there to hold him, but unable to because I hadn't recognized what I'd felt. I think I loved him longer than months. I couldn't remember a time where I didn't feel this connection with him; it was there since the moment we met.

"You love me?" He choked out the question.

"Yes, I love you and our kids more than anything in the world. Is that okay?" He nodded and kissed me tentatively. "I overheard you and Shine talking in the bathroom that night we went to Boss's place. When I asked you were you in love, was I the guy you were talking about?"

"Yes."

"Why didn't you say anything, baby? You stayed in the closet with me."

"It's not that I didn't trust you. I've trusted you more than my entire crew on the streets. It was as if I didn't voice it and it just remained some rumor, then you wouldn't notice the way I looked at you. You were everything I'd ever wanted in our what-if game."

"What-if?"

"Over breakfast or us hanging out to get high, we played this silly game. What if we could get anything we wanted. It didn't matter how silly, hell, most of us didn't remember after we woke up. There I was, Pretty Bosley, a twink-ish sex worker dreaming of a handsome husband and kids." He brushed our mouths together even as he chuckled. "You know, that whole picket fence suburban lifestyle. *Donna Reed* shit."

"Doesn't sound like a bad dream," I said as I gripped his hips and lifted him the few inches to sit on the counter, then I moved between his meaty thighs.

"When you're a homeless kid who doesn't know anything about the good shit, it's like paradise, ya know? We didn't know anything. All we cared about was our next trick, and would it be enough to buy food, maybe a room for the night where ten of us could sneak in and shower, sleep on a real bed?" He studied me a moment in silence. "I don't regret my life, Robert."

"I didn't think you did."

"Most people think I do. Most people think I hated my life. Yes, I loathed aspects of it. I hated holding warm rags against my ass when they were too rough without proper prep and I'd tear. I hated going to the clinic for months after a night where the condom broke. I hated feeling unsafe, but I had something a lot of people didn't have. I was loved by a family of individuals who got me. Who wanted all the things I did, but had sensed that in some part of us, it was always going to be just a game. But for a few hours a night, we were free, high on drugs and dreams, and our bellies weren't eating themselves. We formed bonds that never broke, still aren't even decades later."

"I'm happy you found a family, and to be honest, I like and maybe even love several of the members."

When I met him, he'd shown me a world where blood didn't mean much. DNA didn't make a family. I saw good done for the sake of helping someone. He'd shown the jaded part of me that selflessness existed. His world was fun and colorful even when it was clouded with darkness—the strength of wills shown through all of that. They could laugh and joke even when it looked as if civilized society was collapsing around them.

"They like you, too, even if you're a cop."

"Hey, baby, you're a cop."

"I know, Daddy. But even with my currently shameful profession, I'm still them. I haven't forgotten where I came from.

I'm a law enforcement officer with a lot of gray areas in my thinking."

"I love that about you, too. When you were assigned as my partner, I'd never met someone who'd been on the job as long as you had and still exuded so much joy and compassion. I'm even more amazed since I learned your entire story."

"I love you." He tripped over those three words as if walking over landmines, as if he'd saying them would make the dream collapse. "I really do. I'm terrified, though. It's like seeing the surface of the ocean from under the water, and you're weighed down, and you keep struggling to swim as your lungs burn. And you break the surface taking that first breath only to have the ocean swallow you back up."

"It's okay to be afraid. A certain amount of fear is healthy. It's what we do with that fear that defines us."

"No more fortune cookies for you."

"Brat."

"You love me for it."

"You have no idea how much. I want to fuck you. You think you can be quiet and not wake our guest? I think he's jealous I got you."

"Let him be jealous, Daddy. I ain't looking for second best."

"Good answer."

"I know how to keep my man and Daddy happy."

"You do?"

He hummed and pressed his chest to mine. "Blowjobs."

I groaned. "And, boy, you know I never say no."

"Well, that's not true. You wouldn't let me suck you off the other morning."

"We were in the motor pool."

"Tinted windows." I smirked, and I stepped back dragging him with me.

"Still, I want my baby to be quiet. Those sounds you make are only for me, or do I need to gag you?"

"I trust you to keep me safe."

My chest tightened, and I had no other words as I led him from the bathroom. We parted ways so I could close and locked the door. I turned to find him stretched out on the bed, naked with his legs parted for me. I'd never get tired of seeing how much my Remy desired me.

REMY

COLD CASE
UNIT

I opened the door and was shocked to find Fran stood on the other side. "Hey, we weren't due for a visit."

"Yeah, we're not. You didn't get these from me." She pointed to the file box beside her feet.

"What's that?" I bent and picked up the heavy box and stepped back to allow her inside. Roo was running around in the backyard with Romeo as Robert and I made dinner. We'd taken off early and brought work home. We'd missed too many family dinners the past few weeks as things started moving fast on the case. The captain had reluctantly let us form a small task force, not officially, but we were assigned all the cases and given permission to ask for any and all forensic evidence to be run without question. I would've loved to be there when Coleman got the news.

"Files on all the kids you were asking me about."

I said thanks as she closed the door and followed me to the dining room where we'd set up a workspace. Stevenson and Doc would be by for a scheduled video call with Vega. She'd texted to say she had some news for us.

"But you said most of those were sealed." I placed the box on the table and turned back to her.

"They were, but having seniority helps sometimes."

"Fran, I don't want you getting in trouble because of me."

"I won't. Just make sure those files stay in one piece, and they can be refiled when you return them. But I also have something else to discuss. Is Robert here?"

Social workers and discussions weren't always good news, and her wondering if Robert was there didn't help the sick feeling growing in my stomach. Her expression didn't give anything away, and I reminded myself never to play poker with her at any time in the future.

"Yeah, he's in the kitchen. We were just making dinner."

"Carmen here, too?"

"Yeah, backyard wearing Romeo out. He hasn't been getting his usual runs with me in the evenings, and he refuses to go with Robert in the mornings. Want some coffee?"

"I would love some. Rough day at work."

"Want to talk about it in hypotheticals?"

She chuckled sadly. "I had to remove a boy from very loving parents today. They were homeless and stayed under our radar for quite a while, but, shit, Remy, you know what it's like. They love him, they went without for him, but their car is a death trap. It's barely running enough to get them to and from work. I couldn't find them housing in time, and even both of them working there's just never enough to cover everything."

"What if I said I had a place they could go, free of charge until they get on their feet? Only stipulation is they both maintain employment."

"I'd steal you from Robert."

"Fuck, can people stop trying to steal my man?" Robert's voice carried from the other room.

"He thinks everyone wants me. I have no idea where he got those thoughts from."

"I've interviewed people who know you. Some of the kids on the street mention your name. To everyone who meets you, you're this larger-than-life superhero. Of course everyone would want a piece of that."

"I'm feeling insecure," he yelled again.

"Come on before my man has a meltdown and heads into an annoying midlife crisis on me." I grabbed a legal pad and wrote down Boss's number. "Here, call Boss. He has some empty apartments in his building. Tell him I'm calling in one of the thousand favors he owes me, and then tell him what you need."

"Thanks, Remy, really." I nodded.

We headed into the kitchen to find Robert wearing a Kiss the Cook apron with big red lips right over his crotch. If I'd known I'd be this happy with the man, I would've put my fear aside, but I was a big believer in timing; and we were fine with how it worked out.

"Can we talk without Carmen for a few minutes?" she asked.

"Yeah, she's going to be outside until we yell for her. What's wrong? Did my petition get turned down because I'll fix whatever I need to, I'll buy a different house, I'll quit my job..."

"Remy, Remy, calm down, it's nothing bad. I talked with her counselor, and Carmen is making amazing strides with her recovery. Yes, as you know, she'll deal with a lot of post-traumatic stress growing up, but that's something you're well equipped to handle. It's come to our attention she has a much older sister. She's in college and has no interest in being a mom at twenty-one. She ran into her mom four years ago, and Carmen was a newborn as far as she could tell and was wondering if there was a way she could have visitation. She suffered the same abuse that Carmen did, and she's working through it, but like I said, she just wants to know if she can possibly see about having a relationship with her baby sister?"

I glanced at Robert, and he nodded. "Of course, we can

arrange something or you can. Maybe one of our Sunday dinners."

"That sounds perfect."

"How did she find out about Carmen?" Robert asked as he continued to move around the room.

"She's an exceptionally busy student, with full-time work to help with tuition. She was put in the system several years ago. Her mom dropped her off at the social services office and said she couldn't handle her. She's taking journalism classes and came across some articles about the shooting, location, and the unnamed minor child got her attention. She contacted the office, and they transferred her to me. Like I said, it's nothing bad. She just wants to connect, and I told her about you, what you do, and she seemed ecstatic about the home Carmen ended up in. And on that note." Fran dug into her oversized bag. "I wanted to deliver these myself. Not often I get to give good news." She pulled out a large manilla envelope.

I took it with shaking hands and fumbled with the clasp as Robert wrapped his arms around me from behind. I pulled out the papers and quickly read them. "Court date?"

"Yes. The beginning of the year, you'll meet with the judge for him to sign the official adoption papers. It's rare the system works that quickly, but as I said, you have some very influential friends in your corner. Congratulations."

"She's ours?" I was a dad, the court papers said so, just a few signatures in a courtroom and my daughter was mine and Robert's. I'd been waiting months, stressed over if I would measure up in the eyes of social services and the law to be her parent.

"All yours and Robert's. The signing is still several months away, but family court is woefully backed up."

"Thank you, Fran, I know with me being unmarried and gay, that"—I cleared my throat—"I tried to be positive but, ya know?"

Robert rubbed my belly to soothe me, and I turned to find a smile as big as mine on his face.

"I know, honey, it's fine. Right now, it's not sinking in that you're a dad, but that's what the paper says. No matter what trauma you went through, what still lingers, you came out on the other side stronger, and Carmen will, too. Because she has someone in her corner that more than understands the bad days and knows how to cherish the good ones."

"Thank you so much. When I asked you in the hospital, I swear I didn't think I'd end up here."

"A lot of changes in a short time, but all very good changes. Look what parading around half-naked all the time got you." She smirked.

Robert tightened his arms around me and took the papers to read them around my arm. "Could, well, can we both be on her new birth certificate?"

"It does allow for same-sex parents to have both names on the birth certificate, but you'd both have to adopt her. It's a good thing I'm sneaky, and your name is on the paperwork I filed. So you might want to get started on that white wedding and all that."

The oxygen locked in my lungs as dreams from my past hit me that they could all come true, but were Robert and I at the marriage stage yet? We were practically living together, and our kid called him Papa. But was he ready to get married again? He'd been married to Gladys for over thirty years. That was almost a lifetime.

"We'll discuss that once our brain cells are back working. This case isn't exactly helping out any."

"Well, I pulled the files for the kids you mentioned, there were a few that hadn't been through our office, but most of them had. A lot of them were fosters, and also some with cases filed against the parents. You know the typical stuff, neglect, truancy, living conditions. A lot of the kids were simply put into the system, and they were all headed for reunification until they disappeared."

"Thanks, Fran, we can use the files." Robert handed me the papers I was sure he read a dozen times and went back to rescue dinner before it burned. After he'd done that, he poured Fran a cup of coffee and slid it across the island to her.

"Just let me know if you need anything else, Remy."

"There is something. Have there been any social workers that have been fired or charges filed against them for inappropriate behavior? Maybe just one who's too enthusiastic about his job?"

"We have some that are just out of school and think they're going to save the world doing this job."

"He'd be his thirties or forties."

She sipped at her coffee as she thought. "We've had some fired for pissing dirty or drinking on the job. A few years ago, we had a guy that convinced one of his cases that he loved her, but I'll ask around. Social services has a revolving door and is sometimes a straight road to disillusionment."

"Thanks."

"What's on your mind?"

"There's too many variables. Street kids come into contact with people at shelters and soup kitchens, and outreach programs. They meet social workers and cops, there's too many unknowns in the equation."

"But what's your gut telling you?" she asked.

"That we have a killer with an attachment disorder who's trying to build a family. One he never had for himself. Either he was abandoned, or there was neglect and abuse. He's taking these kids and turning them into a surrogate."

"A surrogate for what? Partner or child?"

"I think a partner. They're high-risk victims. They're homeless and sometimes desperate, especially if they're new. He's getting them at an awkward and impressionable age. Maybe he has a savior complex, and he thinks he can take them in and fix them, train them to follow whatever strict standard he set."

"But these kids know how to handle themselves, talk their way out of dangerous stuff."

"That's all our thought, too. They play along, and when they get tired of the role or they think they have their opening, they take it. Which sends him into a rage. But what I don't get, except for the last victim, there were no marks that can't be explained as happening before. No sign of poisoning. He's killing without leaving a mark. Suffocation doesn't leave marks unless the victim fights their attacker. If he wrapped his hands or something around their throat, they'd have claw marks from trying to get loose."

"And there's no evidence under their nails?"

"No. Manicures and pedicures, they're pampered almost."

"Which usually means remorse."

"What he does to these kids, the way he discards them...I don't know. Like I said, too many variables. Too many people who could be suspects. His DNA isn't in the database, so even with his first kill, he didn't leave anything of himself behind."

"Except semen."

"Yeah."

"Remy, this case is personal. A lot of your cases are. You're pushing your brain and yourself too much. You're going to burn out."

"Well, hello, Daddy." Doc's voice came from the doorway, and I jerked my gaze up to find him with Stevenson close behind him, rolling his eyes. He rushed around the kitchen to wrap himself around Robert.

"Doc, please do not ever say that again." Robert groaned.

"You're such a prude." Doc leaned on the counter and grinned.

"Fran, meet Doc, the lovable and always weird medical examiner, and Stevenson, detective in homicide."

"Nice to meet you, gentlemen, but I need to be going. My daughter set me up on a blind double-date with a co-worker of her husband. If they talk about accounting all night, I may send you a text to call me to help me escape."

"You know how to find us."

"God, I love you two." She huffed as she left the kitchen, and I laughed as I watched her go.

"You two are early."

"Dinner, feed me." Doc batted his lashes.

"You need a boyfriend, Doc," I said.

"Tell me something I don't know. I'm over fifty, and the closest I came to commitment was that guy who I slept with back in college who was mature enough to have extra toothbrushes and folded our clothes before getting nasty. I actually did the walk of shame with minty breath and teeth I didn't brush in a hurry with my finger. Those were the days."

"That's extremely sad, Doc." Stevenson snorted as he took a seat at the island.

"What about you, Mr. Adonis?"

"I was married. He liked me for a year, and then I moved into a studio apartment with everything I came to the marriage with, which constituted two entire totes, and only one of them was full. Next sad story."

It was like that the rest of the time it took us to get dinner finished, who had the sadder story. I won, like always. The guys behaved themselves around Roo, and Doc seemed extra enchanted and even played dolls with her after we'd finished eating. It was a nice night.

Roo complained when it was time for her bath, but we made it through with as little fighting as necessary, and Papa read her an extra book to make up for not being able to play with her new friend. And while he'd done that, I jogged downstairs and checked the time. We had a few more minutes before Vega was due to call.

"You got it good here, Remy." Stevenson came up behind me, nursing a beer he'd had over dinner.

"You want a fresh one?"

"No, no, I'm not much of a drinker. I just take one so I don't get the *are you an alcoholic? I heard people in your profession are prone to addiction* interrogations."

"You wouldn't have gotten that here, I promise. You don't want a beer, we won't ask why. Those bags aren't as bad as they were the last time I saw you."

"Thanks for that...letting me sleep here that night. This job doesn't allow me to have a lot of friends and especially no relationships. It was nice to just hang out, watch TV, hear a kid laughing because they're so happy they can't contain it."

"You're welcome any time. I don't think Robert gets it, but I spent a lot of time living communally, so I adapt to other people quickly in a cramped space."

"Is this hard for you? This case? What you went through, it can't be easy to separate."

"It's not, and I've never been good at compartmentalizing my past from my job. If I didn't say it, I'd like if my past wasn't spread around too much."

"Of course not. That's not my place. Unless you want someone to know, they're not getting it from me. So are you and Robert a definite thing or..."

"I know hundreds of ways to do away with you, Stevenson," Robert said from behind us.

The bratty look on Stevenson's face said he'd known my man was there the whole time. I bumped him with my bicep and turned to find Robert glaring.

"You know I love you, remember, second best."

"Second best, wow, runner up, always the bridesmaid, never the bride." Stevenson put on a show of stomping away like he was a two-year-old having a tantrum.

"We need to find new friends. Wait, how did we become friends with these people anyway?" He pressed several kisses on my lips and hugged me to him.

"I was friends with Doc first. You asked Stevenson for help. You made that friend I didn't."

"Hey! Not nice!" Stevenson yelled from the dining room, and Doc was laughing. "Time to work, Vega is calling."

"Let's get to work. I'm ready to have my Daddy all to myself."

I stepped away and laced our fingers as I led him to the dining room. Hopefully, Vega has some good news.

ROBERT

COLD CASE
UNIT

Vega didn't have good news, but at least no one in the area around Nino's foster home seemed to be on our radar. Bad news was we were stalled until we figured something out. Also, we had house guests again. Stevenson was back in the guest room, and Doc was on the couch.

"Are we going to be hosting the sleepovers from now on?" I asked as I closed the bedroom door and locked it. I didn't put it past Doc to have voyeuristic tendencies or to sneak in for snuggles. Wasn't happening.

"They're fine," Remy said from the bathroom. I stripped out of my t-shirt and jeans, folded the items, and put them on the chair in the corner. I stretched out on the bed with a groan at the feel of cool sheets on my naked body. Since I'd awakened that morning, all I'd thought about was getting back into bed. Maybe it was a good thing we were moving to Cold Case permanently. Yeah, the hours still sucked, and to be honest, the cases were more stress-inducing than fresh ones. But it was nice to be spending more nights at home than in cars that smelled like old grease and occasionally body odor disguised by baby wipes on stakeouts.

I wouldn't mind a slower pace, which meant more time with Roo. A bit of guilt edged into the happiness as I wondered why I didn't think about a different unit or job when I was with Gladys and my older children. I'd always live with that sense that I wasn't around enough, but I couldn't torture myself with hindsight. All I knew was that I was right where I wanted to be. I was in love and happy.

I crossed my arms under my head and waited for Remy to come to bed. I smiled as I thought about him. I didn't picture myself there two years before waiting for him to come to bed while our daughter slept down the hall. Our daughter. Fran had brought the news my baby needed to hear, hell, what we both needed. Waiting on a court date stressed me out, and I couldn't imagine how much it had weighed on Remy.

When I pictured my life post-divorce, I thought I'd spend the rest of my time on this earth working until retirement, eating frozen dinners in front of the TV. Like those sitcoms of divorced middle-aged men learning to survive without their wife and their grown kids never coming around. That wasn't what I got, though. I got a new partner, best friend, and a few years later, a man I loved.

Yeah, part of me still thought there should be some kind of identity crisis, but to be honest, maybe my bisexuality was there all along. It had just been masked in overwork and the devotion I had to my wife. There was nothing I wanted more when I was married than her and our family. The same was true with Remy. I needed him and the family we were building.

I kept my eyes closed as I heard the light click off, and just as I was about to tell him to come to bed, his hot, wet mouth sucked my cock to the back of his throat. Fuck, my boy loved to suck dick. Sloppy and greedy, I'd come down his throat more times than I could count in the few weeks since we'd had sex for the first time. Work, company, and family time had made it impossible for a repeat. Some nights we were just too tired to do more than curl up and go to sleep.

I opened my eyes and carded my fingers through his hair to pull it back from his face. I didn't want to miss a second of the sight of him with my cock buried between his plump lips.

"You can suck my dick, but I ain't coming anywhere but in your ass, you understand?" I pushed the words through my clenched teeth. He worked me until my chest heaved and I held his head, fucking his mouth until sweat beaded on my skin. "No," I ordered as I saw his arm moving as he jerked off. "Not until Daddy's inside you. Hands on my thighs."

He obeyed me, and I marveled at the control I had over him. He trusted me enough to submit and that I'd keep him safe. I cursed as I pulled him off and jerked him upward until he straddled my hips, and I could capture his mouth.

I opened the nightstand drawer without breaking contact with him and found the bottle of lube. Gladys had been my last, and Remy had shown me the results from his last check-up. When he told me it had been five years since he'd been with anyone, I was shocked anyone resisted him.

"You want me on my hands and knees?" he asked me.

"No, I want you to ride me, spread those thighs just a little wider for me." He shifted as I added lube to my fingers and slipped my hand between his thighs, rubbing my fingertips together to warm the slick. "Baby, I want you to relax. Daddy's going to love you so good." I caught his gaze with mine and dropped my focus to his mouth as he drew his bottom lip between his teeth.

I circled his tight wrinkled hole, smoothed down the coarse hair around it, and grinned as my fingers easily moved inside.

"Baby, we're you playing with yourself?"

"Uh-huh, I wanted...needed to feel you fuck me again. So I prepped in the shower."

"Did it feel good?"

"So good, but you feel so much better."

When he whimpered as I spread the lube around inside his relaxed hole, pre-cum beaded in my slit. "Show me how you're gonna ride my dick." I stiffened my fingers and watched him lift to his knees. I wanted him to have power over his pleasure. To take without worry—I wanted him selfish. He rolled his hips as he lifted on and off my fingers. His sweet grunts and whines combined to make me hard enough to fucking hurt. Pre-cum pooled on my lower belly, and I stroked myself lightly, but I wasn't going to come until I was inside him.

I craved the need to mark him inside and out. I tightened my abs and sat up until I could latch onto a sensitive nipple, and his movements stuttered. I inhaled roughly through my nose, I tasted the salt of his sweat, smelled it and the bodywash he used. I took it all in as I bit down hard enough to leave my teeth marks around his tight little nipple. His chest was soft, and his belly was rounded. I craved his softness and sweetness.

I eased from him and felt him clench as if he tried to draw me back inside, but I had something better for him. My only hesitation was to add extra lube, hissing at the chill. It didn't even cool me off. He shifted as I fisted my cock. I placed the broad head to his hole, and he shook uncontrollably as he lowered until he had me buried to the base.

"Now, earn your reward." I tipped my head back as he rode me with a need I'd never experienced. His hard dick rutted against my upper abs. He snapped his hips to take me until there was no more to give and rolled his hips backward. The drag of his slick ass on my bare cock was too much to take. Tight, hot, and his ass was so greedy for me to fill it. Our tongues tangled, and even with him on top, I knew I was still the one in charge. He needed to submit, to know he was safe to give himself into my caring.

I fell back until my head rested on the pillow, and he stopped. I smacked his hip in punishment, and he clenched so hard I hissed curses. I repeated the move, alternated hips and the fleshy curves of his plump ass. I felt the ripple as he sped his movements, bouncing his beautiful body up and down. His softness moved, and he played with his nipples. His pretty dick was slapping on my belly.

"Daddy, I'm not gonna last..."

"Mark my belly, baby, just like I'm gonna do to that tight, wet hole."

He fell forward to take my lips as he arched and rolled, massaging every inch of my cock. He cursed and grunted as I dug my fingers into the scarred skin of his back. We were too loud. The headboard banged against the wall, but I didn't care. Blood rushed through my ears.

He broke the kiss so we could catch our breath, but what he said next made me lose all control. "You're going to be the first to cum in my ass, Daddy."

I hugged him to me and flipped him to his back. I drew his legs upward until his calves rested on my shoulders, and I braced my weight on my hands beside his hips. His skin was hot from his spanking. I pounded his ass as he clawed at my biceps with his short nails. I shifted and hit just the right spot because he stopped breathing and laid frozen beneath me. I aimed for that spot as my muscles screamed and my balls ached. I lowered my gaze to where I was buried to watch my dick stroke in and out of his red, swollen rim. I doubled my speed and strength as I drove him up the bed, bending his body nearly in half as I worked him until the scream broke the symphony of moans, groans, and the slapping of sweat-slicked skin.

He grabbed his cock and aimed it at my belly as he locked down on mine . I forced my way in and out of the vice-like grip, and as soon as I felt and saw, even smelled his release, I shortened my stroked as he whined in sharp high-pitch tones as I used all my strength to hold him down as I thrust one final time and filled him, marked him right where I belonged.

I barely got his legs off my shoulders before I collapsed and hissed as I slipped free before I draped myself over his bigger body.

"Fuck, Daddy." His chest heaved as he tried to calm himself. "You gotta warn your boy if you're gonna try to break him."

I groaned as I found his lips and traced the curves of his smile with my tongue. "As long as you're happy with Daddy trying to break you, we're fine."

"I came so hard I think I almost blacked out, so I'm good."

"The neighborhood probably knows." We chuckled as I rolled to my side, taking him with me. I brought my hand to his cheek. "I love you, Remy."

"I love you, too. I never thought I'd get to say that to you."

"You can tell me any time, and I'll tell you every day how lucky I am."

"You're too good to me, Robert."

"There's no such thing as being too good to you." I kissed him until we had no choice but to get up and clean the mess we'd made of ourselves. I wanted the rest of my lifetime with him, and I hoped he wanted the same.

REMY

COLD CASE
UNIT

Vega, Robert, Stevenson, and I we're packed into a tiny interrogation room that they'd given us to work the case. Vega was seated on a pile of boxes with her laptop balanced on her lap and typing away. Stevenson was going through every file, reading them repeatedly as if he'd missed a detail. Robert was arguing with Coleman, and from the color that highlighted his sharp cheekbones, my Daddy was ready to punch him more than I normally wanted to hit the lab director.

I was in front of the wall that we'd taped every image and note we thought was important. We'd done all the footwork we could, I wanted to speak with Forester, but the man hadn't returned my call or responded to the numerous cards I'd dropped off. I crossed my arms over my chest and mentally marked off the checklist in my head.

"I see you four are hard at work." Graves mocking tone came from the doorway, and I flipped him off over my shoulder without bothering to turn to give him my focus.

"Always so professional."

"Keep it up, you won't have to worry about him being the unprofessional one." The warning was clear in Robert's voice, and

I smiled as I let my gaze move from one image to another, the faces seemingly getting younger from Nino's. There were a few victims that were older than Nino, but they didn't look like it. The profile was still fourteen to twenty-one, but the younger teens basically made up the final four victims. No more than sixteen and still all looked like babies.

"Letting your boyfriend's asshole-ish nature rub off on you?"

The room erupted in laughter more appropriate for a twelve-year-old with their first foray into a dirty mind, but we were all exhausted. We were owed a juvenile meltdown caused by delirium.

"Papa!" I spun in time to Robert on his feet and running out of the room at the sound of our daughter calling his name.

"Roo, what are you doing here?"

I moved a whiteboard to cover the wall, and we all worked to conceal anything inappropriate as he returned with our daughter in his arms.

"Auntie Gladys made food." I smiled as Gladys entered the room with a massive basket.

After Robert saw everything was hidden, he set Roo on her feet, and she went around to say hi. Everyone asked her consent for a hug or handshake, and Roo actually asked Vega for a hug. My friend's faced bloomed into a massive smile and gave my daughter a hug, and then she came to me holding her arms up, and I lifted my beautiful Roo into my arms and settled her on my hip.

"Can't have y'all starving, and she wanted to say goodnight to Dad and Papa. Apparently, I suck at telling bedtime stories even though I'm professional level." We all chuckled at her exasperated tone.

Graves frozen in the corner caught my attention as he stared at us fussing over Roo and Robert giving Gladys a kiss on the cheek. He looked so unsure of himself as if he were afraid to move or get caught. Weird, Graves was the biggest ass in the homicide unit. We'd butted heads since day one.

"Well, we appreciate the food, Gladys." She offered me her cheek, and I gave her a loud kiss as Roo giggled. "Want in on free food, Graves?" I asked and earned an odd look from Robert, but then he rolled his eyes and shrugged his shoulders.

"Honey, did you bring the books you want me to read? And how many?" I knew Robert already knew the number before she held up five fingers in answer. She always had a thing about fives. "You go ahead and eat. My Roo needs Papa time."

I barely steadied Roo as she made a dive for Robert. "Of course, our daughter thinks you're the best."

"Pouting just makes you cute, so you're not exactly making your point."

I mouthed asshole, and he blew me a covert kiss. We hadn't exactly hid that we were a couple, but we also didn't want the heat to come down on us too much in the middle of the case.

"When did you get married?" Graves asked.

"They're not married yet. I do have hopes my ex-husband will get his head out of his ass soon."

"Don't pressure Robert into marriage."

"Why not?" She made a face. "That's what best friends do. It's my right."

"Put some food in your face and be quiet."

"So rude," Gladys muttered as she handed out plates, including one for Graves.

I looked around and didn't see Robert, which meant he'd taken Roo to the breakroom where there was a couch to read to Roo.

"You any closer to an answer?" Gladys asked.

"No, it's all there, except I have one more person to talk to, and I may have to strong-arm my way into his club."

"I know this amazing defense attorney."

"Gladys, my love, you'll be the first I call if I end up in handcuffs in the not-so-fun way."

"Glad to be of help."

"He's here. There was no long gaps between killings. That means no major life changes. He's able to get in and out of an environment where everyone is paranoid, especially recently. Vega said no one tripped any alarm bells in the first case. You find your obsession, you covet this obsession...this paragon that embodied his fantasy had to lure him in somehow. Nico was smart, he was a survivor, and he let this person close enough to take him."

"You're talking about sex workers and hustlers. You walk through those five blocks, and you can see hundreds of people getting in strangers' cars. What if he wasn't a stranger? Regulars foster familiarity and safety. A few dates, Remy. He's a predator, and what do some predators have?" Graves filled a plate as he spoke.

"Camouflage," I answered.

"Exactly."

I glared at Graves.

"What's the best camo in an area like that? You were there, Pretty, you know the game." Vega perched on the table and crossed her legs.

"Undercover cops, but we were always able to clock them. Rookies were the worst. Outreach workers, they were always around, offering space in shelters or meals, handing out cards. Pimps and Madams, they troll for ones to take under their wing. These are all people that we'd know to avoid or to count on as safe. Tricks are different, though. I had regulars, and I never hesitated." I glanced at Graves and got that look again that said I was a puzzle he'd thought he'd figured out, but pieces were missing. "Worst would be authority figures that we'd see as hypocrites. Offer salvation while fucking us."

"I hate to say this, but could we be dealing with a cop...and not a UC, but a uniform? Easily recognizable but still blends in," Stevenson offered.

"It could just be a guy in a cop uniform, easy enough to get, maybe disgraced in some way but kept their uniform and badge." Graves sounded helpful and not petulant over us thinking a cop could be a serial killer. "There's also other first responders, EMTs, firefighters."

"Do you know how many thousands of suspects we'd have to add to our board for that?"

"Just needs to be one."

"You're so helpful, Graves."

"Hey, I gotta earn my free food, and this is a lot better than the frozen dinner I had planned. And y'all seem to be your own little club."

"Vega, any more on the chart?" I asked.

"I made some calls, pretended to be an adopted child in search of my biological parents, and asked did anyone in the family give someone up for adoption. I was vague as fuck, but I asked. Seems the female descendent that we thought was the best fit had passed on, but since times change, they remember their aunt had a son around seventy-four."

"Would put him inside the profile."

"It would, and I thanked them for their help, and I was sorry if I brought up terrible memories. So in that area, I looked for all male newborns born in that year. I cataloged them by race and ethnicity, removed all but the white males. There were forty." Vega grabbed another helping of lasagna.

"Why drop out the non-white newborns?"

"Because, Graves, historically speaking, the highest percentage of newborn adoptions are of healthy white children. I went with males because, *historically* speaking, men want sons, and toxic masculinity is ingrained in patriarchal cultures."

"Could we leave our man-hating to a minimum right now?" Stevenson winked at Vega.

"Most of the present company was excluded from my generalizations. But I came to a dead end. It had to have been a private closed adoption."

"May I make a suggestion?"

"Go ahead, Graves, you already pushed into our little club meeting."

"How much forensic evidence was left behind?"

"Minimal. Semen was left behind, but anything else, hairs, fibers, no-go."

"So we have a forensically aware killer. He knows not to leave anything behind, and because we don't have a DNA match in our systems, that has to mean he knows he wouldn't get popped for leaving behind what he did. Why does he leave the semen? It would be easy enough to use a condom. In a sense, it would be the safest option. Even though I'm sure all our victims used protection religiously, there's still a chance."

"Definitely. He doesn't seem like the type to take a risk like that. He's too damn careful. I mean, there's ones you can find who will go bareback for the right money, but it's rare. My crew wouldn't even give blowjobs without a condom. We went in groups to get tested once a month."

"Remy, he's keeping them to play out some fantasy. What if he's searching for a partner, a husband? Someone to build a life with, to have a family with?" Vega suggested. "These kids are androgynous, makeup, dresses, they could pass for women. What if the woman he wanted was petite, slender? We could be looking for a straight male who's turning high-risk victims into his surrogate."

"That's a stretch, but plenty of closeted men pick up hustlers and escorts to fulfill some down-low fantasy. It would be a threat to them to get exposed. But there's the fact he dresses them like private school kids in cardigans and khakis, and loafers, very opposite what they'd normally wear."

"But what if the condom is the trigger?"

"What?" I glanced at Gladys.

"What's the first thing a couple who's committed decides on besides exclusivity?"

"Getting tested to forgo condoms."

"What if he romances them? Takes care of them? He has their hands and feet done. Pampers them in ways they never were before, and he believes there's a natural progression. And on, for lack of a better word, the honeymoon, his surrogates being street smart and safety-minded kids demands protection. That breaks a sense of trust that he'd been working on for a number of days."

"It would go along with his possible attachment disorder, right?" Stevenson asked.

"Individuals with severe trauma and neglect with the resulting attachment disorder can get violent when rebuked. You see it in stalkers. They live this whole fantasy life with the object of their obsession playing out. To them, they can take a smile as a loving gesture. A polite greeting is consent."

"What if they took the so-called dates as actual dates, and he picks them up one night, and instead of it playing out like normal, he keeps them. Now we're to the playing house stage. That goes on for a week or two," Graves commented as he slowly ate.

"So our killer could be spending months picking them up, which would explain the time between bodies." Still too many variables, but I was getting so sick of saying that.

"The manis and pedis are professionally done. I hate to stereotype here, but men aren't typically giving other men manis and pedis. So he'd have to take them somewhere. These boys are absolutely stunning. Someone would know them."

I'd never even thought about him taking them to have their nails done. Danger of too much exposure, but our killer wasn't good on impulse control. "Gladys, I love your stereotyping right now."

"Marry my ex-husband."

"Not enough to let you plan a wedding." She heavy sighed and snorted. "What did you get from the research on the clothes they were wearing?" I turned to Vega.

"High-quality but in no way unique. Like you said, private school choices for their little automatons."

"We can work out your aggression on the state of our inevitable collapse of society by brainwashing later."

"Fine, there's about fifty stores that purchased those or similar items in the past decade. You won't believe how many people are still doing inventory by hand. It's embarrassing. I digress. I focused on the pattern of the cardigans, and some companies consider patterns proprietary and narrowed those fifty down to twenty-five stores. Still not great, but way easier to work with. There was one company that purchased the items in bulk that included the sweater, khakis, and loafers. I tracked the receipts to a shell company that dead-ended at a post office box that was, no surprise, rented with a fake ID."

"So not helpful," Stevenson said as he rolled his eyes.

"Hey, I found it, and the post office is in the city so we know he's local. The button-down shirts, tightie-whities, and crew socks were generic, could be purchased anywhere. But we can rule out the neighborhood where that branch of the post office is because he wouldn't want to get those delivered close to home."

"How do we find the salon?"

"Legwork. The most important thing to being a detective. So we can rule out the area where the post office is." As I spoke, Vega typed on her laptop. "We'd think high-end because he wants to impress."

"And those places usually keep a computer record of clients to send out mailers and stuff, even if they just ask for an email address, that would still give us IP addresses, but we may hit a roadblock with VPNs. If he frequents the same place, they may have heard his name mentioned."

"Okay, make a list, break it down, and email sections to us."

"Include me. It's not like you didn't take some of my open cases when y'all scavenged."

"Aw, Graves, bucking for entry into the cool kids club?"

"I still don't like you, Bosley."

"You're going to break my heart."

"Don't complain, I'm not. At least there's one less person trying to steal my man." Robert's voice piped up, and I turned to the doorway. "Gladys, our girl is asleep on the couch. She only made it through three books tonight. It is a bit past her bedtime."

"We all know the rule, when she wants her dads, I'm to call or bring her home. You two weren't home, so here I am."

"And I appreciate it. Once this case is over, I'm going to need to buy you something extremely expensive."

Gladys opened her mouth, and I knew what was coming next. "No wedding, something just for you that doesn't end in your ex-husband's nuptials to me."

"Can't blame a woman for trying." She huffed and started cleaning up, Graves and Stevenson pitched in to help, and a full plate was placed on the table in front of me. "You and Robert can share this one, neither of you ate, and vending machines and bad coffee doesn't count."

"Thanks."

"Anything for you two. I'm going to get my girl and take her home to bed. I'll drop her at Mrs. Walton's in the morning before I head to work. What are we doing with Romeo?"

"He's hanging out at Mrs. Walton's. She likes the company at night, and I told her she should think about getting herself a dog. But she said why get herself one when she already has one...mine."

Robert hugged Gladys bye, and I followed her to say goodnight to my daughter. I hated leaving her alone at night because I knew the nightmares still came, and sometimes it was worse when she wasn't in her own bed. I loved my job, I did what I did to make a difference, but when this case was over, I needed to think about making changes. My girl was happy, but I still felt guilty. I understood how Robert felt.

"You're doing amazing things, Remy. This is a blip in a lifetime. Those kids deserve the justice you're going to give them. Yours and Robert's daughter is going to be so proud of her dads for the men you are. A few late nights here and there, but you and him make the effort. One of you is always with her at night, and these where you're both working are rare. But I know even one seems like too much. That's what makes you an amazing dad. Just remember that."

"Thanks. I love you, Gladys."

"Love you, too, and I especially love my honorary niece. And you have no idea how grateful I am that my friend found you."

I choked back the lump that formed in my throat as I accepted a hug, and I crouched down beside the couch, pushed my daughter's curls from her forehead, and pressed a kiss there. When I straightened, I held the basket as she picked up Roo, and handed it back to watch her head to the elevator. I stood there a few more minutes to get myself together and went back to the interrogation room.

As soon as I walked in, Vega was packing up her things. "Each of you has a section of the list split three ways, and I also scanned the images and emailed those as well to show around. I promised my babygirl I'd be at her show tonight, so I have to go or I'll be late. And we don't break promises to our Littles no matter what."

"Thanks, Vega, just call me when you know something more," I spoke as I came to a stop beside Robert.

"We could've taken our girl home."

"We have to be up early to get started on working through the list. We can pop over to Mrs. Walton's to give our girl some love before work."

"I'll start on my section of the list in the morning after I go home to my extremely lumpy fold-down futon."

"No sleepovers. I want my man to myself in an empty house.

Parents gotta take privacy where they can get it." Robert waved at the grumpy man, and I smiled at Stevenson's wink as he exited to head home to his own bed.

We were left alone with Graves. "You trying to turn over a new, nicer leaf, Graves?" I smiled as the man rolled his eyes like a brat.

"No, not nicer, but you two and Stevenson found more on these cases than I did in the months I had them before you added this task force. I won't say I get this do-gooder bullshit you got going on, but I respect it. Don't read too much into it, Bosley. We ain't going to be friends."

"Should I try for some tears or something because I think I can get one to fall." I chuckled as the man flipped me off and disappeared as well.

"Ready to go home to get some sleep?"

"So much sleep."

"Then let's go. Tomorrow will be soon enough to figure shit out."

"Thanks for all this."

"You don't have to thank me. Unlike Graves, I love your do-gooder bullshit. It's one of the main reasons I started noticing you. You cared, Remy. You put yourself fully into a case because you cared about the victim. I'd lost that in the years leading up to you coming into my life. Being your partner definitely made me a better cop."

"Aw, I love you, too, Daddy."

"There's my beautiful brat."

We gathered up our things, and I put a napkin over the plate Gladys made us. I'd heat it up when we got home before I got to go to bed and get cuddled by my sexy man.

ROBERT

I marked another salon off the list as Remy was getting us coffee. We'd barely laid down the previous night before we passed out. We were halfway through our list, and we'd had no hits. Stevenson and Graves weren't having any better luck, and all our phones had been going off all day because of the group text Vega set up for us. How the hell I ended up with all the weird friends I didn't know.

Being with Remy had definitely opened the world to me. I'd been as straight-laced and by the book as a cop could get until him. I wasn't going to complain, he eased the stress of the job, and my last physical showed my blood pressure wasn't through the roof. All I knew was we needed to find the killer because the longer this went on, we were closer to finding another victim, and I couldn't deal with that. Remy really couldn't.

Out of all the cases we'd worked, it was these that pushed him to his limit, and I understood why, but I felt so helpless when I couldn't do anything about it.

"I got us a donut." Remy held out the glazed chocolate cake donut, and I took a bite beside his. I put my phone away as I grabbed the to-go cup of coffee. He had his cold coffee so he could chug.

"The next salon is three stores down. Do you think this was a good lead?"

"Even if it's not, it's still a lead. Gladys is right, though. Think about it. These kids were clean, primped...they were set there to make a statement. If he didn't want to make an impression, he could've just dumped them in the clothes he took them in or naked. I just don't know what he's trying to prove."

We made our way down the sidewalk filled with afternoon shoppers and delivery people, we'd gone casual so we mixed well, but the neighborhood wasn't exactly our kind of place. I glanced at him and tried not to pay too much attention to the dark circles under his eyes and my guilt telling me that I wasn't taking care of him well enough. He hadn't looked that tired since he'd stayed with me after I was hurt.

"Maybe there's nothing to prove. Maybe he's just thinking ahead. He wasn't cruel to them as far as we can tell forensically. He bathed them, dressed them, and combed their hair. He made a full meal that they ate. He cared for them. And that's probably what's going to come out of his mouth during interrogation."

"But they were babies. They felt they had no choices in life. And they sure as hell didn't have any in death either."

"I know, baby, but we've done enough of these cases and interrogations to know killers can come up with any number of excuses. Excuses they think justify what they did."

"I get that. I really do." He took another bite and gave me the last piece before he licked the glaze from his fingertips. "But from a psychological standpoint, I can see that they truly believe that what they did was right in the way their brains processed it. But from the cop standpoint, I really hate them. And more than anything, I'm terrified we're never going to find them."

"That might be true. That's why we have a Cold Case Unit. But think about all that you accomplished. You linked cases that no one even bothered to look deeper into. You developed a team that saw what you did. You gave these kids a voice, an advocate. It's not enough to help the sting if we don't find them or he kills again, but you did good. And I'm very proud of you." I stopped talking as we paused outside the next salon on our list.

"That does mean a lot, Daddy. Okay, serious faces on."

"We got this, baby." I opened the door for him, and we stepped inside. They must be in a afternoon lull. The door sensor chimed.

"Hello, welcome to Impressions. How can I help you two today? Couple massage?" A young woman with electric blue neon hair approached with a beautiful smile.

"No, thank you, Detective Bosley." He showed his badge. "Detective Kaufmann." He pointed over his shoulder at me. "We're working a case, and we wanted to show you some pictures and see if you recognize any of them." As he put his badge away, he pulled out his phone. I watched as he pulled up the pictures of our victims, starting with Nino.

"Of course."

"Thank you so much. Just take a look, and if you recognize even one, that would help a lot." He handed over his phone, and I studied her expression as she stared at each one before scrolling to the next one.

I held my breath; I really didn't want to have to go to another salon. Each one we, Stevenson, and Graves ticked off, started to kill all our hope.

"I don't recognize the ones in the beginning, but I've only been here a few years, but the last ones look familiar."

"Did they come in alone?"

"Hold on." She called over a few others and an older woman, who went through the images.

My heart picked up pace, but decades of practice kept the excitement out of my expression.

"Most of them are familiar, but the last ten I definitely

remember." The older woman spoke up, whose name tag read Celeste.

"Did they come in with anyone?" I asked as she went back through the images and the other ladies wandered off.

"They said their husband, but I've been around long enough that was classic sugar daddy, and unless this man had a harem, he made the rounds."

"What do you remember?"

"Came in carrying tons of bags, high-end boutique, Daddy spent a fortune. The babies looked a little overwhelmed, kept looking to him for guidance. He kept saying for them to get whatever they wanted. They normally got the full service, massage to waxed to nails. Most of their nails were atrocious. One of them had bitten them back so far they were caked with blood. Other than that, they looked happy and healthy, except for the age difference, nothing made me wary."

"Are you sure something wasn't off?" Remy asked.

"Not really. You get a lot of sugar daddies bringing their babies in. In this business, you see way too many kept barely legal young men and women. They didn't look scared or nervous, but you could definitely tell they weren't used to the treatment."

"What about the guy they came in with? What did he look like? Overhear a name?" I rested my forearms on the shelf of the raised counter and held my coffee cup in my hands.

"Under fifty but definitely had some Botox done, or he just had a smile that didn't quite reach his eyes to cause them to crinkle. Expensive ash-blond dye job. Blue eyes but probably from contacts or recently had corrective surgery. I caught him a few times reaching up as if he was adjusting glasses, like it was a habit. Impeccably dressed, only a tailor could fit a suit that well. He's just like a lot of guys reaching a certain age trying to hold on to or recapture youth. I get it. I've owned this place and worked in enough salons to know the type. I offered coffee or tea, he insisted they drink some green juice, I loathe the shit, but it makes me a killing selling it. Said caffeine and sugar was bad."

"No name?" Remy asked.

"Julian, but that's all I got. We have a system set up where someone enters their information, and it sends out coupons or specials we have coming up." She typed on the computer and turned the screen around. "Always paid in cash. Again, not unusual when they don't want a wife or husband to see strange things on the credit card statements."

Remy wrote down the address, but I didn't hold out much hope that it was real, but we had something.

"Anything else you can think of?"

"Not really. I mean he was a good-looking, normal guy, like dozens I see every week."

"Do you have a security system?" I was grasping at straws there, but it couldn't hurt to ask.

"We have a basic one. Files get overwritten every twenty-four hours."

"When's the last time he was in?"

"Two weeks ago, the kid he was with, pretty thing, very soft-spoken. Almost shy in an innocent way which didn't fit his usual type. The others were young, but they'd been around."

Which would fit with our last victim being new on the streets and hadn't toughened up. Maybe our killer was his first client.

"Wait, there was something with the last appointment. The daddy leaned down to kiss the boy's neck, but the kid shied away. Not in a bad way, just in the sense that it tickled or something. It was barely a second, but his face kinda went blank, but then it was like it hadn't happened, and I just told myself I was seeing things."

"Thank you so much for your time. If he happens to come back in, could you give me or my partner a call?" Remy handed over their cards, and she took them with a smile. "Maybe I can send a sketch artist by to talk with you, would that be okay?"

"Sure, no problem. If I see him, you'll definitely get a call." She leaned in, and I grinned at her smile. "I saw you two through the window. Your husband is very cute, and men like to be pampered, too. Maybe an anniversary is coming up?"

"I'll keep that in mind." I winked at her as she slipped me a card, too.

We said our goodbyes and exited. Remy was typing away at his phone and sent his notes to our team of misfits and then tucked it back into his pocket.

"We owe Gladys big."

"We do. So, baby, what's the plan?"

"We have a name which may be fake. We have an email address that's more than likely fake. But maybe he screwed up and didn't think about us tracking down a salon in this city that he got his victim's nails done at. I'll send a text to Davian and a few others to spread the word to be on the lookout for the description. That'll spread pretty quickly, and it's still early enough they'll get it when they wake up." He stepped to the side and leaned back against the wall near the entrance of the alley.

"Can I ask you something?"

"Of course."

"Do you miss the life you had then, not the sex work, maybe the sex work, too? But you're still so connected. Is it weird not to be a full-time part of it?" I'd worried I'd overstepped when he was silent a second too long, but then he shrugged.

"It is. Even in my teens, I was there, making connections, and when the host and her husband kicked me out, well, it was sort of like going to a better home. Even homeless, it was better than being in that house. My first real memory of my childhood was my host whispering how much she hated me. How much I ruined her life."

"That's why you call her the host. You've never called her anything else."

"Yeah, she was just the host. There was no connection, no

mother-son bond in any way. She was a product of an affair. When she was fourteen, she found her biological father hoping to find the parental relationship she always wanted. From what I heard, she was in his bed that night, and she stayed there as the wife."

"You said she cheated."

"She did, a lot. He wasn't any more faithful than her, but when she got pregnant, well, that was a constant reminder that another man got what he considered his. Because every part of her belonged to him, he helped create her and that meant..." He took a deep breath.

"You don't have to talk about it."

"And as much as I don't want to, I think you deserve answers because my childhood...my past made me the way I am."

"And you're perfect."

"You're probably the only one other than our daughter who thinks that. When the host told the husband she was pregnant, he told her to keep me. The familial link made it where they decided not to breed, but it was a way for them to have children. His blood ran through my veins, so I was family in a sense."

"When did the abuse start, baby?"

"It was always there. It was my life. I don't remember a time in my first eighteen years that I wasn't hurt in some way. But they never left marks when they thought they'd be discovered. When school was in session, I was safe from the hits and slaps, the whip, but not from the sexual abuse. Summer break, though, they were free to do what they wanted. Sell me to whomever they wanted, and those people could do whatever. You know, they're still alive, my host and her husband."

"Have you ever confronted them?"

"No. But they're never unsupervised. Someone is always watching. I was terrified when I left someone else would take my place. It never happened, though. Her husband is bed-ridden, probably won't last another year. The host is as mean as ever. I don't miss the start of my life, but I miss the camaraderie of it all. The community that you know will never turn their back on you as long as you're loyal. We shared food and shelter without question because other members needed it, even if we went short. Do you know how much a lifesaver a community like that is?"

"It saved you."

"We saved each other. If a certain nice but closeted cop hadn't taken mercy on me, I imagine I'd still be there. Maybe still starving myself to stay thin and beautiful, waxed and pretty."

I frowned as his face changed. "What?" I asked.

"Waxed, starved, pampered, it's what a pimp does. He brings them in, keeps them safe, and promises them the world. Says you're their number one. You're favored above the rest. It's also classic grooming behavior. When a predator meets a mark, they find something to connect over. So he picks up one of our victims. The younger, the better, and maybe they look a little nervous."

When he paused, I picked up. "So he assumes they're new, he gets them in his car, probably something clean and fancy, he offers to buy them food, that he just wants to talk and he won't touch them at all. And he doesn't. All he wants is company."

"We expect someone wants our bodies not to spend time with us. It throws us. We let our guard down because the person is nice and doesn't just want to use us."

"Let's get everyone back to the office or to one of our houses and go over what we have. Maybe if we lay everything out, one of us may hit something we're missing."

"Sounds like a plan, and I need food. I require sustenance."

"And what my baby wants, he gets. Text everyone, which should be easy with the damn group text Vega set up."

"She just misses us."

"Uh-huh. How many people are we going to add to our immediate family circle?"

"Well, let me set your mind at ease. Graves won't be one of them."

I chuckled at his bratty grin, and I grabbed his hand to lead him back to the SUV. We still had a lot of work to do, and I needed to feed him.

REMY

COLD CASE
UNIT

You'll be fine, baby, just don't kill him. I kept those words running through my head on a constant loop after we'd separated into three groups. Vega and Doc, Robert and Stevenson, and Graves and myself. Robert had a pass because he was mine, but Graves wouldn't get any information without me. I felt like a macabre tour guide through the hellscape of my past; Graves already knew too much.

"Hey, Cherry," I yelled and raised my hand to wave.

"Pretty, slumming again?" The tall, absolutely gorgeous blonde moved with a seductive sway as she strolled toward us. She hadn't changed much in the ten years since she'd stepped onto that corner a decade before. She'd gotten harder, earned respect, well, more like demanded it. She always took the newbies under her wing and tried to steer them. Sometimes that even meant she tried to talk them into going home.

"You know I don't consider visiting my family as slumming. Gorgeous as always."

"Daddy does take good care of his girl." Her Dominant and boyfriend annoyed the fuck out of me, but it wasn't my life to live. "You got something for me to look at?"

I reached into my pocket for the sketch we'd gotten done from the salon owner's memory. "Have you seen him hanging around? Maybe spent some time or picked up our mutual friends."

A smile tugged at the corner of my mouth as she posed just right, back arched, breasts thrust forward, and ass on perfect display. It was unconscious. Her muscle memory knew she was on the clock, even talking to me. She tilted her head in that way men found charming on young submissive women. That action was very much deceptive. She studied the sketch.

"He looks familiar, always dismisses any of the ladies that go up to his car. His voice is very cultured and condescending, but he was less likely to send the petite underaged girls away."

"Anything else?"

"You know we don't pay too much attention. He has a car that doesn't match the area, and I haven't seen him around in a while. I figured he changed hunting grounds. It was just after you sent out word to move in groups and take plate numbers."

"Did anyone get his?"

"If no one gets in a car, we didn't see the point. Maybe hit up our precious Zero. You know he's always lurking about."

"Zero still hangs out? I thought he went back to Harvard." The kid showed up about five years ago, working on some anthropology thesis about modern urban tribal cultures and how they related to underground communities, including homeless and sex workers. He was a brilliant young man, but he'd immersed himself so deeply he hadn't wanted to leave.

"You know this place is sometimes like an addiction. It grabs ahold and doesn't always let you go. Look at you. You can't stay away from this place, making sure your family stays safe." Her crimson lips twitched. "And we really appreciate it, Pretty."

"And I'd appreciate it if the family would stop calling me that. The beast I am, it doesn't fit."

"Oh, but, Pretty, hairy, bearded beast or not, you're still pretty."

I playfully growled at her as she handed back the paper and went back to work. I shoved my hands into my pockets, occasionally stopping to ask if anyone knew where Zero or anyone else I thought could help me.

"How the fuck did you become a cop?" Graves had been quiet so long I could've almost pretended he wasn't there at all.

"Because of my shameless past, I couldn't want to be a cop?"

"That's not what I meant. All this shit you do, it's all selfless. It's not hard to see everyone down here respects you. Why not a social worker or running one of those outreach programs?"

"Social workers and people who work these outreach programs already sympathize with what happens down here. Knows what a majority of kids go through to end up here. Don't get me wrong, there's people of all backgrounds and socio-economic levels. Cops aren't trained for this. They're trained to enforce arbitrary laws without thinking about context or the psychological reasons."

"Again, why are you a cop? Arbitrary laws? Laws are laws."

I shook my head as I stopped by a group of teenagers I recognized from me handing out cards to the free health clinic and condoms. They didn't recognize the sketch, and they may know something, but they hadn't known me long enough to trust me. That was fine. I didn't push in case they could be of help later. I reminded them about the clinic and returned to where Graves stood several feet away.

I began the conversation right where we left off. "No they're not, the judicial system is inherently racist and classist. You have good white kids who don't go to jail or suffer any consequences for sexual assault. But you have young, black men who are serving life sentences for non-violent drug offenses where they were sentenced as young as sixteen."

"Then why not play advocate to get sentences overturned, make stiffer penalties for—"

"You don't get it, *racist* and *classist*," I spoke the two words as slow as possible and earned an eye roll. "And I've been a victim advocate for twenty years. I'm not going to change an entire system with hundreds of years of legal precedence. There are still Blue Laws on the books, but since they're so idiotic, no one has thought about amending them, but technically they're still laws of the land. I don't make a huge change, and like Robert has told me so many times, I can't save them all, but I do what I can."

"You're an idealist when you have every right to be a realist."

"Not so much, don't paint me as selfless. I found a way out, but that help came with assistance. I offer my help, but people are happy or complacent just like anyone in life. So I offer safety in times they need it, but they're ultimately in control of their choices. For the first time for some of them, they were offered a choice. It's no one's business if it's the right one. I have no right to police morality unless that ends in the injury or death of another person."

"God, you're fucking weird."

"Cree, love," I called out to an outreach worker handing out bagged dinners. I grabbed Graves and dragged him behind me until we reached her.

"Remy, what are you doing down here? It's Friday night, you usually have a Chinese date with that very sexy mature man, Robert."

"We're both working tonight. He took the other strange face. This is Graves."

"Too pretty, so not your type." She didn't hide her expression that she wasn't impressed with the buzzed hair and cheap suit.

"Robert will be very happy with that."

"You're on a case, so not this Sunday, but the one after, you have to come to dinner, and I won't take no for an answer. We're still your family."

"I'll bring Robert and let y'all meet our daughter. She's amazing."

"Congratulations!" There was a squeal, and I had an armful of hippie. "So happy for you, Remy. You so deserve it and no skipping the next dinner, even if it's just for a few minutes."

"I promise."

"Okay, you're on the case of our kids disappearing and turning up murdered?"

"Yeah, I have a sketch I want you to look at. Can you do that?"

"Anything for you." She held out her hand, and I passed her the sketch. Just like with Cherry, she studied the image. "I know him. What the hell was his name...Julian." She hissed the word like it tasted nasty on her tongue.

"What can you tell me?"

"Nothing really, um, the past three years he's volunteered to hand out food and personal care kits. You know these people come and go."

"These people?" Graves asked.

"You know, it's like they feel guilty for being rich. He wore jeans and t-shirts, combat-like boots, but you know the ones, the type that people spend money on to make them look like they're old. Designer vintage. He was only assigned to me a few times. His intentions weren't altruistic. I know a predator when I see one."

"Did any of the kids complain?"

"No, but they mentioned a few times that they were uncomfortable with him. I think Boss told him that we were over budget and needed to cut down on our community work until our next grant came through."

"Can you describe him to me?"

"White. Five-ten. Blond hair, totally from a salon. Hair like that doesn't happen in nature. Glasses, wire framed. Body only a gym could create. We shook hands, smoother than a babies. Southern drawl that he let it slip a few times when he seemed to get irritated when some of our people flirted over handovers. His regular voice is very cultured and clipped."

"Any personal info?"

"No, but he worked for us, and Boss is protective. He makes volunteers fill out forms. He'll have those."

"I worship the ground your hippie sandals walk on."

"You're not my type, although, you do give good cuddles."

I shook my head as she smirked, and Graves snorted. I said goodbye and promised to see her at Sunday dinner. As I turned back to get to where we parked, I pulled out my phone and sent a text for Robert, Stevenson, and Vega to meet us at Boss's place. We were so close. We just needed one good fuck up, something he didn't think anyone would pay attention to. That's all.

ROBERT

"**Y**ou neurotic, little shit! Your dick doesn't even have to hit the seat. You could've pissed at a dozen public bathrooms," Remy was yelling as I heard the door of Boss's apartment bang open. "It's down the hall."

I wasn't the only one staring at the entryway to the living room as Remy appeared, rolling his eyes and pushing his hair back from his face.

"Graves is definitely not in our family."

He looked so frustrated, but Vega started giggling and everyone else followed, including me. At least Graves survived the evening with Remy. I'd have to give my baby a reward. He hadn't wanted to split up.

"He's had to pee for an hour but refused to go in a public bathroom. Stevenson, he's all yours next time. I'm not dealing with it." He stomped across the room until he seated himself on my lap, and I tipped my head back for a kiss. Aww's erupted around us, and they turned to laughter when we both flipped them off. After a quick kiss, he settled against my chest.

"I always knew Graves was weird and not in a good way, but you two are so adorable," Vega announced from where she'd settled in at the kitchen table and set up her workspace. "What do we have?"

"Julian."

As soon as he said the name, hope filled my chest that we'd find the bastard before he left another body for us to find. If he used his real name, he had to think it couldn't possibly be traced back to one person. How many people volunteered every day? How many of these community outreach programs were publicly run with fundraisers? He might've thought there was no way to trace it back to him, one man in a city of hundreds of thousands of people.

"So, real name?" I asked Remy.

"He used it at the salon and at Boss's outreach. Boss, what can you tell us?"

Boss crossed the room to a cluttered desk and started riffling through papers. "Total predator. The first day he showed up, I told him we were full of workers that day, but to fill out a volunteer form and a release form and we'd call when we were shorthanded. Wouldn't fill out either but said he would when he came back next time. Set off some warning bells for me. He never got an assignment from me, but he came in on days where I wasn't working or in the building. I never noticed until I saw the sign-ups for that day." He seemed to find what he wanted. "You know the type, Pretty. Psychopaths. They integrate into an environment to find vulnerable victims. This guy totally had narcissistic tendencies. Seemed nice enough on the surface. Said all the right things." He returned to give Remy the paper, and Boss started a pot of coffee.

Remy held the paper. "Same email address. This home address doesn't exist, though. But could be close enough. How do you keep a lie believable?"

"Give it an edge of truth. More truth, less chance of slipping up." Graves answered as he appeared. "Same goes with interrogations, short, simple answers, but again enough honesty, any odd gut feelings, and a detective could normally just push it aside as nerves on being questioned."

"Well, at least Mr. Shy Bladder is good for something." Vega winked at Graves as she tore the paper from Remy's hand and went back to her computer.

"There's nothing wrong with not using a petri dish of a public restroom. Just stepping into a public bathroom should require a hazmat suit."

"Not only is he an asshole, but he's a drama queen asshole. We're definitely not keeping him," Stevenson announced.

"Boss." Remy glanced around. "Where's Shine at?"

"Gladys. They came home after dinner at your place, packed her things, and she went to live with her. Said it would be good for her to change geography for a while."

"Did she tell you?" Remy looked at me.

"No, and Roo hasn't mentioned her Aunt Shine being around. But it doesn't surprise me she packed her up. We'll ask her next time we talk." I smiled as Remy nodded. I was honest with Remy. I wasn't shocked my ex-wife had taken in Shine. Remy and my ex-wife were identical in temperament; they both wanted to do good and save as many as they could.

"Got you, you son of a bitch," Vega cheered. "Julian Fellows, forty-three, married, two sons, investment banker with a portfolio that would make a millionaire insecure. Online bio is complete bullshit. Philanthropist. Recent tax filings show his charitable ass likes to give to right-wing nutjobs intent on destroying anyone brown, poor, and or queer."

"Shit." Remy hissed.

"What?"

"We have a rich, white man with attachment and narcissistic personality disorder, and enough money to be innocent in the spotlight."

"He committed a crime, several actually. He's a serial

murderer." Graves said from across the room where he was leaned against the wall.

"Let's play hypotheticals," Remy said as he got up from my lap. "Say you get a call from twelfth street, children are screaming, caller says there were some loud bangs. What do you do?"

"Call in and rush over. Prepare entry with backup if no one answers."

"Now, what if that same call came in, and it was from Hylen Estates, *same exact call*? What would be your response? Would you match the one from twelfth? Don't hesitate. Admit your bias."

"Just because someone is rich doesn't mean they'll get special treatment."

"And you said I was an idealist. What if you arrived at Hylen Estates and the man of the house said that his kids were just playing, knocked something over? Would you insist on being allowed in? Would you knock the door down like you would at the twelfth street call?"

I watched Graves expression harden, and I knew Remy had pushed the knife in for the kill shot.

"We're inherently biased. Poor equals bad. Rich equals good. The twelfth street address had happy children playing while dinner was being made. Hylen location, he'd just beaten his wife and or kids, but they just fell down the steps because they were clumsy. We must acknowledge our own bias. If someone says they're not, they're lying."

"But aren't you biased against the rich and instantly on the defense?"

"Of course I am. I lived at the Hylen address. Welfare calls were rarely made, but when someone showed up, the nice officers would say thank you for my host's husband's time and be gone. Two minutes of respite before the next wave of rich men were let into my room for whatever they paid for or high-powered promise they offered." No one in the room looked shocked, but Graves's face went pale as he stared at Remy.

"Fellows thinks he's untouchable, and he could be right, but not on my watch. He might be rich, but I know where all the skeletons are buried. And I made sure certain people knew it. I'm biased, but I'm smart. I also know when to plan ahead. Worst case scenario, he doesn't pay in the courts for what he did, but if he doesn't pay legally, there are more ways to destroy someone. And I have all the tools to take him down publicly and professionally."

"Fuck, he's sexy when he gets all Godfather Crime Boss," Stevenson said to break the sudden quiet. "Kaufmann, you sure you two are solid?"

I tensed but didn't acknowledge Stevenson. I kept my attention on Remy. Waited for even a hint that he needed me to support him, but him and Graves were locked in a stare-down. Graves' years of preconceived notions on who or what Remy was were slowly being chipped away to nothing more than dust. Seeing another person, who you've had nothing more than an adversarial interaction with was more than what was portrayed on the surface—it forced you to destroy and rebuild your beliefs of said person. It was seeing a stranger exposed and standing before you, waiting to submit.

"How did you survive?"

"He had us," Vega, Doc, and Boss all spoke up. Doc had appeared from Boss's bedroom. He'd taken a nap because he'd been awake almost two days and Vega forced him to sleep.

"What?" Graves looked past Remy's shoulder.

"He volunteered with my outreach program at sixteen when he was walking the streets and came across one of my vans. We were handing out bagged lunches and giving safe sex practice talks. He became a regular, permanent figure when he turned eighteen, and he was kicked out." Boss refilled coffee mugs and poured fresh ones for Remy, Graves, and Doc.

"I was at the local college when I was fourteen. I ran into him one night. I'd gone for a walk and got lost. He took me under his wing and tried to talk me into going home or he could find me a safe space. He was the first one I told I was a lesbian. He bought me coffee and a meal, even though he hadn't made much that night, but he had it, and he shared. I owe him a debt of gratitude for giving me my first real home...him." Vega spoke as she cuddled Doc on her lap.

"I ran an unauthorized clinic, and he'd come to me to get stitched up. He started bringing kids to me who were afraid of going to a hospital, and he became my go-between with the street kids. Almost became a regular at the office, he'd come in to talk, debate. I tried to talk him into becoming a doctor."

"You see, your life is very black and white, Graves. That's where you're wrong. There's a ton of gray areas, and people aren't inherently good or bad. We're shaped from experience. Remy learned compassion through unbelievable pain. I learned I wasn't a freak because my brain worked differently by finding a way to help bring the unknown justice. Doc, well, he learned there was more to a body than what was done to it before it ended up on his autopsy table. Some of us are born with a moral compass. It tells us that something is wrong because it'll hurt someone else, but in cases of men like Fellows, his moral compass always points south. He hurts people because, unlike a person who judges right and wrong correctly, he was either born without conscience or he learned that through society's treatment of those considered lesser than, he could get away with everything, even murder." Vega's lips curved into a small frown.

My baby had an amazing circle of people, family, and since our relationship shifted, I'd learned just how wide and varied that was. I'd always assumed he spent all his time alone except for his outreach work, but in the past months, I'd seen he hadn't ever truly been alone. He may have experienced loneliness, but that was from people's bias toward his need to do good. He was a compassionate and loving man, who would go without to make sure others had more, even to the detriment of himself. How I got him, I don't know. But I was exceedingly grateful every day that he agreed to be mine and share a child with me.

"So what's the plan? If we can't hit him like we normally would, what do we have?" Graves asked.

"Recon, stakeouts…we have to account for his movements, Vega, I need information on all properties owned inside and outside the city. I need an account of the last six months of his financials. He may pay cash for his second life, but he had to use a card somewhere. We just need to find him in an area that he wouldn't normally frequent. I also need call logs, emails, and I want to know what type of toothpaste he uses. I also want activity on his wife's accounts and phone. I don't want to think she was in on it, but if she is an abuse victim, she could be actively helping or at the least aiding and abetting without prior knowledge."

"You got it, Pretty."

"I'm not taking Graves," Remy announced. "He'll probably be doing the pee-pee dance the entirety of our stakeouts."

"Hey, I said petri dish, sorry. It's learned behavior. My mother has a germ phobia. Are we doing this officially?"

"No, Remy is right. We need everything we can get on him before we take this to a judge for a warrant. Even one fuck up, and we've lost our way in. Boss, can you keep a lookout for him?" I asked.

"Yeah, I'll speak to my team. We'll keep a close eye on him and assign him when he comes in, but we'll call as soon as he enters the building. This fucker needs to be taken off the streets and away from our kids."

I nodded at Boss and looked at Doc.

"My mobile clinic is pretty regular around there. If I get word he's on the streets just give me a location, and I can park nearby. I have some personal time to use. Just let me know if you need me to take it."

"Um, thanks, everyone for this. I know this isn't going to be an easy case, and in a realist mindset, we might be banging our heads against a brick wall, but, just thanks." Remy turned to me, and I offered a smile.

"I'm going to take up residence in Boss's kitchen to get started on the searches you need from me. Cash is at an out-of-town gig with her band."

"Doc can come home with us to catch up on his beauty sleep," Remy ordered. Doc bounced, and Stevenson groaned.

"That's my room," Stevenson whined.

"We have two guest rooms." As soon as the words were out, Stevenson hissed a yes and fist-pumped. "And you need to get a new bed."

"Why? I rarely sleep on it."

"Everyone who's having a sleepover, converge on my place. I have Mrs. Walton staying there with Roo so she could be in her own bed. Everyone be quiet when we get there."

"In the morning, we'll go over shifts for the stakeouts while we have breakfast. We get all the info. I want detailed reports, and I don't care if it's down to the man taking a piss. I want his movements documented. This has to be as by the book as we can make it. Every decision we make is going to be scrutinized."

After everyone agreed, Doc left with Stevenson to get to Remy's house, and Vega popped in her earbuds and checked out. Graves said he'd be by in the morning and left without much more to say.

"Pretty, you holding up?" Boss asked, and I went to Remy, wrapping my arms around him from behind and kissing his scars through the cotton of his t-shirt.

"I'm doing okay. You know this shit is hard on me." My man shrugged his shoulders.

"I know that, Pretty. I've known you since you were a pretty, punk kid who thought their only value was their ass. You're doing so many good things, you show our kids there's other ways…ways out. I'm proud of you, honey."

"Thanks, Boss. And thanks mostly for being there, for putting up with this shit. I know you've got so much on your plate. You didn't need more."

"But you're wrong. I'll take an overflowing plate as long as our kids survive. Nothing more important than that, not even a little extra stress. Just get this bastard, and that's payment enough, and get him by any means necessary."

Boss hugged Remy, and I was caught in the squeeze too, and then I led Remy from the apartment. I could tell he was done for the night. He let out a heavy sigh and stretched his tensed shoulders and cracked his neck.

"Let's get home, a bath and bed for you."

"I'll appreciate it, Daddy. Robert, you know…"

"What, baby, just say it?"

"I wanted to say I was sorry."

I frowned at his apology as I opened the passenger door. "Sorry for what?"

"Keeping this part separate from you. I judged you, and I was biased just like Graves said. I wanted to keep you in any way I could, and I thought this would drive you away if you knew…if you saw the real me."

"I love the real you, and that won't change." I leaned up slightly to kiss him, and then I helped him into the seat, buckling him in as I sensed more than saw his stiff body collapse as he let go of the night and the cop persona. He knew he was safe with me, and he could break without judgment.

34

REMY

COLD CASE
UNIT

The house across the street from Fellows's place was under contract for sale, and we'd conned our way into using the empty house for surveillance. Rich neighborhoods were always considered hotbeds for break-ins and home invasions, crime brought down real estate prices, and realtors got nervous. We'd claimed we'd received some tips that a crew had been casing the area, and she'd jumped at the chance to help. But that had more to do with her commission than any goodwill toward her fellow humans.

"Daddy, did you bring the snacks?" I asked as I settled into the collapsible chair.

"I thought you brought the snacks?"

I turned to him in horror and glared at him. "I put the bag next to your stuff so you would bring the snacks."

"Baby, like I'd forget my boy's snacks." He reached into his backpack and handed over a bag of sour gummy worms.

"I'll add another check to your blowjob reward card."

"You know, that's a long list of Blowjob I.O.U.s, right?"

"It's for both of us. I like giving, and you're very enthusiastic about taking."

"Could you give it a break? Us single people are going to get jealous." Stevenson's voice came over the laptop we set up. They were on standby to follow if our suspect left the residence.

"Can't help it I got a man, and you don't. You and Graves having fun?"

"Man, he brought vegetarian for dinner and gluten-free snacks. I shouldn't have put him in charge of provisions. Cardboard has more flavor. What did your Daddy bring you?"

"Sandwiches and candy, lot of sour gummy worms." I snorted as Stevenson cussed.

"We're switching partners tomorrow night."

"Not a chance, Stevenson. No one watches Remy but me. The only reason you came with me the other night was because you and Graves wouldn't have gotten any info without us."

I twisted to stretch my legs over Robert's lap, and he draped his arms over my calves. He winked at me and relaxed into his chair as he stared out the window.

"Well, I'm shopping for tomorrow." The man was whining so bad I felt sorry for Graves.

"Then it's every man for himself because I probably won't be able to eat what you bring. Can you imagine what the food you eat does to your insides?"

I cut the connection to let them argue without us being made to listen to it. "I'm so glad to be staying in Cold Case. I don't think I can deal with them full-time."

"They're not that bad, baby. Could be worse. Us still bitching at each other at every turn. Stevenson needs to cut down on the flirting, though."

"That'll never happen."

"Don't you two look so cute? Would I have gotten a show if I waited longer?" Vega's face filled the screen, and she had her chin rested in the palms of her upraised hands.

I'd have to remember to cover the camera so our adorable

hacker couldn't get a free show. Vega hadn't changed much in the years I'd known her, and to be honest, I wouldn't want her to.

"No, no sexy times on the job, especially not this one. Got something for us?"

"Pretty, when have I ever let you down?"

"Not yet, but my patience is running thin."

"Fine, fine, ruin my fun. Julian Fellows, on paper, looks like a boy scout, a deacon at his church, his sons attend the best prep school, they're Ivy-league bound. He gives generously to charity, as long as you don't look too far past the cutesy names. This guy is so far in the closet he's in another universe. His clients are the who's-who of conservative right-wing extremists. He was profiled in several fundamentalist publications. None of these articles were fact-checked at all. These people were so far out of reality, they were writing fiction."

"So, what did you find that the fact-checkers didn't?" Robert asked as he stole a gummy worm.

"Son of a wealthy evangelist, mega-church level. His old man was pulling in several million a year tax-free, Jesus equals tax break. He was adopted. His old man used it as a pushing point for abstinence-only and female subjugation. It was very Christ-like. They found him abandoned, God blessed them with this unwanted child, blah blah blah, it was a great parable for the pious preacher and his barren wife, again another pushing point. I have no idea what the point was supposed to be, but I had to watch hours of televised sermons. You owe me so much alcohol."

"You can have anything you want. So we have the element of shame for his sexuality. He was held up as a saved child, probably made to feel special and important as a gift from God." The case just kept turning into more and more of a clusterfuck by the minute. Preacher's son, wealthy and respected in the community, I'd looked online to see what a monster looked like, and he was exactly the type that a jury found not guilty on looks alone.

Handsome, polished, and a saint on paper as long as you didn't dig too deeply.

"Ding ding ding, we have a winner. What does our sexy contestant take home today?" An energy drink can came into view as she chugged that and reached for another before she even finished. "I unsealed his record, don't ask me how, because you won't bust me, but I won't put it past Graves. Fellows has one helluva temper. Very much hit first and ask questions later type, but since he turned eighteen, squeaky clean. Not even a parking ticket. I looked into nine-one-one logs since he got married. There's been a few calls, but as we already suspected, no reports or arrests. Both sons are adopted through a Christian organization. I checked medical records for the wife, nothing out of the ordinary. I do love the online medical charts. There's no signs of disease or hereditary conditions that would account for infertility, and she's never been prescribed birth control. Neither were ever tested for fertility issues."

"So either he's shooting blanks, or we're talking a sexless marriage." Robert poured himself a coffee and handed me my soda bottle.

"Sexless arranged marriage, my friends. Their church believes in letting God decide, which means that the preacher and a board of righteous men decide who gets paired and who doesn't."

"Are we talking a very wealthy and respected cult?" I wasn't feeling as confident as I had when we'd discovered Julian was a real person and not just a ghost that a killer created.

"Yep. Listen, I searched. He's made several small purchases in neighborhoods where he shouldn't be. Soda, candy, smokes, which seemed weird to me after the info you shared of him thinking caffeine and sugar are bad, he wouldn't be buying smokes. There's two homes in his name. The one you're currently staking out and another that he inherited from his father about ten years ago. It's sort of retreat-esque."

"Anything odd about the location?"

"No, except for the fact he only turns on the utilities two or three times a year."

"For how long?" Robert asked as we heard her clicking loudly at her keyboard.

"Two to three weeks, and then he has them turned off again. The property is out in the middle of nowhere. I sent the details to your email."

"Is there anything financial-wise that changes in those time frames?"

"Not really, Remy, but there is an interview that claims he takes a retreat to commune with nature and reestablish his spiritual connection with God."

"Does it coincide with our murders?"

"Exact match for the missing persons reports, and this is possibly the nail in his coffin. The last victim, Fellows had the utilities reconnected for just a week. Claimed an emergency, a medical issue, and the doctors urged him to take a break. No medical visits could be found. Not even one of the concierge ones. The lack of security measures are shocking, but I'm forever grateful for their laziness."

"Baby, do you think it's enough?"

"I don't know. Utility turn ons and some man sneaking vices, not really awe-inspiring. Although, the times are definitely suspicious. If we can hit up the right judge, I think we can at least get a warrant to look. We have enough witnesses that I can get to swear statements he was seen in the area. It could help with bringing his credibility and intentions into doubt, but it's also an issue if they'll take our witnesses seriously. D.A. Maxwell owes me one, we could talk to her, and there's a law-and-order judge who's so clean he squeaks who may or may not know me very intimately."

"Is there anyone in this town you can't blackmail with some sort of guilt?" I jerked my attention to Robert as my stomach plummeted, but I relaxed when all I saw was him smiling.

"If I don't know personally, I'm definitely in the know. In the grand scheme of things, it isn't who you know, it's what you know, and I have over forty years of said knowledge."

"Let's get to work. I want to take him down, and I don't want to be called to another crime scene before we put him in handcuffs." Robert looked at the screen. "Could you compile everything you have and send it to us? I don't care how small. We have a huge case to make, and circumstantial is better than nothing."

The screen went black, and I turned to Robert to find him watching me.

"Remy, I never want you to look at me like that again, do you understand? I've given you no reason to doubt me, and my love for you and our daughter has no conditions attached."

"I'm sorry."

"Hey, I don't want you to be sorry. I just need you to trust me."

"I do, I promise."

"I know I'm not like your family, I wasn't there in the trenches when you were pulling yourself out of hell, but I want to be here now, just us. What you did was what had to be done. There is no shame in that. Do you get what I'm saying?"

"Yes, but I can't help my reactions sometimes, especially when it comes to you. I knew when I met you, you'd be the only one with the power to destroy me."

"Baby, I just want to love you."

35

ROBERT

COLD CASE
UNIT

"**D**on't fuck this up, Remy."

That's what the judge said as he signed off on the search warrant that morning. I watched the interaction between them closely, and the longer we were locked in his chambers, the more I saw Remy's hands fisting at his sides. I'd walked behind him to stroke my fingers across his lower back, and as if that's all he needed, all the tension disappeared.

"We have eyes on Fellows?" Remy asked. Stevenson and Graves were waiting for our word to approach the residence, and Vega was tapped in through our body cams.

"Our team sitting on his office said he hasn't moved," Graves answered.

"Tell them to standby to take him down."

"Copy."

"You got this, Remy." The opened doors at the back of the SWAT van hid us from sight.

He gave a jerky nod. I straightened and tightened his vest over his dress shirt and tie, then I waited until he dropped his gaze to mine. *I love you,* I mouthed the words and earned a sweet smile. If it was just the two us patched in to our immediate team, that'd be one thing.

"Bosley," Vega's voice echoed in my ear, and that woman needed to cut down on the caffeine.

"Go ahead, Vega."

"We have eyes inside. I patched in through the security system. The house is clear except for the wife."

"Copy, Vega, keep eyes on everything."

"Recording as we speak, out."

"You're on lead."

Remy signaled for everyone to follow, and I kept close on his six as we made it up the long walkway. I couldn't imagine Remy in a home like that one. Oversized and pretentious, designed and built simply for show. The night before, we'd driven through his old neighborhood, and he'd shown me the house where he'd lived. Fellows's was small and plain in comparison.

He rang the doorbell, and muffled chimes played on the other side. My partner stood strong, shoulders straight and chin up. A lock clicked, and the door slowly opened.

"Mrs. Julian Fellows?"

"Yes, may I help you?"

It didn't escape our notice that her fingers went white with her death grip on the edge of the door. Or the fact she wore way too much concealer.

"I'm Detective Bosley. We have a warrant to search the home." He handed it over. "Maybe you'd like to call your lawyer."

"There's nothing for you to find, Detective. What is this about?"

"Your husband is a suspect in multiple homicides."

"That's impossible." Her brittle and forced laugh told me she may not be lying, but she didn't altogether believe the denial either.

"We still have to look, Mrs. Fellows. If you'd like to take a seat in the living room, a female officer will be in to sit with you while we search."

"Of course, maybe I should call my husband."

She stepped back as she pulled the door all the way open and motioned us in with a graceful sweep of her arm. We entered and stepped to the side as our team of officers and forensic personnel got started. The orders were already issued, and Vega had found us plans of the home to assist in the search.

"This is Officer Bradley. She'll keep you company, and if you need anything, don't hesitate to ask her." Remy's voice was softer than I expected. His approach was determined by what I was sure were the bruises and the stiff way she held herself.

The warrant gave us access to search the entire property, and that included garages and any storage buildings—sheds. The warrant also allowed us to search the property outside the city. The home was sterile. Nowhere I looked even showed a speck of dust. He stopped as Remy hesitated, and he stared at a portrait in the entryway. The images that came with frames had more warmth. The two sons wore almost exact replicas of the outfits we found our victims wearing.

"Talk it out."

"From looking at her and the way she moved, she's nursing busted ribs. There's a fingertip bruise above the ruffled high collar of her blouse, and when she took the warrant, she had restraint marks around her wrist. Not to mention under the almost professional level of her cover-up, she has a black eye that's maybe a week old."

"You noticed all that?"

"I'm a victim's advocate even when they don't want me to be. I want this fucker."

"I know, and let's make sure we find something to take him down."

"We have to because we found who the surrogates were for. Sooner or later, replacements aren't going to be enough."

Techs and officers filled evidence bags, carefully documenting them for the chain of custody. Remy had told them we couldn't afford fuck-ups. One slip and the type of lawyer Fellows could afford would have the evidence thrown out before anyone could plead the case.

As we moved through and searched, I noticed a disgusting theme playing out. The only image of the wife was in the foyer. All the other images were only of the sons, or them and Fellows. We went to check out the kids' rooms, and something stood out as we went.

"There's deadbolts on the boys' rooms and the master bedroom."

"Not a surprise, Robert. He wants absolute control and submissiveness. There is nothing of the wife and kids outside the bedrooms. There's no clutter that would show that two teenage boys lived here. What did your house look like when RJ lived at home?"

"His sports equipment was everywhere. Laundry that would stink up the entire house. During baseball and football season, his room was a biohazard."

"These kids lined up everything." He laid a gloved finger on a shelf of academic and sports awards. They were each perfectly aligned, not even a centimeter of deviation.

"Vega, you copy?"

"I'm with you, Remy. What's up?"

"Call Fran at Social Services and see if she can come to do a welfare check."

"I'm on it. Out."

"You think he's already started the process, Remy?"

"Maybe not overtly, but it doesn't start off with anything out of the normal. A hug that goes on too long. A request to sit on his lap. Children are conditioned to trust a parent. To them, a parent is the savior...protector, but sometimes they're just monsters waiting to attack."

"Remy, Fran is on her way."

"Copy. Robert, you search the other boy's room, and I'll do this one. No matter how well-behaved and obedient a child is, they will rebel. Maybe one of them wrote down something. If you can't find anything, bag the laptop." Remy said as he stepped outside the room. "All computers need to be taken into evidence. I want them checked by Vega."

"Yes, sir."

I left Remy to go across the hall. It was almost identical to the one I'd just left, down to even the awards on the shelf. I tested the distance and shook my head. The only thing that showed me I was in a different room was the bedspread was navy instead of the lighter blue on the other bed.

I opened the laptop on the small desk and wasn't surprised to find it wasn't password protected. I checked files and search history, nothing that wouldn't show up for homework research. As I bagged the computer, I noticed checklists of the usual chores.

The clicking of a camera caught my attention to a tech in the room. "Hey, could you take pictures of this wall and also the one in the other kid's room."

What felt odd about the list was the words were perfectly straight as if a ruler was used. That isn't how a kid would do it. Hell, my checklist had everything on a slant. Exercise, prayers, weigh-ins, salon.

"Vega, the photos in the house don't show the kids younger than maybe seven or so. Can you find out what they looked like before that?"

"Can do. I just have to check in with class pictures. They normally post those on school websites. What am I looking for?"

"Just an idea. When you get them, could you send the images to my phone?"

"For you, boss man, anything." The connected cut.

"What's going on here? Why are you in my home?"

Ah, Mr. Fellows has joined the party, and just like everyone said, his tone was cultured and clipped. I exited the bedroom and passed the laptop off to an evidence tech as Remy and I made it down the staircase.

"Mr. Fellows, I'm Detective Bosley, and this is my partner, Robert Kaufmann."

At the mention of my name or maybe my dark skin, the man snarled his nose before he caught himself, and just like the salon owner mentioned, his face went blank.

"As we explained to Mrs. Fellows, we had a warrant to search your properties. Your wife is waiting in the living room, and obviously she needs comfort at this time."

"She's a sensible woman, she doesn't need to be coddled."

Remy had tested him, and Fellows failed. Any husband would go to comfort their wife. Even if it was just an act, they'd pretend to care. Remy had also wanted to see the wife's physical reaction to her husband arriving. No matter how controlled someone thought they were, survival instinct would kick in; fight or flee, the primitive brain was geared to self-protection.

"In that case, Mr. Fellows, we'd like you to come down to the station to answer a few questions. You can call your attorney to meet you there."

I was proud of Remy for staying calm, he would fake it until he broke, and I'd be there to put the pieces together. He needed to stand on his own. My baby was strong without me, but I'd only allow it for so long.

"Fine, I will call my attorney, and we'll meet you at the station. I just want to get this ridiculousness over with." Fellows turned on his perfectly polished shoes and left without another backward glance.

Remy glanced at me and then turned to head to the living room. "Mrs. Fellows?"

"Yes, Detective?"

"Do you have anywhere to stay while we continue to search... a friend perhaps?"

"No, but I will need to pick my children up from school. I'll take them to dinner. Would you be able to inform me when the search is finished?"

"Yes, ma'am, I'll have someone call you. A social worker is coming by to speak with you and will probably want to have a talk with your sons as well. She's excellent at her job and will help you in any way you need." Remy held out his hand, and she hesitantly took it out of conditioned politeness. "Mrs. Fellows, I mean in any way." I didn't miss the way he took her hand in both of his, and his fingers stroked along the bruise.

She pulled away quickly and pulled down her sleeves to hide the marks.

"Mrs. Fellow, Detective Bosley and our team will finish up as soon as we can with as little mess as possible."

"That's appreciated, Detective Kaufmann."

We got to work, and Stevenson and Graves showed up to let us know they were going to the station and would put Mr. Fellows into an interrogation room. The longer nothing obvious jumped out to us, the more myself and Remy started to lose hope that we'd be able to take Fellows down. No one could afford for him to stay free.

REMY

COLD CASE
UNIT

Fellows sat in the interrogation room with his legs crossed and his hands on his knee. He appeared as if he didn't have an issue in the world. Just another business meeting to attend, and I hated him. I didn't just want to lock him up; I wanted to destroy him. Part of me, the kid I was and, in some way, would always be, wanted him dead. Maybe I should've felt ashamed of that fact, but I couldn't muster the remorse.

He was like hundreds of men I'd known in the past, clients and perps alike. But where some clients had wanted companionship, a night where they didn't have to hide what they desired, Fellows was nothing more than a predator. A man who viewed those kids as the ones he couldn't touch, a surrogate for his deviancy.

Vega had sent me the before and after images of Fellows's sons. He recreated them in his image, their black and brown hair was dyed to match his blond, and they wore contacts to change their eyes to blue. Every one of the boys he'd murdered was older replicas of his sons before he'd morphed them into clones of himself. Maybe the fact his victims were persons of color made it more justifiable at what he'd done. He could pretend he wasn't using them so he didn't touch who he considered the chosen ones, just like his father had.

"You ready?" Robert asked as he stepped up beside me.

"Yeah, his lawyer here yet?"

"Just arrived. He's being led—" The door opened, and the lawyer entered. "And all the combatants are on the field of battle."

"Oh, this is going to be fun."

"What? Okay, the smile scares me because you're up to something."

"I know him. A little shocked the submissive is Fellows's attorney especially attached to someone so conservative."

"That it's not who you know, it's what you know again?"

"Yep. Let's go."

A lot of detectives went with the good cop/bad cop routine, one to push and one to sympathize, but that didn't work for us. I played the game as well as anyone, in some cases better, but men like Fellows went with divide and conquer. It hadn't escaped me that the bigot hadn't liked Robert. For that, I wanted to destroy him more. I grabbed the folder and exited the viewing room with Robert behind me, and we both took a few deep breaths before we entered.

"Mr. Fellows, so sorry to keep you waiting." For most of my life, I'd perfected the act, so I could pretend to be polite until he gave me the opening not to be.

"I've been waiting here for hours. I pay my attorney quite a bit to be more prompt in his handling of my affairs."

"Gerald, how are you today? It's been a while since we matched wits."

"I'm well, Detective Bosley. I thought you worked Special Victims?"

"I did. I transferred into the Homicide unit a few years ago. Detective Kaufmann, this is Gerald Summerton." I went through the small introduction. Refusing to look or acknowledge Fellows, he was a man who didn't handle disrespect well. And that was definitely something I was counting on.

"Could we proceed with the farce so that I may return to work?"

"Of course, Mr. Fellows. You're being investigated for the kidnappings, sexual assaults, and murders of twenty-seven teenage boys. We're in the process of testing any biological evidence seized by the search warrant, and once it comes back to the semen you left in each victim, I can officially arrest you. So why don't we stop playing games, and you tell me your side of this twisted story." As I spoke, I threw down each image onto the table and watched his expression. Not once did it change, but I didn't miss that his hands tightened around his knees as if he wanted to touch the images. Have another link to the lives he'd taken; relive it.

Robert took up a post in the corner and let me have lead, and I appreciated it because I had more than an upper hand. I was too familiar with men just like him.

"What evidence do you have that proves my client in anyway perpetrated these killings?"

"Eyewitness statements. He was seen with these boys at several businesses. Security tapes are a great thing. And my tech person is exceptionally brilliant at what they do. All we have to do is have your client tell me why? Although, I'm pretty sure I know why."

"If you're so brilliant, Detective Bosley, why do you even need me to tell you? It appears you've already—" Summerton tried to make his client shut up but Fellows held up his hand. "Made up your mind. I'm a rich man, well-respected, the son of a much-loved Pastor. I have no criminal history."

I shrugged. "Your father and your supposed wealth, let's just say, has no bearing on the fact you murdered these boys." I placed my hands flat on the table and leaned in. "What was it, Fellows, you were tucking your sons in one night and the goodnight kiss didn't go as far as you hoped? Maybe they didn't look at you like you looked at them? Maybe one too many nights seated on your lap? Because you're the person you are, you found boys that didn't matter so much, didn't rate even an ounce of the humanity that you lack."

"They meant...mean nothing." Score one for Bosley. "Just whores probably, no one to care about them. I have no concern over what you believe I did."

"That's where you are wrong. There were plenty of people to care. You see, Fellows, I'm a victim's advocate. I've spent most of my life helping boys like this. You may not think you care about these boys, and as far as I'm concerned, that's the only true statement you've made. But you are concerned. It's in the way your pulse kicked into double-time, the sweat that's starting to bead at your hairline, and that white-knuckled grip you have on your knees." I straightened and started pacing. "We're trained to observe and to prove theories. So let me tell you what you did and when I'm done, you can agree with me."

I kept my arms relaxed, slipped my thumbs casually in my front pockets, and I caught Robert hiding a smile behind his hand.

"You get off work one night, go down to the strip in your big fancy car, and you drive checking out the young boys hustling to survive. Doing nothing that would hurt anyone, just living. You're welcome to stop me at any time if I don't get the story right." I took a deep breath and locked eyes with Fellows. There was nothing in his expression, either from his psychopathic personality or the Botox he used to remain handsome and youthful. Yet, eyes never lied, and there were micro-expressions that were inherent to being human. A snarl of the nose or the curl of the lip. The way they looked right or left as they decided on what lies to tell or if they were tapping into their memories.

"From your lack of response, I can assume you're not going to step in. That's fine with me. You invite one of these boys, perhaps we can use Nino for an example." I used a single finger to slide the image closer. "Nino is a straight-A honor student who's going to age out, so he just wanted to make money to survive. You get him into your car, promise you just want to talk. You spend a month or maybe more grooming him, luring him in, and then you take him. You pamper him. Give him things he'd never afford on his own and still, well, no sex, you're biding your time, comfort equals safety. But soon that's not enough, so you make a fancy meal and then something goes wrong. You look at them, and they're not the ones you wanted. Only your sons will do, but you push forward. You rape them, murder them, clean away all the evidence, but then you make a stupid mistake. Something you should've known better than to do."

"If you're so smart, then what is that mistake I supposedly made?"

"You didn't douche them when you were done. You left semen. Why no condom, Fellows? Some possessive move, some leftover alpha male instinct to mark? Maybe you just like how dirty it looked when it leaked out? Your wife never let you do it, and your sons never—"

Fellows surged to his feet, and I smirked as his face went from collected to mottled red. From the corner of my eye, I saw Robert standing at the end of the table ready to intervene. Summerton already had a look of failure as soon as Fellows ignored every squeeze of his arm to quiet him before he said something.

"They were nothing. I used and discarded with the ease of throwing out trash. Who were they to deny me what I wanted? So after I killed them, I took what I wanted." A cold laugh slipped free as Fellows fell back onto his chair. "But they looked so peaceful, like they were sleeping."

"So you cleaned and dressed them and dumped them, for what, Fellows? What did it get you? Showing remorse after the fact doesn't absolve you. Your God won't forgive you for it. You dressed them like your sons. A tech is waiting outside to take your DNA."

"Did you find the other one? He was the prettiest so far. Just like my sons, perfect, so flawless. I was going to keep him, all safe. I'm done talking."

Robert rounded the table and put Fellows under arrest, and I rushed from the room, pulling out my phone. "Vega, he took another one. Have our techs gone to the second location yet? Have any new missing persons tripped our alarms?"

"No, they're just finishing up. The next shift was about to head that way. Nothing in that area or that meets any of our established parameters. I'll do another search of all males missing in the past week." I heard clicking. "The utilities are on."

I didn't wait to respond as I disconnected the call, and I turned to head back to the interrogation room as Fellows was led out, still as superior as he was when he first arrived.

"We have to go." It's all I had to say before we were off running, and Stevenson and Graves checked in to say they were right behind us. "I can't find another body, Robert."

"But if we do, Fellows will pay for it." He squeezed my hand, and I nodded as we hopped into the SUV and took off to Fellows's second home.

37

ROBERT

COLD CASE
UNIT

S irens were blaring, and the farther we got from the city, the more time passed too quickly, and it was as if we stood still. Remy had been on the phone with Vega, Stevenson, and Graves. Doc was on his way, too. Remy was trying to hope for the best, but the tone of his voice told me he wasn't holding out much optimism. I'd seen him in action countless times in interrogations. With his psychology degree and experience, he knew where to hit them and make it count.

When Fellows had jumped from his chair, all I thought was to put myself between Remy and him. My baby could take it, he was called the best for a reason, but these cases weren't like the others. I'd worried it would push him too far. He was intelligent and compassionate, which made him a great detective, but he also had decades of trauma, too.

"Vega, I need a name, something," Remy demanded, and I took the phone from him, putting it on speaker.

"Either no one has reported him missing, or he went off script for this one. We have four possible matches, but they don't match the established victimology."

He cursed under his breath. "Which ones would match his sons with the makeovers?"

"We have a fourteen-year-old white male, blond hair, blue eyes, reported missing from Hylen Estates." I grimaced as she mentioned the area. "Physically, he's a perfect match. He also attends the same school. FBI is involved as a possible kidnapping/ransom case."

"What's his name?"

"Francis Mopson, goes by Frankie. He's been gone a week."

"Any info on what area he disappeared from?"

"His mother and father are on several charitable organizations. They were touring our turf for possible grant recipients. Fellows could have spotted him then, and he thought it was a gift."

"Thanks, send me his picture. Once we arrive and if we find him, standby to call the Feds. Let's hope we have some good news for them."

The GPS chose that moment to announce I take the next left, I barely turned in time, and my back wheels fishtailed on the loose gravel. I corrected as I noticed the long line of vehicles behind us. The SUV skidded to a stop throwing gravel as we pulled up to the cottage-type house that was a mile off the main road.

We jumped out, and there were no sounds. It was quiet and isolated. City kids wouldn't know how to escape even if they'd had a chance. It was desolate. Before any of the other vehicles came to a stop, Remy was already on the porch. He identified himself and kicked in the door. We all converged on the house with weapons drawn.

"His name is Frankie. I don't care what you tear down, take this place down to the foundation if needed."

Furniture was turned over, and area rugs thrown away from the hardwood floors. Frankie was a frantic chant throughout the house. People knocked on walls in search of hidden compartments. I lost track of Remy at some point, but I heard him yell my name, and I rushed to the back of the house. I saw him crouched down in front of a small door, one of those hidden storage compartments that blended into the wainscoting along the lower wall.

"Hey, Frankie, I'm Remy. I'm a detective. Are you hurt?" His tone was soft and soothing, the same one he used when Roo had a nightmare. He lowered to sit on the floor to make himself smaller. The space he stared into was dark, and I couldn't see passed the entry. "It's okay. We can take as long as you need."

He silently said to call Vega to contact the FBI. I stepped to the side and made the quick call as Doc entered the room.

"Remy, you need me?"

"I have a doctor here. Do you need him to check you?" He waved Doc over, and the adorable, small man wasn't threatening in the least, and may make the boy comfortable.

"The man who did this to you was arrested. It's safe to come out. We just want to make sure you're okay before you see your parents."

A small, slender hand attached to a thin arm appeared and then a mop of blond wavy curls, and every inch Frankie advanced, Doc and Remy retreated. They allowed him space and gave him a choice. He squinted as if he'd been in the dark long enough for his eyes to adjust to being locked up.

"He-he's gone?"

"He was placed under arrest not long ago. You want to see?"

He nodded, and Remy pulled out his phone. "Vega, show me the arrest of Fellows, but without audio."

Frankie stared at the screen, and Remy watched him for any reaction. Fear leaching from the boy's body was visible in its abruptness. Then the tears started, and he threw himself at Remy's chest. And just like with our daughter, he buried his face in the boy's hair. Allowed Frankie time to process, but from the look Remy gave me, he knew that a good cry and the knowledge the man was in custody was only the beginning.

Doc asked permission to touch him, to check for wounds, but he clung tighter to Remy. It seemed as if hours passed as Doc examined the kid around Remy. Doc told Frankie step-by-step what he was checking for and where he would touch before his hands even reached the spot.

To Remy and Doc, even Vega, the world came down to consent and choice, safety fostered in victims. Too much of the world viewed what was taken in terms of what a victim did to cause their own pain; forced from you by people who believed themselves more powerful. Then it all hit, years of murders solved, months of half-assed investigation or no one caring at all. All that was left was a trial, but that didn't bring back so many innocent boys that should've lived to find themselves—have lives with all the normal things. Boyfriends and heartache, maybe college and jobs far from the strip.

"Detective Kaufmann, the FBI flew in with the parents. They're waiting outside for word." An officer I vaguely recognized whispered from the doorway.

As a unit, Remy, Frankie, and Doc came to their feet. Frankie was clutching Remy as tightly as his thin arms were able. I cleared the way for them to make their way to the front door. The two men were shielding the boy from both sides.

"Frankie," a high-pitched scream had the boy pulling away and taking off at a run.

He ran into the arms of a petite woman with a kind face and a larger man who held them protectively. Tears were streaming as quickly down his face as the ones wetting his wife's. Remy stumbled back, and I caught him, wrapping my arm around his waist as I offered what strength I could.

"It's over except for the trial. You did an amazing job, baby. You should be so proud of yourself."

"I thought I'd open the panel and see another body, another set of empty eyes."

"We can't do anything about the ones we lost, but this one, it's the best outcome. Look at him. He's home with parents who love him."

Remy nodded and leaned into my side.

"Detectives?" A forensic tech walked out onto the porch.

"Yeah, did you find something?"

"There's a ton of receipts, all cash purchases. There's several more of the outfits neatly folded in one of the back bedrooms. We're going to be here all night just taking samples from the storage space he was locked in."

"Thanks."

"Congratulations, Detectives."

I nodded my thanks, and we got to work. We helped in the search, filled the agents in on what we had already, and had Vega send over what we had on the case. Typically, we didn't share with the Feds and vice versa, but with this case, to get the bastard convicted, we'd play nice.

Fellows had remained free for so long, but serial killers always screwed up in some way. That was what happened, a mistake, but even before that, he'd committed the biggest mistake in coming up against Remy. My man wouldn't have given up until he found the killer.

"Remy, okay?" Doc asked as he leaned his shoulder against my bicep.

"Not right now, but I'm sure he will be. I'll make him take the weekend off, and we and our girl can go away."

"Do that. You're good for him, Robert. You allow him to let someone else take care of him. He's always needed that but never trusted anyone to take control. Just keep doing what you're doing. I'm going to head to the hospital. Check in on Frankie to make sure I didn't miss anything. I wasn't able to do a thorough exam with him attached to Remy."

"I'll call later to give you an update on what we found here."

"Appreciate it."

Work to do, then I could take Remy home, and we could have a quiet night until the chaos of the next day started. The investigation was only one phase of the case. Then it was time to make sure every piece of evidence stood up in court. We had a long way to go before we could completely relax, but until we could officially mark this off with a conviction, I'd do what I could to take care of Remy as much as he'd allow.

38

REMY

COLD CASE
UNIT

"To the new and extremely Queer Cold Case Unit." Vega held up her beer bottle, and we all toasted.

Earlier that day, the homicide captain had called all of us into his office. I thought it was about mine and Robert's request to move units permanently. The old-timers down there had already put in for retirement. What I hadn't expected was to find out Stevenson and Graves had requested to move as well. Losing four of his best detectives hadn't sat right with him, but at least for me and my man, we weren't giving in.

Everyone toasted and took a drink as Vega sat down on Cash's lap. Doc was tucked between Stevenson and Graves. He'd already been several drinks ahead when we arrived, so I was taking him home with us and tucking him into bed in the guest room.

"How's Mrs. Fellows and the kids?" Stevenson asked.

"In a very nice tropical off-the-grid place for a bit. I set her up with a therapist for her and the kids. She seemed to be doing well when I talked to her last. She's just waiting to hear if she has to come back for the trial. She's already filed for divorce." I shifted on Robert's lap as he loosely held my waist.

"Do you think he's going to go to trial?" Graves picked up his beer.

"His father has broken off all contact. His clients and employees jumped ship. They're offering him a deal that will put him behind bars the rest of his life, but he still thinks he can get off. Trial by media isn't in his favor. Especially since this received national attention. His best option is to take the deal or have a judge instead of jury determine his fate. Either way, he's going to jail, and our kids are safe."

"Enough of the Fellows trial, everyone excited about being in charge of an entire unit?" Vega asked.

"I can't believe I put in the damn request. I should kick Stevenson's ass."

"Aw, you cranky little shit, you know you'd miss us. Remember, cool kids club." Stevenson's ruffled Graves' hair that had started to grow out a bit. He was looking almost scruffy.

"I can deal with being unpopular."

We all threw popcorn at him from the bowl in the middle of the table. If someone had told me that I'd be hanging out with Stevenson and especially Graves, that they'd be regular residents on my couch or in my guest rooms, I'd have told them they were idiots. Excitement at what the future held and the difference we could make in investigating the forgotten, I couldn't wait.

Finally, I'd reached a point in my life where I didn't have to keep the two sides separate. Until Robert, I hadn't realized how much I'd kept to myself. I smiled as I leaned back against my man's chest, and he hugged me tightly. My phone chimed, and I picked it up from the table, and I answered the video call from Roo.

"Hey, Roo, you ready for bed?"

She waved at Robert and I, and then we had a crowd saying hi. I rolled my eyes, but I loved how my daughter's eyes got so wide at seeing some of her favorite people. She was at a friend's house for a sleepover, one of the girls that went to daycare with her. It was her first overnight with a friend, and I'd barely contained my pride when I helped her get ready earlier that evening.

"Dad, Papa, you're picking me up tomorrow?"

"Of course, sweetie, we're going to have lunch and go to the park. I promise, and you know Papa doesn't break promises."

The untrusting, traumatized girl we found in that apartment transformed into a happy child, who used her voice, and I got lucky enough to share her with Robert. I smiled as he offered to tell her a story for bed, but she said the mom was going to read them books. The call ended too soon, and I set my phone aside.

The night went on with celebration and conversation. By the time we'd all had enough, Robert and I were sober, and Doc was giggly. Vega led Cash to the door after hugs and goodnights. Stevenson drove Graves home since they came together, and we took Doc.

"Is he always this friendly when drunk?" Robert asked as he batted Doc's hand away from his crotch.

"Poor, undersexed man, we need to find him a boyfriend." I got my friend buckled in the backseat.

Quickly, Robert drove us home as Doc's little laughs switched to soft snores, and I turned to glance into the backseat. He was adorable for a man of fifty, with his soft rounded features and shocking silver hair.

"Thanks for tonight, Daddy."

"You're welcome."

"No, really, I know you didn't really want to come out to celebrate."

"Baby, any way I can spend time with you, I'm happy." He took my hand and laced our fingers. "Yeah, we have like months of sleep to catch up on, but you needed a night out with our friends. I still don't know how we got a few of them."

"Stop, get used to me collecting strays. I do it a lot."

"I've noticed, and Boss and Shine have told me plenty of stories."

"Maybe we should have you make less friends."

"Ouch, way to hurt Daddy's feelings."

I snorted as we talked quietly so as not to wake Doc but figured that was kind of pointless. I was looking forward to getting back to my volunteer work. Romeo and I were going to the hospital. I was just ready to get back to my life before Fellows.

I must have dozed off because the next thing I knew, Robert was whispering for me to wake up. He whispered that he'd carry Doc inside. I went through the motions of opening the door, letting Romeo out in the backyard. And when Robert didn't come to find me, I followed Romeo upstairs, where he headed straight for the room where Doc was. I ducked into my room to find Robert next to the bed stripping.

"Hey, Daddy." I closed the door and leaned back against it. I sighed taking in the quiet.

"Time to recharge, baby?"

"Beyond time." I started to push away from the door.

"No, stay there." He approached me in nothing but his jeans. He placed his hands on the door on either side of my shoulders. "I want us to move in together."

"We already kinda live together."

"Exactly, we're either here or at my house, but I want to make a permanent home for us and Roo either here or my house. It's up to you."

"I really love your house. It's where we became a family the first time. The first home Roo ever had." As I spoke, he pushed his lips to mine, soft kisses that just showed me he cared, not to seduce. The thing was, his smile was enough to make me want to submit. The way he called me baby.

I moaned as he jerked at my buckle, slipping the leather free, and then undid my pants. The rasps of my zipper barely registered over the harsh increase in our breathing. I wrapped my arms around his neck and pushed our mouths together as he freed my cock and stroked the length too softly.

"Tighter, Daddy."

"No, baby, I know what you need."

I panicked as he pulled away, but I followed him with my gaze as he lowered to his knees, and he swallowed my cock. My head fell back with a thud against the door, and I fisted my hands in his hair.

"You were made to suck my cock, Daddy." I whimpered as he kept the slow pace. I lifted my head to look down at him, and his fingers dug into my hips. He tapped my hip with his thumb to signal he was ready, and I fucked his mouth, felt the release and contraction of his throat as I bottomed out.

His left hand released me, and the harder I face fucked him, the louder his grunts and groans. My clothes stuck to me as I started to sweat. My ass cheeks clenched with every thrust, and I could see him jerking off as he sucked me off.

"Fuck, Daddy!" I curled my hand around the back of his head as my sac started to draw up, and the ache and pleasure became almost too much to handle. I jerked him forward until his nose was buried in my pubes, and I shot down his throat with a shout. I rubbed my free hand across his sweaty back as he bowed, and he gagged hard as he found his own release.

He pulled back, licking my softening cock as he retreated and tongued my slit, suckled the sensitive head as I jerked. He was also too much and not enough. He placed a gentle kiss just above my bush of pubic hair, and then he got to his feet. He roughly kissed me as our spent, spit and cum covered cocks rubbed together.

"I love you so much, baby."

"I love you, too," I whispered as I tried to catch my breath.

"Let me strip you and tuck you into bed. My baby needs his rest."

"Robert, you take such good care of me."

"It's my pleasure to make sure you're okay. That's what a good partner does for his man. Makes the world and problems a little less heavy because I'm there to help carry them."

I nudged his lips with my tongue, and he opened. He sucked and backed up, leading me away from the door. The kiss turned desperate and rough, and hands brutally gripped my bare ass as he dipped into my crease. "Maybe I don't need rest right now."

"Baby, I was so hoping you'd say that."

I smiled against his lips as he fell onto the bed and brought me with him. This was what I always wanted and was terrified to demand. But Robert made it so damn easy.

EPILOGUE

ROBERT

COLD CASE
UNIT

A year later...

The only real sounds in the house were the television playing in the other room as I cleaned up from dinner. Remy had gone upstairs to bathe Roo and get her ready for bed. When she was tucked in, he'd yell for me. Fuck, I loved being a family with him and our daughter. I grunted as my boy wrapped himself completely around me and held on tight as I finished up the dinner dishes. He buried his face against the side of my neck.

"What's wrong, baby?"

"We've turned into an old married couple. I get no Daddy cuddles anymore," he whined, and I recognized the tone—it was the one he used on bad days. They didn't happen as often, but I'd become familiar with what he needed from me. And I was more than willing to give.

"How long has it been since I cuddled you?"

"Six whole hours, not one cuddle or grope, nothing. You're not attracted to me. You can tell me."

"You're earning spankings." I turned my head to brush a kiss to his temple.

"You say that like it's a threat."

I spun in the circle of his arms, grabbed his hands, and twisted them until they were trapped at the small of his back. He was shirtless, his skin was warm and hairy against mine, his jeans a little damp from bath time. Our Roo started fighting bedtime a few months ago and would turn her baths into a water fight. "You know I love you more than anything, and you get all the cuddles and kisses. Are you feeling insecure, baby?"

"We're coming up on a year. That's my cut-off. That's when my men start getting bored."

"Remy, I want you more today than I did a year ago when I had you and our Roo move in. Do you actually think I would believe another man was better than the one I have? Because if you do, I'll spank you on principle alone."

"Quit being so nice. I want to pout."

"You are awful cute when you pout."

"Fuck, I've gone from sexy to cute."

I chuckled as he made himself heavy, and I tightened my arms around him. I'd saddled myself with an adorable brat, and I had to admit I loved that. When our Captain assigned me the new guy, I thought it would be like any other partner I'd had, but he'd changed how I viewed my work and life. After three years of partnership, he'd made me a better and more compassionate cop.

We had our rough patches. Our daughter had more better days than bad ones. My baby still had his nightmares where he woke me crying in his sleep, but I wouldn't give up Remy and Roo for anything in the world.

"I think you're sexy and adorable, like you think I'm sexy and nice, but I want to know why you're feeling insecure, baby boy. Come on, tell Daddy all about it." I smirked as he groaned. I relaxed back against the counter and pulled him until he rested his weight on me.

"I don't know. Our anniversary is coming up. I will not be giving you a trip anywhere."

"I wouldn't go without you or Roo. I know your past colors

your perception of me and our relationship, and I understand that...I accept that. Although, you also have to accept that I'm not going anywhere. You and Roo are important to me, my gorgeous husband and our beautiful daughter."

"Husband? You haven't even gotten me a gumball machine ring yet."

"Are you ready for the ring?"

"Really? You're not joking, right?"

"That's something I would never joke about. I have the ring upstairs. It was my plan for our anniversary, but I think you need the security of that ring and the commitment. You and Roo are my family, I love you both, and I want to make sure that you know that you and her are it for me. I love her as much as Carol and RJ and the grandkids."

"Even the bad days where I get tired and the flashbacks hit, or when she wakes up screaming in the middle of the night not remembering where she is?"

"Especially the bad days, because when I make you two feel better, I know you trust in me to make sure you two are okay. And what could a man want more than my husband and daughter feeling secure with me?"

"I'd let you fuck me for the sweet factor alone. It's like Remy Kryptonite. I'm a total slut when you say things like safe and secure, oh, oh, don't get me started on husband, I think my jock went up in flames."

"I knew you were a brat, but, fuck, how did it get worse."

"You said you love me and want to marry me. You can't take that shit back."

"I would never want to. So you going to make your man and Daddy extremely happy and say yes?"

"You haven't asked me a question yet. I mean, I haven't even seen the ring. What if you actually got it from a gumball machine? That would just be so embarrassing."

"Stay right here, baby." I quickly kissed him and ran to the stairs and ascended, heading for our bedroom. I went to the closet where we kept our safes for our weapons. I'd hidden the ring I'd bought months ago inside. I used my fingerprint to unlock the safe and opened the lid. My heart sped up as I saw the box that held our rings.

Gladys had gone with me to pick them out and promised her she could plan the whole thing if she kept her marriage talk to a minimum. She'd been talking about marrying me off to her new bestie for over a year.

I rushed back downstairs to find him seated on the counter. He tensed as he saw the box as if he were expecting a joke.

"What did I say, baby?"

"That you wouldn't joke, but you actually have a ring."

"Of course I have a ring. I've had it for months. I've been terrified to ask."

"Robert, what do you have to be scared about?"

I stayed silent as I rounded the island and moved between his thick thighs. "You're an intelligent, compassionate, gorgeous man, and it doesn't escape my notice that you get a lot of offers."

"And those offers get denied when I tell them I'm married." He smirked.

"Well, why don't you do me the honor of actually marrying me...wear my ring so everyone knows you have a man, a husband, who loves you." I opened the box and showed him the rings inside. "I got myself one. I want everyone to know I belonged to you, too."

"Daddy..." His voice broke.

"No tears unless they're happy ones. I spent decades of my life married to a woman I loved, made a life with her, and raised children. When she divorced me, I thought that was the end for me. I threw myself into my job because that's all I had until you. And now I want to spend the rest of my life with you, raising our daughter. I want this second chance more than anything, Remy. Please say yes."

"Yes."

I took his ring from the box and slid it onto his finger as I brought my mouth to his. Everything I wanted in life was the man seated on our counter with our sleeping daughter in her room upstairs. I'd never believed in second chances until a beautiful man named Remy became mine even before I realized he was.

ABOUT THE AUTHOR

Two time USA Today Bestselling author J.M. Dabney is a multi-genre published writer of Body and Fat Positive Romance & Fiction. They live with a constant diverse cast of diverse characters in their head. They live for one purpose alone, and that's to make sure everyone gets the happily ever after they deserve. There is nothing more they want from telling their stories than to show that no matter the package the characters come in or the damage their pasts have done, that love is love. That normal is never normal and sometimes the so-called broken can still be beautiful.

The author is Non-Binary and uses the pronouns They/Them.

ALSO BY J.M. DABNEY

Sappho's Kiss Series

When All Else Fails

More Than What They See

Dysfunction it its Finest Series

Club Revenge

Soul Collector Prophecy

Twirled World Ink Series

Berzerker

Trouble

Scary

Lucky

Brawlers Series

Crave

Psycho

Bull

Hunter

Executioners Series

Ghost

Joker

King

Sin & Saint

Trenton Security

Livingston

Little

Gage

Pure

Masiello Brothers

The Taming of Violet

3 Moments Trilogy

A Matter of Time

The Men of Canter Handyman

Black Leather & Knuckle Tattoos

Chance at the Impossible

Bloody Knuckles Bar & Grill

Clipping the Gargoyle's Wings

New West City Universe

Co-written with Davidson King

The Hunt

Standalone

By Way of Pain (Criminal Delights - Assassins)

Christmas, Bloody Christmas (By Way of Pain Xmas Story)

Waited So Long

An Odd, Little Girl

Cold Cases and Second Chances

Claiming Whisper

Adoring Beast (Included in Dirty Daddies 2021 Anniversary Anthology

A Yuri Sorenson Mystery

Not Another Statistic

Permanent Freebies

Has the Honeymoon Ended? (Brawlers Short Valentine's Story)

Once Upon a Bear Claw

The Scars She Bears (Executioners Short)